MURDER
IN FOUR
PARTS

▼

MURDER
IN FOUR
PARTS

▼

BILL CRIDER

MINOTAUR BOOKS ≈ NEW YORK

This is a work of fiction. All of the characters, organizations, and events por-
trayed in this novel are either products of the author's imagination or are
used fictitiously.

A THOMAS DUNNE BOOK FOR MINOTAUR BOOKS.
An imprint of St. Martin's Publishing Group.

MURDER IN FOUR PARTS. Copyright © 2009 by Bill Crider. All rights
reserved. Printed in the United States of America. For information, address
St. Martin's Press, 175 Fifth Avenue, New York, N.Y. 10010.

www.thomasdunnebooks.com
www.minotaurbooks.com

Library of Congress Cataloging-in-Publication Data

Crider, Bill, 1941–
    Murder in four parts : a Dan Rhodes mystery / by Bill Crider.—1st ed.
      p. cm.
   ISBN-13: 978-0-312-38674-0
   ISBN-10: 0-312-38674-5
  1. Rhodes, Dan (Fictitious character)—Fiction. 2. Sheriffs—Fiction.
3. Murder—Investigation—Fiction.   4. City and town life—Texas—Fiction.
I. Title.
   PS3553.R497M855 2009
    813'.54—dc22

                                              2008036246

First Edition: February 2009

10 9 8 7 6 5 4 3 2 1

To Members of the Alvin Crossroad Chorus

MURDER
in FOUR
PARTS

▼

1

▼

Sheriff Dan Rhodes couldn't sing very well.

It wasn't that Rhodes didn't like music. He did, and he could hear songs perfectly well in his head, every note in tune, every tone rounded and full. When he opened his mouth and tried to sing, though, the sounds that came out didn't match what he heard in his mind. They sometimes came close, but not in a good way.

Which explained why Rhodes had never before been asked to join a musical group. He'd been asked to join just about everything else: civic clubs, book groups, political parties, record clubs (that had been a while back), and even a softball team or two. Lately AARP had been making persistent overtures.

Rhodes, however, wasn't much of a joiner, and he'd resisted all the opportunities presented to him so far, including the latest one, as he explained to Hack Jensen, the Blacklin County dispatcher.

"Well, you oughta think about joinin' the barbershop chorus, anyway," Hack said. "It's a kind of thing that might get you some votes. There's an election comin' up, whether you want to admit it or not."

Rhodes didn't want to admit it. He didn't like elections, and he especially didn't like campaigning.

"It's more than a year until the election," he said. "Besides, nobody's announced to run against me."

"You think it'll be easy, then?"

Rhodes wondered if Hack knew something he didn't. It was possible. Even likely. For a man who hardly ever seemed to leave the jail, Hack knew a lot about what was going on in the county.

"It's never easy," Rhodes said.

"If you lost the election, you'd miss this place," Hack said, waving a hand to indicate the big room they were in.

Rhodes spent a lot of time at the jail, all right, more than he should have, he sometimes thought. The room where Hack sat at the dispatcher's desk was as familiar to Rhodes as his own living room. That might not have been such a good thing.

The open area was also the room where people were booked into the jail and where most people came if they were looking for help from the county's law enforcement. There wasn't a lot to recommend it, but Hack was right.

"I'd miss it," Rhodes admitted, "but I could get used to being a private citizen."

Hack snorted. "I bet. You been sheriff for so long, you wouldn't know how to do anything else. And half the county'd still be lookin' for you to take care of 'em."

"Which half? The half that voted for me?"

"You wouldn't get half the votes. You lost, remember?"

Things had moved fast, a little too fast for Rhodes. The election was more than a year away, Rhodes didn't even have an opponent, and he'd already lost.

"What does all this have to do with me joining the Clearview Community Barbershop Chorus, anyway?" he said.

He and Hack had been arguing about the chorus off and on for more than a week, and Rhodes was getting a little tired of the whole thing.

Hack gave Rhodes an exasperated look. "Like I said. Bein' in the chorus gets you some votes. Lets folks know you're a part of the community that's havin' a good time and that you're not just out on the street arrestin' people who have overdue parkin' tickets."

"When's the last time I arrested anybody for an overdue parking ticket? Or even gave a parking ticket?"

"That ain't the point."

"Anyway," Rhodes said, ignoring him, "arresting people is my job. I'm the sheriff, not a barbershop singer."

"Well, you oughta be glad they asked you to join the chorus. They might get their feelin's hurt if you turn 'em down."

Something in Hack's tone clued Rhodes in to the real subject under discussion. He said, "I think they should've asked you to join. You have a nice baritone voice."

Hack nodded. "I sure do. You'd think they'd have invited me, but they invited you, instead."

"You don't need an invitation, you know. They don't have try-outs or anything. You can just go down to the community center and join. They'd be lucky to have you."

Hack grinned. "Yeah, but who'd run this dispatch board? The county needs me."

"But not me?"

"You got plenty of deputies." Hack paused. "You ever think

they might have a reason for askin' you to join the chorus besides your singin' abilities?"

As often happened, Rhodes knew he'd been wrong at least twice now about the actual direction of the conversation.

"What would the reason be?" he asked.

Hack shook his head. "I don't know. It was just somethin' in the way Berry asked you."

Lloyd Berry was the director of the chorus, and he'd come by the jail a bit earlier to talk to Rhodes about joining the group. Berry was a local florist, and singing was his hobby. He'd been enthusiastic about the benefits of belonging to the chorus. He'd also seemed a little nervous, as if he might be worried about something, though he'd said nothing about what that might be.

"Could be he wanted you there to referee any fights that broke out," Hack said.

"Why would there be fights at a chorus rehearsal?"

"Well," Hack said, "there's some strange folks in that bunch."

Rhodes knew who Hack meant: C. P. Benton and Max Schwartz, both of them relative newcomers.

Benton, better known as Seepy, was one of the bass singers in the chorus. He played guitar and drove a Saturn. That qualified him as strange by Clearview and Blacklin County standards.

Max Schwartz sang baritone. He'd given up his law practice in Kentucky and moved to Clearview with his wife, Jackee, to open a music store. He was devoted to the music of the Kingston Trio, not a group known for their barbershop arrangements. Rhodes didn't know why Schwartz was in the chorus. Maybe he just liked to sing harmony. At any rate, a man who'd give up a law practice to open a music store in a small town would certainly be considered odd by most people in the county.

Then lately he'd gotten into the restaurant business. Nothing strange about that, at least Rhodes hoped not. The last man who'd had the restaurant hadn't come to a good end.

Schwartz and Benton had a few other peculiarities, too, but that didn't make them troublemakers. Both had been involved in one of Rhodes's previous cases, but they'd been on the side of the angels.

Hack wasn't talking about those two, though.

"It's Cecil Marsh and Royce Weeks that'd worry me if I was the director of that bunch," Hack said. "Those two never have liked each other, and now they're both singin' tenor in the chorus. They're on opposite sides in the chicken deal, too. Could be a problem."

Marsh and Weeks currently had two problems, including what Rhodes liked to call "neighbor trouble." Others might have called it an ongoing feud. It had started when Weeks had moved next door to Marsh more than twenty years earlier. Weeks insisted that Marsh move three or four ornamental shrubs that were over the property line. Marsh said they weren't over the line, and he wasn't going to move them. Weeks called a surveyor, who found that the shrubs were indeed on Weeks's property, by about six inches, seven at the most. Weeks told Marsh to move the shrubs or he'd chop them down.

That was the beginning. Over the next twenty years, Rhodes or one of his deputies had been called to one house or the other to settle problems with barking dogs, uncut lawns, rogue sprinklers, suspicious smells, terroristic threats, garbage that was improperly disposed of, allegedly stolen newspapers, disturbances of the peace, and any number of other things that Rhodes couldn't recall at the moment.

"They haven't killed each other yet," Rhodes said.

"That was before the chickens," Hack said.

Clearview was in the midst of a great chicken controversy. For as long as the town had been there, some of its citizens had kept chickens in their backyards. Weeks was one of them.

Now, times were changing. Some people objected to the chickens, saying they were a health hazard, that the roosters disturbed the peace way too early in the morning, and that civilized people didn't need chickens anyway. Marsh was one of that group, though Rhodes thought his real objection was to Weeks rather than to the chickens.

"Could be just a matter of time before one of 'em does the other one in," Hack said. "The way those two go at it, I'm surprised it hasn't happened already. Just think about 'em sittin' by each other ever' week and singin' the same part in that chorus. Tenors are kind of nutty anyway." He paused. "Or so I've heard."

"I'm not a tenor," Rhodes said.

"Never said you were. I was thinkin' of Lawton."

Lawton was the jailer, the Lou Costello to Hack's Bud Abbott. It wasn't that Hack and Lawton were a comedy team, at least not intentionally. They did, however, bear a certain physical resemblance to the long-deceased vaudevillians, whom Rhodes had often watched in black-and-white movies on television. Now those movies seldom turned up anymore. Ten years or so down the line, Rhodes thought, hardly anybody would even remember who Abbott and Costello were, which Rhodes thought was a shame.

"Lawton might be a baritone," Rhodes said. "Like you."

"Baritone?" said Lawton, coming into the big room through the door that led to the cellblock. "Who you callin' a baritone? I'm a lead, if I'm anything. I been thinkin' about joinin' that barbershop chorus they've got and givin' 'em the benefit of my vocal cords."

Hack rolled his eyes, but before he could start an argument, Rhodes said, "Lloyd Berry just came by and asked me to join the chorus. Hack thinks he had an ulterior motive."

"That bunch needs somebody to keep an eye on 'em, all right," Lawton said. "Darrel Sizemore, for one."

Sizemore owned a junkyard where he bought and sold scrap metal, and he got a lot of jokes about his name because he was, as he liked to put it, height-challenged. His lack of height didn't keep him from being a bit more pugnacious than most people. For all Rhodes knew, the lack of height was the cause of the assertiveness. Whatever the reason was, he didn't take kindly to the jokes. He'd had a little legal trouble once, but it hadn't amounted to much.

"I was comin' to Darrel," Hack said. "Sings bass. You wouldn't think it to look at him, but he can drag the bottom. Must have a hollow leg or something to get a sound that big. Anyway, he's a fight waitin' to happen. He's fine as long as nobody argues with him or says anything about how short he is, but if you cross him, it's Katy bar the door."

"We oughta invite the chorus to the jail," Lawton said. "Let 'em sing to the prisoners."

"I don't think they're that hard up for an audience," Rhodes said.

"Maybe not," Lawton said. "You gonna join?"

Rhodes shook his head. "I don't have time. I have to be out there busting crime twenty-four hours a day."

"You'll be sorry you didn't join if a fight breaks out and somebody gets hurt," Hack said.

Rhodes wasn't worried. Some of the people involved in the chorus might be a bit odd, and some of them might be overly aggressive, and some of them might be bad neighbors, but that didn't mean there was any danger of a fight breaking out. Rhodes thought that singing in harmony together might bring everyone to harmony in other ways.

It was nice to think so for a couple of seconds, but Rhodes forgot all about it when they got the call about the alligator.

2

▼

THE ALLIGATOR SQUATTED ON THE MUDDY BOTTOM OF THE drainage ditch that ran along the county road in front of Seepy Benton's house. The gator was partially covered with windblown leaves, and it looked a lot like a log. Benton claimed he had no idea how it had gotten into the ditch, not that it mattered. The immediate problem was how to get it out without getting hurt.

It had been a long time since Rhodes had seen an alligator. There weren't a lot of them in Blacklin County. None, in fact, as far as Rhodes knew.

The last time he'd seen one, he'd been just a kid. He and his parents had been on a family vacation, headed down to the Gulf Coast to visit Galveston, and they'd stopped at one of those roadside attractions that was advertised for miles with billboards promising spectacular exhibits: SNAKES! JUNGLE BEASTS! FEARSOME CREATURES OF THE SWAMPS!

As far as Rhodes remembered, the exhibit had turned out to be a couple of snakes that might have been defanged rattlers or maybe just hog snakes, a flea-infested monkey or two, and an alligator. The gator hadn't been a very big one, certainly smaller than the one Rhodes was looking at now.

This one was at least seven feet long from the tip of its snout to the tip of its tail. As far as Rhodes was concerned, that was plenty big enough.

"Maybe it's a crocodile," Deputy Ruth Grady said.

"No, it's an alligator, all right," Seepy Benton told her.

Benton looked a little like an out-of-place rabbi. He had blue eyes, a salt-and-pepper beard, and curly hair that stuck out from under the narrow brim of his hat. He taught math at the local branch of a community college, but he knew about a lot of things not related to mathematics. Strange things, mostly, and that included alligators.

"How do you know?" Ruth asked.

"For one thing, you can't see its teeth," Benton told her. "You can see a crocodile's teeth even when its mouth is closed."

Rhodes was glad he couldn't see the animal's teeth, but he didn't mention it.

"Also, the snout's wider than a croc's," Benton continued. "An alligator's got a lot more crushing power in its jaws. It even eats turtles. A croc's snout is narrower and kind of comes to a point."

Rhodes would just as soon not have heard the part about the crushing power of the jaws, but he didn't mention that, either.

"All we have to do is clamp its mouth shut," Benton said. "Alligators have the crushing power, all right, but the muscles that open its jaws are a lot weaker. I could hold its mouth closed with one hand. Then it couldn't bite anybody."

Rhodes believed him about the mouth, but he wasn't relieved

by the information. The alligator seemed to be sculpted out of pure muscle.

"Who's going to hold the rest of it?" Rhodes said.

Benton smiled. "You're the sheriff."

Rhodes wouldn't have been surprised if Benton had jumped into the ditch and wrestled the gator. The math teacher had been interested in Ruth Grady for a short time before falling for Mel Muller, a Web site developer. Benton had helped Mel do a beautiful site for the county. The site had pleased the commissioners, but Benton and Mel's relationship had ended when the site was completed. Rhodes didn't know why, and it wasn't any of his business.

Now Benton was interested in Ruth again. That wasn't any of Rhodes's business, either, but he couldn't help being a bit curious.

Benton gave the gator a speculative look.

"I'll wrestle it," Benton said to Rhodes, who wasn't surprised at all, though he knew the remark was intended to impress Ruth. "You can hold its mouth shut. I do a hundred push-ups every day. I'm pretty strong."

"You may be strong," Rhodes said, "but you're not deputized. This is county business."

"I'm the one who found the alligator."

"Right, and you called us to take care of it. Which is what we're going to do."

Benton might have argued the point, since Ruth was listening to every word, but just then Alton Boyd drove up in a dusty white van with the county insignia on the side.

Boyd pulled the van off the road as much as he could and parked behind Rhodes's county car. Boyd, the county's newly appointed animal control officer, was a bandy-legged man with thinning blond hair concealed by a gimme cap. He had broad shoulders and a thick waist, and his face was seamed with wrinkles, though he wasn't much past forty.

Boyd's job ran to rounding up stray cattle, dogs, and cats rather than capturing alligators. Lately Rhodes had been sending him out to corral Vernell Lindsey's goats, which were notorious for jumping her fence and getting into the neighbors' yards.

"What we got here?" Boyd said around the unlit cigar he had clamped in his teeth.

Until Boyd had been hired, Rhodes had thought there were no more cigar smokers in Blacklin County. In fact, maybe there weren't. Rhodes had never seen Boyd actually smoke anything. Apparently Boyd was satisfied just to have something to chew on.

White Owl was the brand he preferred. Boyd took a lot of kidding about that, but he always insisted that you didn't have to pay a lot of money for a quality cigar.

"We have an alligator," Rhodes said. "In the ditch."

Boyd took a look. "Sure enough. I thought Hack was about halfway kidding me." He studied the gator for a couple of seconds. "Could be a crocodile, I guess."

"No," Ruth said. "It's an alligator, all right. You can't see its teeth."

Benton smiled. Rhodes kept quiet.

"Sure enough," Boyd said, as if he'd known it all along. "So Hack was right."

Hack had probably enjoyed relaying the information about the alligator to Boyd, Rhodes thought. Hack got a kick out of the unusual.

"Let me get my stuff," Boyd said.

"You have stuff for alligators?" Rhodes said.

"Duck tape."

Boyd opened the back of his van and stepped inside. When he returned, he had a roll of duct tape in one hand and a couple of coiled lariats in the other.

"Rope him, tie him up, tape his mouth shut, throw him in the back of the van," he said.

Somehow Rhodes didn't think it would be that easy. He wasn't confident about Boyd's ability with a rope, not when it came to alligators.

"Don't you have some kind of pole with a loop on the end to catch animals with?" he said.

"Nope. Just use the straight old lariat rope."

"I can rope," Benton said.

Rhodes should have been expecting that. He said, "You can't help. You'd open the county up to a lawsuit if something happened to you. The commissioners would have my hide if you got hurt."

"I wouldn't get hurt. I can do a hundred—"

"We know," Rhodes said. "A hundred push-ups. It doesn't matter. You might be strong, but you're still a civilian."

"I'm more than a civilian. I went to the academy."

That was true. Rhodes had started a Citizens' Sheriff's Academy, and Benton had been one of the first graduates. The academy had seemed like a good idea at the time Rhodes thought of it. Since then he'd had some second thoughts. Several of them.

"There's nothing official about the academy," Rhodes said. "You'll just have to watch."

Benton moved aside, but Rhodes could see he wasn't happy about it.

"We know you could handle the gator by yourself, Seepy," Ruth told him, and Benton brightened. "It's just it's our job."

"All right," Benton said. "But if you need my help, just say the word."

Boyd handed Rhodes one of the lariats. "You want to rope the head or the tail?"

Rhodes looked at the rope. He'd last handled a rope about the time he'd last seen an alligator.

Ruth Grady took the rope from Rhodes's hand. "I'll rope the head," she said. "When he starts thrashing around, Alton can get the tail."

"Sounds like a plan," Boyd said, as calm as if he were about to rope a fence post.

He tossed Rhodes the duct tape. Rhodes caught it cleanly.

"Soon's we get him secured," Boyd said, "you tape that snout of his shut. You be careful. These fellas are stout. Not to mention mean."

"I'll help get him secured," Benton said. "Did I mention that I know several alligator-wrestling techniques?"

"Probably," Rhodes said, "but you'll still have to stay out of the way. If I get in trouble, you can yell advice."

"I have some right now."

Rhodes nodded. He wasn't surprised. "What is it?"

"Don't try to tape the snout until they have the tail secured. That tail is powerful enough to break every bone in your body with one swipe."

"Thanks," Rhodes said. "That makes me feel a lot better about this."

"I'm always happy to assist the law," Benton said.

"Assist by standing a little farther away, then," Rhodes told him.

Benton moved another couple of feet away from the edge of the ditch, and Ruth Grady moved in on the alligator, shaking out a loop in the lariat with her right hand.

The alligator might have been watching her, but Rhodes couldn't tell. It didn't move, and its snout was flat on the ground. It could as well have been a statue for all the animation it displayed.

"I'll get his attention," Benton said, moving forward.

"Stop right there," Rhodes said. "We just want him to lift his head, not attack us."

Benton looked insulted. "I wasn't going to agitate him."

Rhodes suspected there was a fine line between getting the gator's attention and agitating it, and he didn't trust Benton not to cross it.

"You just stay where you are and let us handle this. That's why the county pays us the big bucks."

While they were talking, Ruth walked along the top edge of the ditch to a spot where she could look down at the gator. The ditch was only three feet or so deep, and she dropped the loop of the lariat down in front of the gator's snout.

The gator paid no more attention than if a gnat had landed nearby. Ruth dragged the loop right up to the snout, ready to slip it on at the first opportunity.

Rhodes didn't think the gator would cooperate, and it didn't. It just sat there, still as a stone. Ruth waited, but Rhodes had a feeling that when it came to waiting nobody in the group was as good as the gator.

Alton Boyd couldn't do anything at his end of the gator, either. The gator's meaty tail lay flat against the ground.

"Now what?" Rhodes said.

"He has to move sometime," Boyd said, but Rhodes wasn't so sure of that.

"I could get his attention," Benton said.

He opened his mouth, and Rhodes thought he was going to yell. Instead, he made a high-pitched noise that sounded like a flying saucer in one of the bad old movies that Rhodes used to watch on TV.

Whatever the sound was, it worked. The gator raised its snout an inch or so above the ditch and moved its head to the side. Ruth slipped the loop over the snout and pulled it tight.

Rhodes wasn't sure what happened after that. It was as if he'd been watching a paused picture on a TV screen when someone had suddenly switched it to fast-forward.

The gator rolled over and over. Leaves flew up from the ditch, whirling as if caught in a tornado. Something white as snowflakes circled wildly among the leaves. Clods of dirt and grass spattered the sides of the ditch.

Ruth struggled to hang on to the rope that twisted in her hands, while Boyd juked around on his bandy legs, attempting to get into position to lasso the thrashing tail.

Benton yelled something that Rhodes couldn't hear because of the commotion in the ditch.

Boyd threw his loop and missed. The gator continued to flip itself. If anything, it was flipping faster than before.

Boyd retrieved his loop and tried again. This time, whether by luck or skill Rhodes couldn't tell, Boyd caught the tail. He pulled the loop tight and ran backward to pull the rope taut.

The gator, as if it sensed what was about to happen, stopped flipping and planted itself firmly in the bottom of the ditch. Just as

Boyd tightened the rope, the gator whipped its tail up and to the right. Boyd's feet slid out from under him. He yelped, and the White Owl flew out of his mouth. It spun through the air and landed somewhere in the grass near the ditch.

Boyd hung on to the rope, and the gator flicked its tail to the left, dragging Boyd through the grass. Rhodes dropped the duct tape and ran to help. He grabbed hold of the rope a few feet in front of Boyd just as the gator slung its tail again. Rhodes dug in his heels, and with the weight of Boyd behind him was able to keep the muscular appendage from moving more than a couple of feet.

Boyd, still hanging on, pulled himself upright. He and Rhodes together were able to draw the rope tight and immobilize the tail.

Now that the gator wasn't flopping around, Ruth was able to tighten up on the rope she held. The gator struggled against the ropes but found that it couldn't flip itself now. It kept trying for a minute that seemed to Rhodes more like a quarter of an hour.

Seeing that it wasn't getting anywhere, the gator subsided into a sullen stillness, turned half on its side.

"I told you I could get his attention," Benton said.

"What was that noise you made?" Ruth asked.

"Just a noise. Alligators hear best in the thousand-hertz range, so that's what I tried for."

Ruth looked impressed. Benton tried to look modest, which Rhodes thought was an effort for him.

"You think you have him?" Rhodes asked Boyd.

"Sure. He's not going anywhere."

Rhodes hoped not. He let go of the rope and located the duct tape. He picked it up and walked to the gator's head. The gator didn't seem to care that he was there, so Rhodes bent down and wrapped its snout with the sticky duct tape. He rounded the snout at least ten times. He didn't care what Benton had said about the weakness of the muscles. He wanted to be sure the gator's mouth didn't come open when they took the rope off.

When he was sure the tape wasn't going to come loose, he straightened and said, "What next?"

"We gotta get him in the van," Boyd said. "You want to hold this rope?"

The answer to that was *no*, but Rhodes said, "Why not?"

He went back to where Boyd stood and took hold of the rope, careful to keep the tension on.

Boyd left him there and looked around for his cigar. When he found it, he brushed it off against his pants. After a brief inspection of its surface, he stuck it back in his mouth. Then he got two more ropes from the van.

"What are those for?" Rhodes said.

"Gotta tie his legs up with something."

Rhodes looked at the claws on the gator's feet. They looked capable of slashing a small tree in half. Or of opening a man's belly from top to bottom.

"Just how did you plan to do that?"

"It's easy," Seepy Benton said from his place well away from the action. "Alligators tire easily. This one's probably so tired he can hardly move."

"It better be," Rhodes said, but he needn't have worried.

Either the gator was tired or it just didn't care anymore. Boyd bound the feet without much trouble and went back to the van again. This time he returned with a stout wooden pole.

"Is that a ten-foot pole?" Benton asked.

"Wouldn't poke a gator with anything shorter," Boyd said. "Just kidding," he added when he saw Rhodes's look of alarm. "We're gonna use this to carry him."

First he tied the rope Rhodes held to the pole while Rhodes kept the pressure on. After Boyd was satisfied with the knots, he tied Ruth's rope to the pole.

"Now we hoist him up and get him in the van," Boyd said. He looked at Rhodes. "I think we should let the civilian help with this part."

"I can handle one end by myself," Benton said.

"You'd better just help me instead," Rhodes said. "I need somebody strong."

With the gator trussed, helpless, and not much interested in fighting, they hoisted him up with Benton and Rhodes at one end of the pole and Boyd and Grady at the other. It wasn't easy, but they managed to struggle up out of the ditch and get him stashed in the van. When they laid him on the floor, the gator gave a couple of halfhearted flops and then lay still.

"Now what?" Rhodes said.

"I called a zoo in Waco on the way here," Boyd said. "They told me if we really did have a gator, they'd take him. I'll just run him over there right now. Prob'ly take the rest of the day to get 'er done, though."

Rhodes didn't think the county commissioners would mind if Boyd spent his day getting rid of the gator.

"Go right ahead," he said.

Boyd nodded and slammed the doors on the van.

"I'll call in if I get back early," he said.

Rhodes nodded, and Boyd left.

"A job well done," Benton said as if he'd handled it all by himself. "What I'd like to know is, where did that alligator come from?"

"I'd like to know what the white stuff flying around was," Rhodes said.

"Oh, I can tell you that," Benton said. "It was chicken feathers."

"Uh-oh," Rhodes said.

3

▼

SEEPY BENTON'S HOUSE WAS JUST OUTSIDE OF TOWN AND nowhere near the homes of Cecil Marsh and Royce Weeks. However, Marsh owned the property just across the road, where there was a dilapidated old house and a barn that listed far to one side and seemed about to fall down. On the other side of the barn was a stock tank. The stock tank was just about the right size to keep an alligator comfortable. Rhodes figured there'd be plenty for the gator to eat: turtles, mudcats, maybe a few little perch.

But no chickens.

"Where do you think a chicken came from?" Benton said. "I don't keep chickens, and I don't know of anybody who has them around here."

Rhodes didn't think the chicken had come from around there.

"Cecil Marsh owns that land across the road, right?" Rhodes asked, just to be sure.

Benton nodded, and Rhodes told Ruth to get Hack on her

shoulder radio and ask if there'd been a complaint from Royce Weeks.

"What kind of complaint?" she said, and then, "Oh."

Rhodes didn't think Cecil Marsh was the kind of man who'd steal his neighbor's chickens and transport them to his little place in the country to feed them to an alligator. Still, with the way things were going in the Great Chicken Controversy, it could have happened.

Ruth engaged in a crackly conversation with Hack. Rhodes could hear Ruth's side of it, but he couldn't make out what Hack was saying.

Ruth listened to Hack's final comments and signed off. She grinned at Rhodes.

"He hasn't heard anything from Weeks," she said. "He wanted to know why you were asking."

Hack and Lawton couldn't stand not knowing what was going on, and in fact they liked nothing better than finding out things before Rhodes did. Then they'd make Rhodes wheedle the information out of them. Rhodes was glad to have the upper hand for once.

"You didn't tell him, did you?" he said.

Ruth shook her head. "I told him it was confidential."

Rhodes liked that. "Good."

"I hate to interrupt," Benton said, "but what's going on?"

Ruth explained about Marsh and Royce Weeks being on different sides regarding the keeping of chickens within the city limits.

"I heard something about that," Benton said, "but I didn't pay much attention since I don't live inside the city. I think getting an alligator out here and feeding a chicken to it would be going a little far to make a point."

Rhodes thought so, too, but you never could tell what people might do to prove a point or just to antagonize someone else. Marsh and Weeks had pushed the limits for years.

"Have you ever seen an alligator around here before?" he asked.

"No," Benton said, "but there are plenty of tanks around here where one could hide out. An alligator could live in this climate. He wouldn't be very comfortable in the winter, but he could survive."

It was a warm day in April. The alligator had survived the winter in good shape, it seemed to Rhodes.

"Somebody would notice an alligator if it was in a tank," Ruth said.

"Maybe not," Benton said. "They're pretty quiet, and most of the stock tanks are out of sight of the road."

"What about Cecil Marsh's place?" Rhodes said, gesturing with his thumb. "Anybody ever visit over there?"

"I haven't seen anybody, but I'm not at home all the time."

Rhodes supposed it was possible that the alligator had been somewhere else, miles away, and had just wandered to the ditch in front of Benton's house, but that didn't explain the chicken feathers. It didn't seem likely that the meeting of the chicken and the gator had been a coincidence, although it was possible. There were chickens all over Blacklin County, and one might have wandered into the gator's path.

Rhodes wanted to know what that path had been, but it wouldn't be easy to track. It hadn't rained for a while, and if the gator had flattened any grass in its travels, it was no longer obvious. Rhodes supposed the reptile had been in the ditch for a while.

"You didn't see the gator yesterday?" he said.

Benton shook his head. "But then I wasn't looking for him. I just happened to glance over that way when I was leaving for class this morning, or I wouldn't have seen him at all."

"You didn't go to class, did you?"

"No, I called your office, and then I called the college to let them know I wasn't coming in. I told them it was an alligator emergency."

Benton said everything with a straight face. Rhodes was never sure when he was joking.

"Do they get a lot of those calls at the college?" Ruth said. "Alligator emergencies?"

"I think mine was the first," Benton said. "But now that it's over, I'd better go on to work. I can just about make it for my eleven o'clock class."

He went back to his house and drove away in his Saturn. Rhodes told Ruth that she could write up the report on the gator incident, though he wasn't sure it was over.

"I'll stay around and see if I can turn anything up," he said. "A clue, maybe."

"You're going onto Marsh's property without a warrant?"

"I have reason to suspect that the alligator might have come from there because of the stock tank. Anyway, we're not even sure a crime has been committed. You might say I'm paying Marsh's property a friendly visit."

"We might say that," Ruth said. "If we were ever asked."

"And I don't think we will be."

Ruth nodded. She got in her patrol car and left, and Rhodes walked across the road.

Marsh hadn't had any work done on his barbed-wire fence in years. The posts tilted and the wire sagged. There was no gate, just a cattle guard, and that wasn't needed, since Marsh didn't have any cattle or any other kind of livestock. Rhodes crossed the cattle guard, careful not to get his foot caught.

The rutted road, which hardly deserved to be called a road, led past the remains of the old barn, so Rhodes turned aside to have a look inside what was left of the building.

There was nothing much to see. The door to the little storage area had fallen to the ground, and most of it had rotted away. The rest of the barn had a dirt floor, upon which lay some pieces of wood that might once have been part of a hayrack. Rhodes couldn't see any signs that an alligator had been in residence, so he went on up to the house.

The screen door no longer had any screen in it, and all the windows were broken. A spiderweb hung suspended between the posts on either side of the top step, and Rhodes brushed it away, wiping the sticky webbing on his pants.

The view wasn't improved by the removal of the web, and Rhodes didn't trust the porch not to collapse beneath his weight. So he walked around and looked into the house through the broken windows. He saw trash on the floor of one room, some cans with no labels and a few mildewed magazines, and thought maybe someone had stayed there for a while, but if so it had been long ago, and certainly the room hadn't been home to an alligator.

Having found no clues, Rhodes strolled down to the stock tank. The low dam was almost bare of trees. A couple of straggly willows sprouted from the yellowish dirt, their green leaves stirring in the light morning breeze.

Rhodes walked around the dam and stood on the edge of the tank. It was no more than thirty yards to the other side. Green algae floated on top of the water around the edges of the tank, and a turtle poked its head up to look at Rhodes with a beady black eye.

If there had been an alligator there, at least one turtle had escaped his jaws, Rhodes thought. He couldn't see any claw marks
in the earth along the sides of the tank or on the dam. There was
no slick place where a gator might have slid into the water after
spending a quiet day on the bank while soaking up the sun. Maybe
the gator hadn't ever been there at all. It was nothing more than a
random alligator that had encountered a random chicken.

How likely was that? Rhodes wondered. Not likely at all, really. The alligator had come from somewhere. So had the chicken.
Well, as long as nobody complained about missing chickens or
about being menaced by an alligator, there was no reason the sheriff had to worry about it.

At one time Rhodes might have had his fishing rod in the trunk
of the county car. Over the last couple of years, however, he'd
pretty much given up fishing. Otherwise, he might have made a
few casts into the tank, just in case there were some fish worth
catching. Not that he thought there were. The water was muddy,
and there was too much algae.

Rhodes went on back to the county car. He tried to put the alligator out of his mind, but he couldn't help but wonder about it and
where it had come from. Sooner or later, he thought, he'd find out.

Back at the jail, Rhodes found that Hack and Lawton had already
figured out why Rhodes had wanted to know if there had been any
complaints from Royce Weeks.

"You thought that alligator came from Cecil Marsh's place,"
Hack said. "And you thought maybe Cecil was gonna set it on
Lloyd's chickens."

That was close enough, so Rhodes didn't bother to go into the details. He just nodded.

"That was too easy," Lawton said. "There's more to it, I'll bet."

Rhodes shook his head, a gesture almost guaranteed to drive Lawton and Hack up the wall. They'd be sure he was keeping something back from them.

"Anything going on that I should know about?" he said.

"Maybe," Hack said, and Rhodes realized he'd made a mistake. He'd given them back the upper hand.

"Better tell me about it," he said.

"Got a call about a man gettin' him some exercise," Hack said. "Nothin' wrong with that, I guess."

Rhodes knew better. No one would call about a man getting exercise.

"Jumpin' jacks," Lawton said. "I never could do those when I was a kid. Didn't have any coordination to speak of."

"Me neither," Hack said. "Couldn't chew gum and walk down the street at the same time."

Lawton nodded. "Speakin' of the street . . ."

"What about the street?" Rhodes said.

Hack frowned. He didn't like being brought back to the subject too quickly.

"That's where the man was exercisin'," he said. "In the street."

"Traffic hazard," Lawton said. "Right downtown."

Clearview didn't have a police department to patrol the downtown. The city contracted with the sheriff's department to enforce the law in the city limits, while also taking care of the county. Rhodes had more bosses than anybody needed.

"Not a lot of traffic downtown," Hack said, "but he was still a hazard."

The sad truth was that not much was left of Clearview's downtown area. Most of the businesses that had been there had long since closed their doors. Some of them had migrated out on the highway near the giant Wal-Mart, while others had simply faded away. Many of the old buildings had fallen down or been demolished.

"Where downtown?" Rhodes said.

"Out in front of the Lawj Mahal," Hack said.

Rhodes had given the name of the Lawj Mahal to the big new law offices of Randy Lawless, the most successful attorney in the county. The offices were located in what had once been the heart of downtown, and the sparkling white building that housed them occupied about half of an entire block, the rest of which was given over to a paved parking area.

"So he *wasn't* in the street," Rhodes said.

"Parking lot," Hack said. "Same thing. Still a traffic hazard."

"Private property."

"Endangerin' the public, no matter where he was," Lawton said. "Not to mention endangerin' himself. Especially since he wasn't dressed right."

Rhodes was afraid to ask what that meant, so he said nothing. Hack and Lawton looked at him, waiting to see how long it would take him to break. He lasted about half a minute. Maybe less.

"All right, I give up. Tell me the rest of it."

Hack grinned and leaned back in his swivel chair. "Well, when Lawton says he wasn't dressed right, he's kind of exaggeratin'. He was hardly dressed at all. Wasn't wearing anything but a jockstrap."

"Weather's a little too cool for a man to go buck naked, I guess," Lawton said.

"And a fella can run faster if he's not wearin' pants," Hack said. "You take Tarzan. He never wore pants, and he could move pretty good."

"Who responded to the call?" Rhodes said, hoping to get things back on track.

"Buddy," Hack said. "Didn't catch the fella, though."

"Lucky for him," Lawton said.

Buddy might not have been descended from Cotton Mather, but he held some of the same views, and the exerciser would have gotten quite a lecture had Buddy caught up with him.

"How did he get away?" Rhodes asked, trying to visualize a nearly naked man running through the nearly deserted streets of downtown.

"Must have had a car parked somewhere close," Hack said. "Time Buddy got there, he was long gone. What you think he was doin' those jumpin' jacks for?"

"Some kind of protest, maybe," Rhodes said. "Or just trying to get in shape. We'll have to ask him if we catch him."

"Don't think we will," Hack said. "He won't try it again."

"You never know," Rhodes said.

The phone rang, and Hack answered.

Rhodes could hear only one side of the conversation, but he could tell it was about something a lot worse than a nearly naked man doing jumping jacks.

Hack turned around and said, "It's Lloyd Berry. He's at his shop, and he's dead."

"Heart attack?" Lawton said.

"Nope. Looks like somebody's killed him."

4

▼

BERRY'S FLORAL WAS IN A STRIP SHOPPING CENTER THAT A COU-
ple of optimistic local businessmen had built years earlier in the
belief that Clearview would grow toward the west, just a short distance north of where two highways intersected. They'd made a
drastic miscalculation, though they'd had no way of knowing it at
the time. Their mistake had been to build on the side of town opposite the one where Wal-Mart would put up the big box that attracted shoppers the way a bright light attracted insects. As a
result, the shopping strip had been home to a number of failed
businesses over the years.

The floral shop, however, had managed to hang on through the
bad years, and now things were improving. A community college in
another county had established a branch campus in Clearview, and
their new buildings weren't far south of the strip. A restaurant belonging to the late Jerry Kergan and now owned by Max Schwartz

wasn't far from the college campus, and it helped draw people to the area as well.

The strip itself was home to the floral shop, which anchored one end; a check-cashing enterprise that also sold money orders and did small loans; a nail salon; Tom's TomToms, which sold and rented GPS receivers; and Rollin' Sevens, which behind its blacked-out windows housed a number of what were called eight-liners, near cousins to video slot machines. The machines were legal in Texas under certain conditions, and Rollin' Sevens was the busiest place in the strip. Rhodes had received quite a few complaints about the place, but so far he hadn't been able to prove it wasn't playing by the rules.

As far as Rhodes was concerned the main problem wasn't with the gambling itself, whether it was legal or not, but in the occasional robbery that occurred near the place. People going in always had money, and they were often careless.

At the moment, however, Rhodes wasn't interested in gambling or robberies. The death of Lloyd Berry was a considerably more serious matter.

Rhodes parked the county car in front of Berry's shop in a spot marked FLORAL CUSTOMERS ONLY on the curb in faded black paint. Next to him was Darrel Sizemore's little blue Chevy S-10 pickup. Business wasn't booming. The only other cars on the center's parking lot were clustered at the other end, where Rollin' Sevens was located.

The floral shop was unique among the strip's buildings in that it was the only one to have a second story. Berry had gotten permission from the owners and added it just after moving in. He'd once told Rhodes he needed living quarters because he'd found himself working so late at certain times of the year: just before the high school prom, the week of the football homecoming game, and before big weddings and funerals. Instead of going home at one or two o'clock in the morning, Berry would just go upstairs, where he had a bed, a TV set, and a small kitchen and bathroom. Rhodes had driven by there more than once late at night and seen a light in the second-story window.

No light was on there now, but the fluorescent lights inside the shop were on. Rhodes went through the front door. A bell rang in the back.

The shop was filled with Easter decorations, baskets with plastic eggs of all colors and pink and yellow bunnies, crosses with ivy twined on them, even some inflatable bunnies.

There were also potted plants and flowers, most of which Rhodes couldn't identify. He was familiar with ivy and chrysanthemums, and there were some roses in a cooler. The place smelled of earth and the sweetish mingled odors of the flowers. Darrel Sizemore stood by the counter in the back of the shop.

"Hey, Sheriff," he said.

His deep voice quavered, which was unusual for a man as confident as Sizemore was. Rhodes figured the feet sticking out from behind the end of the counter were the problem, or rather what the feet were connected to.

"Hey, Darrel," Rhodes said. "Want to tell me what happened?"

Sizemore took a deep breath. He was about five and a half feet tall, but he looked smaller in the shop, standing next to the high counter. He had a high, wrinkled forehead and ears that stood out from the sides of his head.

"I'm the treasurer of the Clearview Chorus," he said. "Lloyd asked you to join, I think."

Rhodes nodded. He believed in letting witnesses tell things their own way, even if it took them a little time to get started.

"I came out here to talk to Lloyd about some of the money matters," Sizemore said. "We don't have a lot of money, and it seemed to me that Lloyd was spending too much on music. It's expensive, and . . ." He paused and waved a hand in the air, dismissing what he'd said. "That doesn't matter, though. When I came in I didn't see Lloyd. Sometimes he's in back, working on arrangements, so I started to go look for him. When I came to the end of the counter, I saw his feet."

Sizemore turned and looked at the feet that Rhodes assumed belonged to Lloyd Berry. They were wearing running shoes with a big *N* on the sides.

"I thought maybe he'd had a heart attack," Sizemore said, turning back to Rhodes. "Or a stroke. Something like that. I went behind the counter to see if I could help, and then I saw him."

Sizemore paused again, but this time he didn't look at Lloyd's feet. He kept his eyes on Rhodes.

"One look and I could tell he hadn't had a heart attack. It's a lot worse than that."

"You told Hack somebody had killed him."

"That's right. You'd better have a look for yourself."

"All right."

Sizemore moved farther down the counter, getting out of the way as Rhodes passed him.

Berry's body lay on the floor on a black rubber mat that ran the length of the counter. Rhodes knelt down beside it. One look at Berry's head and Rhodes could tell how Sizemore knew Berry hadn't died a natural death. The left side of the head was crushed and bloody. Beside the body lay a heavy metal pipe cutter wrench.

Rhodes wondered what something like that was doing in a floral shop.

Lloyd Berry had been alive, and now he was dead. In an instant. The deaths he investigated always made Rhodes sad. The waste of life bothered him in ways he couldn't really explain, and it put a little hard knot of anger in his stomach, a knot that wouldn't go away until he'd found out who'd committed the crime. Rhodes never let the anger surface, never let it interfere with his investigation, but it was always there.

He stood up and looked at Sizemore over the top of the counter.

"Did you see anybody else when you got here?" he asked.

Sizemore shook his head. "Nobody. Why would anybody kill Lloyd?"

Rhodes didn't know the answer to that, but he knew there was a reason. There was always a reason, though never a good one. Maybe even Sizemore had one, but now wasn't the time to bring that up, not yet.

"You know anybody that uses a pipe cutter like that?" Rhodes said.

"Oh, that was Lloyd's. You'd be surprised at some of the things he used around here. He has all kinds of tools. He's got knives to cut rose stems with, and he uses hammers to mash the stems of the mums. They last longer in the vase that way. That wrench was to cut some of the artificial bushes he uses in cemetery arrangements."

Sizemore stopped talking and looked at the floor for a second. When he looked up again, he said, "Lloyd talked to me about his work sometimes. I didn't mean to ramble."

"Did you call anybody besides my office?" Rhodes said.

Sizemore shook his head.

"I'll call for an ambulance," Rhodes said. "And a deputy. You can wait outside."

"Thanks," Sizemore said.

He went outside and seemed glad to go. Rhodes followed him out and got Hack on the radio. He told Hack that Berry was dead, all right, and told him to send a deputy.

"How about the JP and an ambulance?" Hack said.

"Better wait on calling the ambulance," Rhodes said. "I have to work the scene."

"So you'll call the ambulance?" Hack said.

Rhodes said he would and signed off. Sizemore had let down the tailgate of the pickup and sat with his short legs dangling off. His feet were as small as a child's. Sizemore's head was down, as if he might be praying or thinking hard, but he looked up when Rhodes approached.

"Would it be all right for me to leave?" he said.

"Sure. You and Lloyd didn't have any problems, did you?"

Sizemore stiffened. "What's that supposed to mean?"

"Not a thing. Just wondering about that music business you mentioned. About how Lloyd was spending too much of the chorus's money."

"That was nothing. I didn't even get to talk to Lloyd about it. Why did you bring that up?"

"Just wondering," Rhodes said. "You can go on back to work now if you want to."

"I do." Sizemore jumped down off the tailgate. "Lloyd was my friend. I hope you don't have some crazy idea that I had anything to do with that in there."

"I always have to ask questions," Rhodes said. "That's my job.

I may want to talk to you again, but don't say anything to anybody about this just yet."

Sizemore didn't respond to that. He got into his truck and slammed the door.

Rhodes stepped aside, and Sizemore backed out of the parking spot, hardly looking to see if Rhodes had moved out of his way. He didn't wave good-bye to Rhodes as he drove away, but Rhodes's feelings weren't hurt.

Rhodes started to go back into the shop, but he stopped when he saw the justice of the peace drive into the parking lot.

Rhodes had met his wife, Ivy, when she was running for the office of justice of the peace. She'd lost the race, and Rhodes thought the major reason was that in Texas it was the job of the JP to make the declaration of death at the scene of a crime, auto accident, or other fatal event. Rhodes believed that at the time Ivy had run, most of the people in the county weren't ready to elect a woman to do that kind of job. Things had changed, maybe even enough so that Ivy could win if she chose to run again, but so far she hadn't mentioned giving it a try.

Gerald Elsner was the man who'd defeated Ivy. He was a former cattle rancher who'd decided he'd had enough of worrying about too much rain or too little, putting out hay and feed in the winter, wondering if beef prices would ever go up enough for him to make a decent living. He'd sold his cows, moved to town, and run for office. He still liked to wear jeans, boots, and a Stetson, and that hadn't hurt him in his political career, short as it was.

"What you got, Sheriff?" he said, getting out of his big Dodge pickup. He left his Stetson on the seat. "Something wrong with Lloyd?"

"That's for you to say," Rhodes told him and led the way into the shop.

It didn't take long for Elsner to declare that Lloyd Berry was indeed dead.

"Lloyd was a good guy," Elsner said as he and Rhodes stood outside the shop. "Can't imagine why anybody'd want to do that to him. That barbershop chorus he organized was really popular. You ever heard them?"

Rhodes said that he had.

"I love that harmony stuff," Elsner said. "I hope they don't stop singing now that Lloyd's gone."

Ruth Grady's car came into the lot.

"I guess you won't be needing me anymore," Elsner said. "You catch whoever killed Lloyd, Sheriff."

"I'll do my best," Rhodes said.

"Election's next year," Elsner said.

Rhodes thanked him for the reminder, wondering if a western-style hat would improve his popularity. Not that it would matter, since hats made Rhodes look more like Buck Benny than Roy Rogers.

"Are you thinking about the election already?" Ruth asked, having overheard Elsner's final comment.

"I'm trying not to," Rhodes said. "Seems like everybody else is, though."

"Not Lloyd Berry."

"No, Lloyd's not thinking of anything."

"We'd better see what we can find out, then," Ruth said, and they went inside.

5

▼

"YOU HAVE ANY IDEAS?" RUTH SAID AFTER THEY'D GONE OVER the scene carefully.

"Just one," Rhodes said. "I think Lloyd got into an argument with somebody. Things got out of hand, and whoever was arguing with him picked up the wrench and hit him."

"Must have been a pretty good argument," Ruth said, "considering the way it ended. But there wasn't a fight."

Rhodes agreed. The plants were all in their places, nothing knocked over other than a small ceramic pot of ivy that lay not far from Berry's head. Rhodes figured it had been on the counter and had gotten swept off when the killer grabbed the wrench. The pot had landed on the mat and was unbroken. Dirt had spilled out around the edges and onto the mat.

"It wasn't a robbery, either," Ruth said.

They'd looked in the cash register. There wasn't much money in it, but there was enough to convince them that none had been taken.

"Do you think Darrel Sizemore killed him?" Ruth asked.

"It's a possibility," Rhodes said.

"He's kind of short, don't you think?"

"You mean too short to swing that wrench up and hit Lloyd in the side of the head? I don't think so. The handle on the wrench is long enough for Darrel to swing it like a baseball bat. He's got enough reach to do the job."

"Would he have called it in after he did it?"

"Sure," Rhodes said. "Remorse can set in pretty fast."

Ruth nodded. "Maybe. What about the Rollin' Sevens?"

"What about it?"

"Do you think there's a connection?"

Rhodes thought about that for a couple of seconds before answering. "You mean Lloyd might have known something he shouldn't have?"

"Well, you never have found out who runs that place, have you?"

Rhodes had to admit that he hadn't. The space was leased from the owners of the strip center, but the signatory of the lease was merely a legal representative of whoever the real operator was. Finding that out had so far been more trouble than it had been worth. Berry's death might have changed that.

"Or it could be that he saw something," Ruth said. "One of the robberies, maybe, when he was staying here at night. He could have seen a face, gotten a license number."

"If he did," Rhodes said, "he never called it in."

"All right, but what if somebody just *thought* Berry had seen something. It might amount to the same thing."

"We'll have to keep that in mind," Rhodes said. "Anything else?"

Ruth said there wasn't, so they worked the scene, looking for anything that might be a clue. Aside from the wrench, which they tagged and bagged, they found nothing.

"There're going to be fingerprints all over this place," Ruth said, "but maybe nobody touched the wrench except Lloyd and whoever hit him. That doesn't mean we'll get any usable prints, though."

Rhodes knew that. He didn't put much stock in prints anyway, because they were no help at all unless other prints that matched could be found in some database somewhere. That wasn't often the case.

"You can dust the counter and the cash register while you're here. I'll call Hack and let him know he can send the ambulance. Then I'm going to take a look upstairs."

The wooden stairway to the second story was located on the outside of the building, in the back. Rhodes went through the plant room and out the back door to reach it after calling Hack. The paved area behind the buildings was bare except for the trash bins. A fence ran along the edge of the paving and separated the strip center from the fields beyond. There wasn't much to see. A few cows grazed about a hundred yards away, but they had no interest in Rhodes, if they even noticed him at all. He suspected that they didn't. Cows weren't among the most alert creatures he'd dealt with. Certainly not as alert as the alligator had been.

Rhodes climbed the stairs and tried the door at the top. The door was unlocked. That was no surprise. It wasn't likely that anyone would break in with Berry working downstairs.

The door opened onto a room that held a single bed, a leather recliner, and a TV set. The TV set was a new flat-screen model.

Rhodes hadn't noticed a satellite dish on the roof, but he was sure there was one. Otherwise, Berry wouldn't have had such a fancy set. A short nightstand stood by the bed. A clock and lamp sat on top of it. The bed was made and the room was clean. Rhodes looked through the nightstand. The drawers held only a TV schedule and a paperback book, something by Joe Lansdale. Rhodes remembered that someone had mentioned Lansdale to him when he was working another case, but he didn't remember what had been said. At any rate, he was sure the book wasn't a clue.

The little kitchen and bathroom were equally clean, and there was no sign that anybody had used either of them for a while. If Rhodes had been hoping for some kind of clue, it quickly became obvious that he wasn't going to find one. He went back downstairs. The ambulance was parked in front, and two men were removing Berry's body. Rhodes stood outside with Ruth and let them do their job.

"What about the next of kin?" Ruth said. "He wasn't married, was he?"

"Not now," Rhodes said. "His wife died a long time ago in a car wreck. They didn't have any kids, and he never remarried. We'll find out if he had any kin that we need to notify. You can look into that."

"The chorus will miss him."

"Darrel will tell them." Rhodes thought about his warning to Sizemore. "Maybe he already has."

The EMTs loaded Lloyd's remains into the ambulance and left.

"Who gets to do the interviews?" Ruth said.

"We both do."

"You're not going to be a sexist and ask me to take the nail salon, are you?"

"No. I'll start at Rollin' Sevens, and you can start next door at the check-cashing store. Whoever gets to the nail salon first gets to do the interviews."

Ruth thought it over. "I guess that's fair. You aren't taking Rollin' Sevens because you think there's going to be trouble, are you?"

"Not me," Rhodes said. "You know I don't like trouble."

"Right. Neither do I. Have you had any lunch?"

"No. It won't hurt me to miss it."

It wouldn't hurt him, and he'd missed a lot of lunches over the years. When he got the chance, however, Rhodes liked to sneak away and have a burger at McDonald's or the Dairy Queen. Maybe even a Blizzard with little bits of a Heath Bar mixed in. Ivy liked for him to eat healthy, and he made an effort at home, most of the time. When he was working, it was a different story.

"I had something earlier," Ruth said, "so we might as well get started."

During the time Rhodes had been there, only a few cars had come to the strip to visit the other businesses. Nobody had come to Berry's shop to see what was going on, and nobody from the other places had come out to see what was going on. Maybe they were too wrapped up in their own jobs to care, or maybe they weren't curious.

Ruth went into the check-cashing store, and Rhodes headed down to Rollin' Sevens. He felt bad about Lloyd's death. Berry had, as far as Rhodes knew, been a good citizen, never in trouble, always willing to pitch in and help out when the town needed him. Now he was gone. It was a waste and a loss, or so it seemed.

Rhodes knew well enough that sometimes in the course of an investigation, he'd uncover things that would change his picture of the people involved, and not for the better. He hoped it wouldn't be that way this time.

The sidewalk was cracked where the ground had shifted under it. A plastic cup lay next to the curb in one spot, and a white paper napkin scooted across the parking lot. A couple of cars drove past on the highway and went on by the big pond that locals called the Brickyard Tank.

No other signs of anything resembling a brickyard remained, and for that matter Rhodes didn't even know what a brickyard was. He guessed it was a place where bricks were made, and he supposed he could have asked somebody, but he'd never even thought about that. When he was a kid, what interested him was fishing, and he'd often gone to the Brickyard Tank with a cane pole and some grasshoppers that he'd caught in the tall grass nearby. He remembered clearly the time he'd caught a two-pound bass that had seemed much bigger. He didn't recall that there had ever been any alligators spotted nearby. It was too bad, Rhodes thought, that life couldn't remain that simple.

But it didn't. Now any parent who let her son go fishing at a place like that without a life jacket and a couple of adult supervisors would probably get turned over to the CPS within minutes.

Rhodes found himself standing at the front door of Rollin' Sevens. He wasn't under any illusions about the place. Although he hadn't seen anyone go into it or come out, he knew that everyone inside was well aware that he was around. If he'd been a gambler, like the people playing the eight-liners, he'd have bet ten dollars that everyone even knew that he was just about to join them. The blacked-out windows didn't matter. They knew, and they'd all be on their best behavior. There'd be no signs of anything that wasn't completely innocent. For some reason Rhodes thought of the scene in *Casablanca* where Captain Renault expressed his shock that illegal gambling was going on in Rick's Café Améri-cain.

The interior of Rollin' Sevens didn't resemble Rick's in the least. There was no piano player, no orchestra, no happy couples sitting at tables enjoying a meal. All Rhodes saw under the harsh fluorescent lighting were people, most of them over fifty, sitting on tall red stools with short backs, staring at the big video machines that looked for all the world like slots. There were no clocks visible. The players ignored Rhodes as they fed coins into the eight-liners and hoped that Lady Luck would smile on them.

Little Las Vegas, Rhodes thought.

The machines had colorful screens and names like Bonus 9, Cherry Master, and Pirates of the High Seas. On the walls above the machines, a couple of signs proclaimed that there would be A DOOR PRIZE EVERY HOUR!

The law was never simple when it came to eight-liners, but a door prize was an acceptable way to get people into the place as long as the players didn't get additional entries into the drawing according to credits they'd won on one of the machines.

When it came to prizes awarded on the machines, things got a lot more complex. As Rhodes understood the Texas Penal Code, the prizes awarded, like stuffed toys, had to be worth less than ten times the cost of a play, or five dollars, whichever was less expen-sive. The five dollars had to be awarded in coupons, which had to be redeemed inside the place of business. Some owners tried to get away with giving a five-dollar coupon to be used at Wal-Mart, so the winner could go to the store, buy a pack of gum, and put the rest of the money in his or her pocket. That was illegal. Redeeming a coupon for a fuzzy animal at the place you'd won it, however, was acceptable.

Rhodes thought it was all too complicated and open to interpretation. It led to all sorts of clever attempts to get around the law, some of which were probably going on right in front of him, even though he was unable to spot them.

He stood in front of the closed door. Everyone continued to ignore him. He listened to the soft *bings* and *bongs* of the machines, the coins sliding into the slots, the murmur of people talking to themselves and their neighbors. After a minute or so, a door opened in the back of the room, and a man came out. He crossed the floor and said, "Afternoon, Sheriff. I'm Guy Wilks. What can we do for you?"

Rhodes wasn't sure where the *we* came from, since Wilks didn't have anyone with him. Wilks wore dark blue jeans that looked new, a white shirt, and white canvas shoes. His thick black hair was combed straight back from his forehead, which had a pasty pallor like a frog's belly. Rhodes figured Wilks didn't get outside much during the daylight hours, and he looked as if he'd had more than one mug shot made in his lifetime.

"We need to have a talk," Rhodes said.

Wilks's white forehead wrinkled. "What about?"

"Another tenant of this center."

"I can't help you there. I don't know any of them. I keep pretty much to myself. Running this business is all I care about. I got to be on top of everything, be sure everything's on the up-and-up, you know?" He grinned. "In case the law ever decides to drop in on me."

He continued to smile to show that he was just kidding. Rhodes didn't smile in return.

"Come on, Sheriff," Wilks said. "Lighten up."

"One of the other tenants has been murdered," Rhodes said.

Wilks stopped smiling. "I guess that's not so funny. Come on back to the office."

He turned, and Rhodes followed him, feeling as if everyone in the place turned to watch as he passed by them. He could almost feel their gazes boring little holes in the back of his shirt. Rhodes wondered if they noticed how his hair was thinning out on the crown of his head. A hat like Elsner's would make him look funny, he thought, but it would at least cover the incipient bald spot.

Beside the doorway of the office stood a wire bin about four feet tall. It was full of small stuffed animals: cats, dogs, bears. Rhodes knew he was supposed to believe that everyone in Rollin' Sevens had a lifelong dream of going home with several of the animals in the backseat of his car, but somehow he couldn't quite picture it.

"Those are the prizes?" he said.

"You bet," Wilks said without turning around. "People love 'em. It's like those Beanie Babies were a few years ago, I guess. They collect 'em."

"Right," Rhodes said.

Wilks stood aside and let Rhodes pass by him. Then he closed the office door.

"You don't believe me?" he said.

"I believe you. That's not why I'm here anyway."

"Yeah. You said something about a murder."

Wilks moved around Rhodes and sat behind his desk, an old oak model that looked as if it had come from a thrift shop. The only things on it were a computer monitor and keyboard. There were a couple of other doors, one in the back of the office and one in the wall to Rhodes's right.

"That's right," Rhodes said. "Lloyd Berry."

"Runs the florist shop," Wilks said, showing nothing. Rhodes thought he'd be a good poker player. "Who killed him?"

"That's what I'd like to find out."

"Well, I can't tell you. How'd it happen?"

"I can't go into details right now."

"Secret lawman stuff, huh? Have a seat, Sheriff. You look tired."

The only chair other than the one Wilks sat in was a wooden folding chair. Rhodes hadn't seen one of those in a while. He didn't feel tired, but he sat down and took his reading glasses from his shirt pocket. Then he got out a notepad and a ballpoint pen.

"You knew Berry?" he said.

"I knew who he was. Spoke to him a time or two, but never went in his shop. He ate lunch sometimes at Max's Place. I go there now and then."

Max Schwartz hadn't gone in for originality in renaming the restaurant after he took it over. He'd told Rhodes that he might change the name when he decided what kind of restaurant it was going to be, but so far he hadn't. What he'd decided on as a specialty was barbecue. It would be hard to compete in that market, Rhodes thought, but Max was going for a more upscale customer than the other two barbecue spots in town, so it might work out for him.

"Know anybody who had it in for Berry?" Rhodes said.

"Sure, everybody's heard about it."

"Not me," Rhodes said.

"I meant everybody around here. Maybe word hasn't gotten out to town yet."

"Tell me who it is," Rhodes said.

Wilks leaned forward. The desk chair squealed.

"Somebody named Cecil Marsh," Wilks said.

6

▼

RHODES HADN'T EXPECTED TO HEAR THAT NAME. HE'D PLANNED to talk to Marsh about the alligator, so this would give them another topic of discussion.

"What about Marsh?" he said, jotting in his notebook.

"It's a pretty good story," Wilks said. He leaned back in the chair, which squealed again. "You know how a quartet from that barbershop chorus goes out every year on Valentine's Day and sings to people's sweethearts?"

Rhodes nodded. He'd had the quartet sing for Ivy. He knew he wasn't very romantic, so it was something different for him. He'd thought she'd like it, and he'd been right. The quartet not only sang a couple of songs but also gave her a rose and a card.

"You have to pay," Wilks said, "but I hear it's worth it."

"It is," Rhodes said. "What does it have to do with Cecil Marsh and Lloyd Berry?"

"Well, Marsh paid the quartet to sing to somebody, but it wasn't his wife. He said it was just a friend, and maybe it was. Anyway, Berry told Marsh they'd do it on the q.t., but apparently he let the cat out of the bag, and Marsh's wife found out. Marsh got into quite a screaming match with Berry at the shop yesterday."

"You were there?"

"I heard about it from Kasey down at the Check-In."

That was the check-cashing place. Rhodes figured Ruth would be getting all the firsthand information if Kasey was on duty, so he moved on.

"Who did Marsh have the quartet sing for?"

"I didn't hear that part of the story. Sure wasn't his wife, though."

Marsh was more careless than Rhodes would have guessed, and he trusted his friends more than he should have. Or maybe Berry hadn't been his friend.

"Did Lloyd ever come down here and try the machines?" Rhodes asked.

"I just told you the only times I ever saw him were at Max's Place."

"That's not exactly what you said."

"Well, it's what I meant."

Rhodes made a note. "So he's never been here."

"I didn't say that. I said I never saw him here. I'm not here twenty-four hours a day, and I don't stand here looking at people all the time when I'm here, either."

"Do you know if Lloyd ever witnessed any robberies here?"

"We haven't had any robberies."

"Not inside, maybe, but there have been some outside. The department's investigated them."

"I don't know what Berry saw or didn't see. I told you I only spoke to him a couple of times. And I don't keep up with what goes on outside. That's not in my job description."

He'd kept up with the gossip on Berry and Marsh, but there was no need to mention the contradiction to him, Rhodes thought. He talked to Wilks for another ten minutes but got no further information. He stood up, tucked his notebook and pen back in his pocket, and thanked Wilks for his time.

"If you think of anything that might help me out," Rhodes said, "I'd appreciate a call."

Wilks stood, too. "Sure, anytime I can help, I'll let you know."

Wilks tried to sound as if he meant it, but Rhodes knew Wilks wouldn't call him even if the murderer walked into Rollin' Sevens and confessed. He opened the door and let himself out of the office.

He was surprised to see that hardly anyone was left in the gambling room. People must have thought he'd start taking names when he came out of the office.

He looked around. All three people still in the room were men, and Rhodes knew all of them. Lance and Hugh Eccles were cousins, but they looked enough alike to be brothers, with their red hair that stuck out from under their Astros caps, their freckled faces, and their broad shoulders.

The third man was Travis Fair, and he was even bigger than the cousins. All three were gypsy truckers. Hugh and Lance owned their rig together, and Travis had one of his own. Rhodes assumed they were relaxing on one of their days at home by doing a little gambling.

The problem was, they didn't look relaxed.

"Hey, fellas," Rhodes said as he started across the room.

Lance and Hugh moved in front of him. Travis stayed where he was, off to the side.

"What's the problem, Sheriff?" Hugh said.

"Nothing about gambling," Rhodes said. "You don't have anything to worry about."

"We weren't worried. Were we, Lance."

"No," Lance said. He grinned at his cousin. "We weren't worried."

They might not have been worried, but they weren't moving, either.

"You know, we don't do anything wrong in here," Hugh said. "Ain't that right, Lance?"

"That's right," Lance said.

Travis didn't say anything. He didn't move. He didn't grin. He just stood and watched.

"It's like family here," Hugh said. "All of us get together and have a little fun, not bothering anybody, not hurting a thing. Just having a nice sociable time. I can't see why the law doesn't allow that."

"It does allow it," Rhodes said. "As long as that's all that's going on."

"Well, then, you ought not to come here and scare folks off," Hugh said. "It's not right. It's not good for the business. Some of those folks you scared might not ever come back."

Rhodes wondered if Hugh had been hired as the new PR man for Rollin' Sevens or if he was upset about something.

"You work here?" Rhodes said.

"That's pretty funny, Sheriff. Right, Lance?"

"Right," Lance said, but he wasn't laughing.

Neither was Travis, who might as well have been a statue for all the moving or talking he'd done so far.

"Well?" Rhodes said. "Do you work here or not?"

"No," Hugh said. "I don't work here. I got my own rig that I hire out and drive. I bet you knew that, Sheriff. I just come here on my time off. But I don't like it when you chase away my friends."

Rhodes could have said that he hadn't chased anyone away, but it would have been like talking to one of the video machines. Hugh took a step toward him.

"You don't want to start any trouble, Hugh," Rhodes said.

"Trouble? I'm not starting any trouble. I'm just relaxing in the Rollin' Sevens, or I was until you came along. You sure messed up my day, Sheriff."

Rhodes wondered if Wilks was watching from his office. If he was, he wouldn't be making any calls for help. He was probably enjoying the show.

"If you'd take off your badge," Hugh said, "Lance and I could show you a thing or two about having a good time."

Rhodes's badge holder was on his belt, and he had no intention of taking it off, not that he was averse to having a good time.

"What about Travis?" he said. "He doesn't look like he's having much fun."

"Travis? He won't bother you. He's just here to watch. You gonna take off the badge?"

"No," Rhodes said. "I'm not."

Hugh gave him a shocked look. "I never took you for a sissy, Sheriff."

"I'm sorry if I've destroyed your illusions," Rhodes said.

"Huh?"

"Never mind. If you'll get out of my way, I'll leave and forget you threatened me."

"Now hang on a second," Hugh said. "I don't know what you're talking about. I never made any threats. I asked politely, and you wouldn't go along with me. So now I'll have to try something else. Take his badge off him, Lance. That way I can do what needs doing."

For a second Rhodes didn't think Lance would obey, but then the big man took a step forward and reached out as if to grab the badge off Rhodes's belt.

Rhodes took hold of Lance's wrist and pulled. Lance had already started forward and was too surprised to resist. So Rhodes used the man's momentum and yanked him right on past before letting go.

Hugh didn't seem to know what to do next, so Rhodes turned around and put his foot on Lance's rear. He gave the redhead a shove that sent him stumbling toward the back of the room, then spun back to face Hugh, who had made up his mind to take a roundhouse swing.

Rhodes knocked Hugh's arm away with his left and began a turn as he grabbed the front of Hugh's shirt in his right hand. He kept on turning and threw Hugh in the same direction Lance had been traveling.

Lance had managed to stop himself before he hit the wire bin of stuffed animals, but as he got himself steadied, Hugh crashed into him. The cousins did a clumsy little belly-to-back dance and then hit the bin. It collapsed under their weight, and they fell to the floor with stuffed animals all around.

Rhodes looked over at Travis, who still hadn't moved. But now he was grinning.

"I hope you enjoyed the show," Rhodes said.

Travis gave a fractional nod. "It was better than Bugs Bunny and Elmer Fudd."

He and Rhodes watched the cousins flail around in the pile of stuffed animals before finally getting back to their feet. There was no sign of Wilks. The door to the back room remained closed. Maybe Wilks was playing solitaire on his computer or had gone out into the alley for a smoke. Or maybe he was hoping Hugh would break Rhodes's nose or some other part of his anatomy.

"Are you gonna arrest anybody?" Travis said. "You could charge 'em with assault on innocent animals."

"I don't have time to fool with them," Rhodes said. "Try to keep them out of trouble."

"I'll try, but it's not easy."

Hugh and Lance looked at their shoes, or maybe at the stuffed animals at their feet, and avoided Rhodes's eyes.

"You two should know better than to pick a fight with a trained lawman," Rhodes said. "Don't do it again. Next time I might have to shoot you."

Hugh's head jerked up. "You wouldn't do that, would you?"

"I might," Rhodes said.

His Dirty Harry act was working better than he'd expected. He decided to leave while he was ahead, without even asking Hugh if he felt lucky. Try as he might, though, he couldn't resist at least one final gesture. He pointed his finger at Hugh and snapped down his thumb.

"Bang," he said.

Hugh gratified him by flinching. Rhodes took a last look at the signs advertising the door prizes, turned, and went outside, where he ran smack dab into the blonde who was standing there and almost knocked her flat.

7

▼

RHODES REACHED OUT AND GRABBED HER ARM, HOLDING ON while she steadied herself.

"You sure are in a big hurry, Sheriff," she said.

"Sorry about that," Rhodes said. "What are you doing here?"

"I think you know," she said.

She was right. He did know. She was Jennifer Loam, a reporter for the *Clearview Herald*. The truth of the matter was that she was *the* reporter, the only one the paper had, and a good one besides. Rhodes expected her to leave Clearview any day and go to work for a bigger paper in a bigger town. So far she'd surprised him by staying. That was good for the paper, and it was good for the town. Rhodes wasn't sure how good it was for his department, though. She was so on the ball that she got the news about crimes almost as fast as he did, and as soon as she got the news, she was on the scene.

"Well?" Jennifer said.

"Well, what?"

"Well, why don't you tell me why I'm here?"

"Lloyd Berry," Rhodes said. "And I don't have any comment."

"What about 'The Sheriff's Department is on the case, and an early arrest is expected at any moment'?"

Rhodes had never said anything like that in his life.

"You know better," he said.

Jennifer smiled. "And you know you're going to have to tell me something sooner or later. I'm going to interview the people in this shopping center first, though. I have a feeling they'll have more to say than you will."

Rhodes looked toward the other end of the center. He didn't see Ruth, who was probably in the nail salon by now.

"Just don't get in our way," he said, feeling a little like he'd suddenly become Hugh Eccles.

"Now, Sheriff, you know me better than that."

"I know you, all right," Rhodes said. "You can start down there at the Check-In, unless you'd like to see what you can get out of Mr. Wilks and his eight-liners."

"I don't think anybody in charge of illegal gambling would want to talk to a reporter."

"It's legal gambling," Rhodes said. "As far as I can tell. That's something you could investigate."

"I might just do that, but I think the murder's more important right now. I'll see you later."

She started toward the other end of the center, and Rhodes went into Tom's TomToms.

Tom was Tom Fulton, a cheerful soul, always smiling. Rhodes wondered if he might not be entirely *too* cheerful. Surely nobody could be that chipper all the time. Take the name of his business.

Fulton sold other kinds of GPS receivers besides TomToms, but Tom's Garmins wouldn't have had the same chipper ring to it. Fulton also sold other electronic gadgets, mainly cell phones. Tom's Cells would have been a terrible name, Rhodes thought. It sounded like the name of a private jail.

"Need to find out where you are?" Fulton asked when Rhodes entered. "Just a little GPS joke, Sheriff. How are you?"

Rhodes said he was fine and asked if Fulton had heard about the death of Lloyd Berry.

Fulton appeared surprised, and his smile turned into a look of sad concern. "Lloyd's dead? What happened?"

Rhodes gave him the short version and asked the same questions he'd asked Wilks. Fulton said he'd heard about the argument between Marsh and Berry from Kasey at the Check-In but hadn't thought it amounted to much. "I passed it off as a little tiff between friends," he said. "They probably got over it in ten minutes."

Rhodes doubted Marsh's wife would have gotten over it so easily, but he didn't tell Fulton that theory. After all, Fulton might even be right. Rhodes would wait until he'd talked to Marsh and his wife to decide.

"How well did you know Lloyd?" Rhodes said.

"Just the way you know anybody else in the shops here. He came by now and then, but we weren't what you could call friends. Just two guys who said hey when we saw each other. He hadn't been by lately."

While Fulton appeared much more willing to help Rhodes than Wilks had been, he didn't come up with any more useful information.

Rhodes had one final question for him. "What about that door prize deal you have going with Rollin' Sevens?"

The door prize being offered on the signs in the gambling room was a free rental of a GPS receiver, and Rhodes wondered about the connection.

Fulton had an explanation ready, as if he'd been expecting the question.

"Good publicity for both of us," he said. "People get to try out a GPS for free, and if they like it, maybe they'll buy one. So Wilks has his door prize, and maybe I get some new customers."

"I thought everybody in Blacklin County knew where everything was."

"Not everybody knows the back roads around here like you do, Sheriff. Besides, people don't use these things just to find out where the roads go or where the Dairy Queen is."

Fulton picked up a small Garmin from the counter and tapped it with his finger. He turned it so that Rhodes could look at the screen.

"See, here we are right here, but what if we wanted to find something that was hidden around here somewhere?"

"Something hidden?" Rhodes said. "Like what?"

"Could be anything. Likely nothing worth anything. More like a prize in a box of Cracker Jacks. The only value would be that you'd get to say you found it."

Rhodes felt as if he'd missed part of the conversation somehow.

"I'm talking about geocaching," Fulton said. "You've heard about it, haven't you?"

"Vaguely," Rhodes said.

"There are Web sites for geocaches all over the place. Last I heard, nearly half a million caches were registered. Lots of people like looking for stuff."

"Hiding it, too, I guess."

"That's right, and they all need something to locate the caches with. That's my business."

"So there are things hidden in this county?"

"Plenty. I don't know for sure about the county itself, but there are close to five thousand caches within a hundred miles of where we're standing. That's at last count. Could be more or less now. I'd guess more."

Somehow, Rhodes thought, the latest fads were getting way ahead of him.

"So you can see why the door prize thing is a good idea," Fulton said. "Heck, I'd give anybody who walked in a free trial if they asked for one, but this way Wilks gets to give a prize that's not worth much, and I get a customer or two. I hope."

"So it's Wilks who runs Rollin' Sevens?"

"I don't know anything about that. He's just the one I deal with."

Rhodes talked to Fulton a bit longer before leaving. He wondered as he did why Jennifer Loam didn't do a story on geocaching. It would be more uplifting than one about the murder of Lloyd Berry.

Ruth Grady came out of the nail salon just as Rhodes left Tom's.

"Want to compare notes?" she said.

"Sure. But let's do it in the courthouse. Jennifer Loam's here snooping around."

"Why not go to the jail?"

"That's the first place she'll look for me," Rhodes said. "I'd rather not talk to her any more for a while."

"All right. I'll meet you at the courthouse. Hack and Lawton won't like it, though. They don't want to be out of the loop."

Rhodes grinned. "All the more reason to talk it over at the courthouse instead of the jail."

Rhodes's official office was in the county courthouse, but he rarely used it. Jennifer Loam had been there, but it wasn't the first place she'd look for him. It was much more private than the jail, and it was where Rhodes went when he wanted a little time away from people. Besides, there was the additional attraction of a Dr Pepper machine, and even if the Dr Pepper was in plastic bottles and didn't have real sugar in it, it was better than no Dr Pepper at all.

Rhodes bought himself a package of bright orange peanut butter and cheese crackers from the vending machine as well, to make up for missing lunch. He offered to buy some for Ruth, but she said she didn't want anything.

"I'm watching my weight," she said, and Rhodes wondered if the attentions of Seepy Benton had anything to do with that.

They went into the office. Rhodes sat behind the desk and propped up his feet; Ruth took one of the other chairs. While he drank his Dr Pepper and ate the crackers, she told him what she'd found out.

It didn't amount to much more than he'd already learned. Kasey Yardley from the Check-In had been an eyewitness to the argument between Berry and Marsh, and she'd spread the word up and down the center. Tran Phuong at the nail salon had heard about it from Kasey, just as Tom Fulton had.

It all added up to nothing: Nobody knew anything about Berry having any enemies, nobody could imagine why he'd been killed, nobody had seen anything at all, not even Kasey, who said she might have been reading a magazine when Berry was killed but that whatever she was doing, she sure hadn't seen anybody go in or come out of the floral shop.

"Typical," Rhodes said.

He crumpled the cellophane paper that had held the crackers, scattering little orange crumbs all over his desk. He threw the paper into the wastebasket under the desk, then pulled the wastebasket out and brushed the crumbs into it.

"Nobody ever sees anything," Rhodes continued. "You'd think that just once in a while, maybe one time out of a thousand, somebody would have a description and a license number."

"Yes, it's funny how that never happens," Ruth said.

The thing was that it did happen now and then—and it should have happened in the case of Lloyd's murder. Rhodes wondered how someone got into and out of the shopping center without anybody noticing. It was possible, but it didn't seem likely.

"How is it that Kasey overheard the argument yesterday but not today?" Rhodes said.

"She told me that she'd gone outside for a cigarette. She's not allowed to smoke inside the store. Anyway, she was out on the walk in front and heard the yelling. Naturally she listened."

"Just our luck she was inside when the fight happened today. We need a witness."

"We catch most of the bad guys," Ruth said. "Even if we don't always get much help."

"Most of them," Rhodes said. "Not all, though."

"Nobody's perfect. Anyway, maybe a witness will turn up."

Rhodes didn't think so. Customers came and went to the center, and the people in the other shops could see arrivals and departures. It was odd that nobody had seen whoever went into Lloyd's, but Rhodes supposed it was possible that everyone was otherwise occupied, as unlikely as that appeared.

"I didn't know Lloyd Berry," Ruth said. "He seems to have been a nice enough guy, according to the people I talked to. Why would he squeal on his friend?"

"I'll ask Cecil Marsh about that," Rhodes said. "And about that alligator, too."

"You think he had something to do with the alligator?"

"I'm not sure. Maybe Lloyd was on the wrong side of the fence when it came to the chicken question."

"Nobody would kill somebody over anything as silly as chickens," Ruth said.

"These days," Rhodes said, "you never can tell."

Ruth thought it over. "You could be right. Marsh must be pretty contentious. He and Royce Weeks have been going at it for a long time."

"Longer than I like to think about."

"But they haven't killed each other. They've never even had a real fight, have they?"

Rhodes hadn't thought about that, but he realized that Ruth had made a good point. As vocal as the two men were, and as often as they'd engaged in arguments, name-calling, and threatened lawsuits, neither had ever laid a hand on the other. They even sang together in the chorus without disrupting the practices.

"You're right," Rhodes said.

He knew that didn't really mean much, however. Whoever had killed Berry seemed to have acted in a single instant of intense anger. Marsh might finally have snapped. On the other hand, Rhodes might be wrong about the way things had happened. It was too soon to know.

Rhodes thought about Berry's attempt to get him to join the chorus. Weeks and Marsh might have been getting along, but had Berry felt threatened by Marsh? That seemed likely enough, given the incident with the quartet.

"So do you think he did it?" Ruth said. "Marsh?"

"It's way too early to start forming opinions. You don't want to let some preconceived notion get in the way of the facts."

"That's pretty good. Should I write it in my crimefighter's notebook?"

Rhodes didn't mind being made fun of. He said, "It's good information, all right. I think I stole it from Sherlock Holmes."

"When are you going to talk to Marsh?"

Rhodes swung his feet off the desk. "Right now seems like a good time. I hope I can get to him before Jennifer Loam does."

"Good luck with that," Ruth said.

8

▼

FINDING CECIL MARSH WASN'T NECESSARILY GOING TO BE EASY. Marsh was a handyman, and a good one. He did painting, both inside and out, light carpentry, and Sheetrock repair. He also built fences and even did a little concrete work. A man of his abilities was always in demand, not just in Clearview but all over the county, and he was likely to be anywhere.

About the only way to locate him would be to ask his wife where he was working that day. Since Rhodes wanted to talk to her anyway, he drove to Marsh's house, which was located in one of Clearview's older neighborhoods but one in which the homes had been taken better care of than in some areas.

Rhodes had heard people say that a handyman's house was often in bad repair because the owner was so busy fixing things for other people that he rarely had time to do anything around his own property. If that was generally true, the Marsh house was an exception. It was a white frame structure with fresh paint, a neatly trimmed yard, and a roof with shingles that couldn't have been more than a couple of years old. The shrubs on the property line, the ones that had started the Marsh-Weeks feud, were still thriving. Rhodes noticed that they were carefully trimmed so as not to extend onto Weeks's property next door.

Rhodes parked on the street and went up the walk to the front door. There was no doorbell, so he knocked on the door frame.

In a couple of seconds, Faye Lynn Marsh opened the door. She was a stout woman with dyed black hair and a pretty face that was just starting to show signs of aging at the corners of her mouth and eyes.

"What's Royce Weeks done now?" she said.

Rhodes wasn't surprised by the question. The only times he'd ever been to the house before had been to deal with the feuding neighbors.

"It's not Royce," he said. "It's something different this time."

"What is it, then?"

"We should probably talk about it inside."

"You're right." She stuck her head out the door and looked at the house next door. "That Royce Weeks is a snoop, and you never know what he'll say or do. Come on in, Sheriff."

Faye Lynn took him into the small living room, where he sat on an old sofa with a coffee table in front of it. A copy of *Southern Living* lay on the table beside a copy of the *Harmonizer* and an oversized yellow candle. Some barbershop quartet was on the *Harmonizer* cover, but Rhodes didn't know any of them. Faye Lynn sat across from Rhodes in a pink swivel rocker. She didn't light the candle.

"If it's not about that Weeks, it must be about Lindy Gomez," she said. "That's it, isn't it."

"I'm not sure," Rhodes said. "It does have to do with the quartet."

"It's Lindy, then. Cecil says it was all just a joke, and I'm sure he's telling the truth."

"A joke?"

"That's right, a joke, and I'll tell you who was behind it. Royce Weeks, that's who."

Rhodes not only didn't get the joke, he didn't know what was going on.

"You should probably explain the whole thing to me," he said. "Just to be sure I know what really happened."

"All right, I will. Cecil never told the quartet to go sing to that Gomez woman, and he never paid them their money. Somebody else did, and used Cecil's name. It was that Royce Weeks who was behind it, you can count on it."

At least now Rhodes knew the recipient of the singing valentine. That was progress of a sort.

"Why would Royce do a thing like that?" Rhodes asked.

"To get back at Cecil, that's why. Cecil always gets the best of him, and he can't stand it. So he saw this was a way to get back at him."

Rhodes saw a lot of things wrong with that theory. For one, how could Weeks have known that Berry would tell anybody that Cecil had paid the quartet to sing to Lindy Gomez? Of course, he was in the quartet, so if no one in the group had let the information slip, Weeks could have put the word out himself. Even at that, however, there had to be some connection between Marsh and Gomez.

"Cecil did know Lindy Gomez, didn't he?" Rhodes said.

Faye Lynn made a face. "Everybody knows her. Her picture's in the paper just about every week."

That was true, along with an article touting the accomplishments of the students at Clearview Elementary School. Gomez, the new principal, was unmarried and one of the town's most eligible young women.

"I didn't mean he'd read about her in the paper," Rhodes said. He thought over what he was going to say. "I mean he must have known her well enough to make the joke work."

"You might say that. They weren't friends or anything. When she moved to town last fall, Cecil did some work at her house. That's all there was to that."

She crossed her arms for emphasis, but Rhodes wasn't convinced she knew the whole story. He decided it was time to change the subject before he got Cecil in any more trouble with his wife.

"Have you been here all day?" he said.

"Me? Yes. Why?"

"Somebody visited Lloyd Berry today. Somebody who must have been pretty angry with him."

"Well, it wasn't me. Cecil blessed him out yesterday, though. He told me all about it. He said that Lloyd apologized for having said anything, and he admitted that Cecil might not have been the one who paid the quartet to sing for that Gomez woman."

"Did he say who paid them?"

"It was Royce Weeks."

"Did Lloyd say that?"

"Not in so many words, but he did say he got the money in a letter with the instructions about singing to her."

At last a detail Rhodes hadn't known about. It could even mean that Faye Lynn was right about Weeks.

"Where's Cecil working today?" Rhodes said.

"Over in Obert. He's helping somebody put in a new driveway."

"Who?"

"Chap Morris, I think he said."

Rhodes knew Morris, and he could check on the new driveway if it became necessary. Of course, Cecil could easily have stopped off at Lloyd's shop before he went to Obert. It would have been only a half mile or so out of his way.

"Why are you so interested in Lloyd Berry, anyway?" Faye Lynn said.

"Somebody killed him," Rhodes said.

Faye Lynn stared at him. "He's dead?"

"That's right."

"I'm sorry to hear it." She sounded stunned, and Rhodes thought she might cry. "You mean you're asking me these questions because you think I killed him? Or Cecil did?"

"It's just my job," Rhodes said. "Something I have to do whether I like it or not."

Faye Lynn brushed at her eyes with the back of her hand. "I think you like it," she said.

Rhodes didn't see any point in arguing, so he changed the subject. "Did Cecil ever say anything to you about an alligator?"

"An alligator?" Faye Lynn was incredulous. "What are you talking about?"

"We got a call about an alligator today. It was in a ditch right across from that property you own out on the county road."

"Who called you? It must have been that Royce Weeks. He's always got something to complain about."

"Royce doesn't have anything to do with this," Rhodes said, hoping he was telling the truth. They still hadn't established the identity of the random chicken.

"It's those chickens of his," Faye Lynn said. "The rooster starts up before daylight, and the hens cluck around all day. They're noisy and nasty, and they stink. Royce could buy his eggs at the Wal-Mart like the rest of us. Chickens don't have any place inside the city limits."

"I don't have anything to do with that," Rhodes said. "It's up to the city council to decide if chickens can be kept in town."

"Ha," Faye Lynn said. "You can't ever get those people to take a stand on anything."

"About the alligator," Rhodes said.

"No, Cecil never said anything to me about any alligator. He wouldn't know an alligator if it came up and bit him. That's the silliest thing I ever heard. Well, not as silly as you thinking he killed Lloyd Berry, but it's still mighty silly all the same. If anybody killed Lloyd, it was that Royce Weeks."

"What makes you think that?"

"Because that's the kind of person he is."

"Would he have a reason?"

"He wouldn't need one."

Faye Lynn stood up, and it was plain that she expected Rhodes to do so as well. He didn't disappoint her.

"Thanks for the tip," Rhodes said. "I'll talk to Royce for sure. I still want to talk to Cecil, too. You can tell him that for me if he gets home before I have a chance."

"You can bet I'll tell him. He won't be any too happy with Royce Weeks when he hears it, either."

Everything led back to Royce Weeks as far as she was concerned. Rhodes wondered if the feud was really between Royce and Cecil after all. Maybe Faye Lynn was behind the whole thing and had been all the time.

After he left the Marsh house, Rhodes went right next door. He thought Royce Weeks would be at home. He usually was. He'd worked in retail for years, selling shoes and men's clothing at a downtown department store until the Wal-Mart had put the store out of business. Then he'd gone into business for himself, selling things on eBay. Rhodes wasn't sure just where Royce got the things he sold, or even what the things were, but he seemed to be making money from them.

Royce's house wasn't as well kept as Marsh's was, and the chickens didn't help the appearance of the property any. They were in a big pen in the backyard, and, sure enough, some White Leghorn hens were walking around, clucking and pecking at the ground. Rhodes didn't see a rooster.

Weeks had a doorbell, so Rhodes rang it. Weeks took longer to get to the door than Faye Lynn had, but he didn't look any happier to see Rhodes than she had been.

"What's that damn Marsh woman complaining about this time?" Weeks said.

Weeks had a deep voice, almost as deep as Darrel Sizemore's. Rhodes had heard that some of the best barbershop tenors were basses. That was because the tenor part was often sung in falsetto, and a lot of basses had just the right falsetto touch for the parts.

Weeks was tall and skinny with a complexion that rivaled Guy Wilks's for pallor. His thin gray hair straggled across the top of his head, and his mouth turned down at the corners.

"She's not complaining," Rhodes said, which wasn't strictly true but accurate enough for the situation. "This is about Lloyd Berry."

"Lloyd's been complaining? He doesn't even live around here."

"Lloyd's not complaining," Rhodes said. "He's not doing anything right now. If you'll invite me in, I'll tell you about it."

Weeks backed away from the door, which Rhodes took as an invitation. He went inside.

It didn't take Rhodes long to figure out what Weeks was selling on eBay. After all, he was a trained lawman.

The room was full of books, books on shelves, books on tables, books on the floor. Books on the computer desk and even in the chairs.

Some of the books were paperbacks that looked like the ones that Clyde Ballinger, a local funeral director, liked to read. They had garish covers and titles like *Bad Ronald, Naked Fury,* and *Hell Is a City.* Rhodes recalled that Ballinger had mentioned something about the old books having disappeared from garage sales and flea markets, where Ballinger had once been able to buy them for nickels and dimes.

"Those are worth plenty," Weeks said when Rhodes picked up the copy of *Bad Ronald.* "Be careful with them. They're old and fragile."

"Where do you find them?" Rhodes asked.

"Everywhere," Weeks said, not giving anything away.

Rhodes set the book back on the table where he'd found it and picked up a hardback by someone named Richard Sale. *Lazarus #7.*

"You really shouldn't handle those," Weeks said. "You might damage one and cost me some money."

"I didn't realize books like that were worth so much," Rhodes said.

"You'd be surprised. And the sexy ones are worth even more."

Rhodes looked around, wondering where the sexy ones were.

"I don't have any of them," Weeks said. "They're hard to find around here. I don't think you came to discuss literature with me, though. You mentioned Lloyd. He probably hasn't read a book in his life."

"Too late now, then," Rhodes said.

"What does that mean?"

"It means he's dead. Somebody killed him."

Weeks didn't say anything until he'd cleared some books off a chair and put them on a table.

"You might want to sit down," he told Rhodes.

Rhodes didn't see any other vacant chairs in the room. "What about you?"

Weeks pulled out the chair from the computer desk. It didn't have any books on it, and Weeks sat down. Rhodes went to the cleared chair, careful to avoid stepping on the paperback copy of *Six Deadly Dames* that lay on the floor nearby.

When they were seated, Weeks said, "So when are you going to arrest Cecil?"

"Why should I arrest him?" Rhodes said.

"Because," Weeks said, "he killed Lloyd."

9

▼

WEEKS, OF COURSE, HAD NO PROOF OF HIS ACCUSATION, BUT HE insisted that Marsh had to be guilty.

"Cecil was really mad that Lloyd let it slip about the singing valentine for Lindy Gomez. He and Faye Lynn had a big fight about it."

"How do you know about that?" Rhodes asked.

Weeks gave Rhodes a quizzical look. "Didn't you happen to notice how close our houses are? I hear a lot of things."

Rhodes thought that Weeks probably made it a point to listen in whenever he could. He hadn't looked at all surprised to see Rhodes at his door, and he'd known Rhodes had already been to the Marsh house.

"Mrs. Marsh thinks you might have had a reason to kill Lloyd," Rhodes said.

Weeks looked like a man who'd just been poked in the back

with a sharp stick. "The woman hates me. Anybody can see that. Surely you didn't believe her."

"Why would she hate you?"

Weeks shook his head and gave a smile that was probably supposed to look innocent. "I don't have any idea," Weeks said. "I've tried to be a good neighbor to her and Cecil, Lord knows, I've tried. But they just never seem to let up with their petty complaints."

Rhodes didn't feel like rehashing the history of the feud or reminding Weeks of his own recollection about who'd started the feuding.

"It couldn't be that you're the one who posed as Cecil and paid for the quartet to sing to Lindy Gomez, I guess."

Weeks's eyes widened. "That's crazy. Why would I do a thing like that?"

"You don't deny that you and Marsh have been feuding for years, do you?"

"No, but that's his fault. I wouldn't pull a stunt like that on him. The only problem we have right now is that he doesn't like my chickens."

"Lots of people object to having chickens in town."

"I don't see why. They're no worse than cats or dogs, and they're a whole lot more useful."

Rhodes couldn't see anything to be gained by getting into that argument.

"I heard that Lloyd and Darrel Sizemore were having some problems," he said.

Weeks appeared glad to change the subject. "That's right. Darrel doesn't like it that Lloyd's spending money on music. There's a legal angle there, you know."

Rhodes didn't know, so he asked what it was.

"It's illegal to copy sheet music. You're denying the writers their royalties. You're supposed to buy the music for whatever you sing. Darrel is one of those 'information is free' types, though. He said the music belonged to everybody and that we didn't have enough money in the treasury to be buying sheet music. Lloyd didn't call him a thief, but he came close to it."

Darrel hadn't mentioned that. Rhodes wondered what Lloyd would have thought of someone who sold used books on eBay, but he didn't ask.

"When did Lloyd and Darrel have that argument?" he said.

"At last week's practice. Which reminds me. Today is Tuesday, right?"

Rhodes agreed that it was.

"So our practice is tonight. I wonder what will happen. If Lloyd's dead, who's going to be our director?"

So far, nobody Rhodes had talked to seemed too concerned about Lloyd's death. Nobody in the strip center had known him very well, and his supposed friend, Weeks, was worried only about who was going to take his place as director. Faye Lynn Marsh had hardly cared, except as the death might affect her husband. Darrel Sizemore had been bothered, but more because he'd found the body than because of any feeling for Lloyd.

"Did Lloyd have any close friends?" he said.

"I don't know. He was the director of the chorus and a good singer, so we all respected him. I'm not sure anybody really liked him, though. Didn't anybody see who killed him?"

"So far nobody's admitted it," Rhodes said. "Somebody could turn up, though, when the news gets around town."

"That won't take long."

Rhodes agreed. Changing the subject again, he asked Weeks if he'd lost any chickens lately.

"I've been wondering if you'd get around to that," Weeks said. "I got a call about it from Hack this morning. What's going on?"

Rhodes didn't like to lie, but now and then he had to stretch the truth a little.

"We've had some complaints about chickens wandering around loose. We thought maybe you'd lost some."

"Complaints? From Marsh?"

"No," Rhodes said. "Not from either of the Marshes."

"Well, I can tell you that none of my chickens are missing. They can't get out of the pen. I've clipped their wings, so there's no way for them to get loose. And I haven't seen any chickens in town. That's probably just a rumor started by people like the Marshes. If you want to do something for the town, you round up all the stray cats and dogs and don't worry about the chickens."

"We have an animal control officer now," Rhodes said. "Alton Boyd. He's doing a good job."

"Then get him after those rogue chickens, if there really are any. And if there are, they aren't mine."

Rhodes was almost sorry he'd brought it up. He had the feeling that Weeks wouldn't admit it even if some of his chickens had gotten out of the pen. White Leghorn feathers all looked pretty much alike, so there was no way to identify the feathers Rhodes had seen in the ditch with the alligator as belonging to one of Weeks's hens.

Rhodes thought about his job. Alligators, chickens, murder, and family feuds. Maybe when it came time to file for election, he wouldn't bother. He'd stay at home and watch old movies on TV and sell something or other on eBay. He'd have to learn a lot more about computers before he could do anything like that, though. It would probably be better to stick with something he knew, even if it was frustrating at times.

"Sheriff?" Weeks said.

"What?"

"Are you listening to me?"

"I'm listening. I'll have Alton look into the problem with the chickens."

The fact that there wasn't really a problem would make it a lot easier to solve, Rhodes thought, wishing that all his problems were imaginary.

He thanked Weeks for his help and left, again being careful not to step on any books.

As he pulled away from the curb, he looked into the rearview mirror and saw Jennifer Loam's car headed in his direction. Rhodes grinned. He was one step ahead.

It was getting to be late afternoon, so Rhodes didn't bother to drive to Obert to look for Marsh. He thought it might be a good idea to drop by the chorus practice that evening and talk to him then. He could talk to some of the others while he was at it.

So instead of looking for Marsh, Rhodes headed for Max's Place. He wasn't sure if Schwartz would be there or at the music store, but he'd be at one or the other. He wanted to talk to Schwartz before the chorus met again.

When he arrived at the restaurant, Rhodes could smell woodsmoke. It made his mouth water. The cheese crackers he'd eaten for lunch hadn't done much to take the edge off his appetite.

Rhodes went inside. Schwartz had redecorated the place with a

Wild West theme. The lobby contained old photos of Texas Ranger units, western movie posters, a couple of saddles, some worn-out boots, and even a dummy of John Wayne, dressed as he'd been in *Rio Bravo*.

Schwartz himself was behind the counter. He was wearing a string tie and a ten-gallon hat that looked like something from an old Hoot Gibson movie. It made Elsner's Stetson look like a child's hat.

"Howdy, Sheriff," Schwartz said. "You lookin' for some good barbecue this afternoon?"

"Maybe," Rhodes said. "I need a little information first."

"You've come to the right place, then." Schwartz leaned on the counter. "When it comes to barbecue, I'm the man to talk to. Let me tell you something."

Rhodes tried to interrupt, but when Schwartz got on a roll, interrupting him wasn't easy.

"It all starts with the smoker," he said. "So I bought the best, the Cadillac of the industry."

Rhodes wondered if the Cadillac was still the standard of any industry. Maybe it was. He drove an old Edsel, himself, so he wasn't qualified to comment.

"Southern Pride," Schwartz continued. "That's the name of the smoker. Bought two of 'em on eBay, and the barbecue's mighty fine. Maybe not great, but pretty danged good. I figure if I start out with good barbecue, people will buy it, and I can make it better as I go along."

Rhodes tried to interrupt again, to ask about the music store, but Schwartz didn't give him the chance.

"I know what you're thinking. You're thinking, 'How can he run the restaurant and the music store at the same time?' It's easy.

My wife's going to handle the music business when I'm not there. She can run a business as well as I can. Maybe better. I'm more of an idea man than a manager. So while I'm getting this one off the ground, she'll take care of the other one."

"I see," Rhodes said, "but—"

"Anyway," Schwartz said, "after the smoker's cooked the barbecue, there's the sauce. I know some people say that you should eat barbecue without sauce, but I'm not one of them. My theory is that the sauce is the key to the flavor, and I've got a secret mixture that'll knock your socks off. Mixed it up myself from my own secret formula. The barbecue might be just good, but the sauce is great."

He stopped for breath and pointed to a small poster behind him. It was a picture of Seepy Benton, who sat on a stool and held a guitar.

"I'm keeping the entertainment, too," he said.

Kergan had allowed Benton to sing occasionally, if singing was the right word. Benton wrote his own songs, and the ones Rhodes had heard were hardly related to the western theme.

"He's writing some cowboy songs," Schwartz said. "One of them's called 'Don't Forget Your Pants When You Strap on Your Chaps or You'll Get Chapped.' "

That sounded like something Benton would write, Rhodes thought, but he really hadn't come to hear about Schwartz's barbecue, his secret sauce, or his plans for the future of the restaurant.

"Cobbler," Schwartz went on, waving a hand as if he were whipping it up right there. "Cherry cobbler and vanilla ice cream. That's what I'm serving for dessert."

The thought of warm cherry cobbler with vanilla ice cream melting on top of it was almost enough to distract Rhodes, but not quite.

"I want to ask you about Lloyd Berry," he said.

"Berry?" Schwartz smiled. "You're a hundred percent right. Berry cobbler would be great. Blackberry. We'll have that, too."

"Not blackberry," Rhodes said. "Lloyd Berry. The director of the barbershop chorus."

Scwartz gaped. Rhodes waited for him to grasp the idea that they weren't talking about his plans for his restaurant any longer. It took a few seconds.

"What about Lloyd?" Schwartz said at last.

"He's dead," Rhodes said. "Murdered in his shop."

Schwartz pushed his hat up on his head. "Are you kidding me, Sheriff?"

"No kidding," Rhodes said.

"Damn. He was in here just yesterday for lunch. He and that Wilks fella that runs the gambling den."

Rhodes remembered what Wilks had said about eating at the restaurant. "Wilks and Berry were together?"

"They sat at the same table, if that's what you mean."

That wasn't exactly the way Wilks had told it. Rhodes wondered what that meant.

"Was the restaurant so crowded that they had to sit together?"

"Crowded? We don't have crowds yet, but we're still in the planning stages. We're still in the brisket stage. Just wait till I start cooking ribs. Wait till everybody's heard about my sauce."

Rhodes held up a hand. "What I should have asked was, did Wilks and Berry look friendly? Did they talk?"

Schwartz shrugged. "How do I know? I'm too busy at lunch to watch people. Speaking of which, how about dinner? We should be getting some customers in here anytime, but if you want to eat right now, I can give you any seat in the house."

82

"Maybe I'll come back later," Rhodes said.

He'd have to ask Ivy what she wanted to do. If she hadn't planned anything for dinner, she was always ready to eat out, and she rarely planned anything because of Rhodes's irregular hours. He never knew when he'd be getting home.

"You do that," Schwartz said. "You give my food a try, and you won't be sorry."

"Don't you sing in the chorus on Tuesday nights?"

"Yeah, but Jackee will be here. She can run this place, too, when I'm gone."

"What about a director for the chorus?"

"Damn. Lloyd's dead." Schwartz was another one who didn't seem exactly torn up about Berry's death. "How did you say it happened?"

"I didn't say."

Schwartz winked. "Cop stuff, right? Withhold the information so that if the suspect slips up and tells you, you can book him."

People watched too much TV, Rhodes thought. "No, I just didn't say. Have there been problems with the chorus? Anybody have it in for Lloyd?"

"Cecil Marsh did because of that valentine business. I guess you know about that."

"I've heard the story. What about Darrel Sizemore?"

"Yeah, Darrel and Lloyd argued about the music. You'll notice there's no music playing in here."

"Why's that?"

"Because I have to watch out for the law, that's why. Not you, not the local law, but it's illegal now to play commercial CDs in a place of business. That's why Seepy's playing his own songs. He can't play music by other people."

"I thought you played Kingston Trio music in your store."

Schwartz looked around as if spies from ASCAP and BMI might be lurking behind the John Wayne dummy.

"I used to, but I stopped when I found out it was illegal. Well, not exactly illegal, but you have to pay a big fee if you play music like that. So I don't. Now it's very quiet in the store."

Not if you're there, Rhodes thought. "Did Lloyd have any other problems with people in the chorus? Or anywhere else?"

"Not that I know about."

The front door swung open, and a couple came in.

"Gotta get busy," Schwartz said, coming out from behind the counter. "Howdy, folks. Lookin' for some good barbecue? You've come to the right place." He led them toward the dining area. "I've got the best smokers and the best sauce in Texas."

Rhodes didn't wait to hear the rest of the spiel. He let himself out.

10

▼

To get back to the jail, Rhodes had to drive across the old overpass that curved above the railroad tracks on the west side of town. The overpass was a town landmark. It had been there all of Rhodes's life, and he'd thought it would be there long after he was gone.

He'd been wrong about that. The state highway department had decided that the overpass wasn't up to standard and was making plans to build a new one. Rhodes supposed it was necessary. He didn't like to think of the overpass collapsing and dropping cars and trucks, not to mention their passengers, all over the railroad tracks below, but at the same time he was sorry to think of the old structure's being demolished.

Sometimes it seemed to him that everything he remembered about Clearview was disappearing. Many of the fine old houses he'd known in his youth were gone, and others had fallen into disrepair. Most of the buildings in the downtown area had either fallen down or been torn down after most of the businesses were sucked into Wal-Mart's orbit farther out on the highway that Rhodes was driving on.

The elementary school he'd attended was gone, and houses had been built on the playground where he'd stumbled through touch football games and many innings of softball.

The railroad tracks below him still carried trains, but none of them stopped in Clearview. The depot that had served the town had been torn down so long ago that Rhodes didn't even remember it, though he'd heard some of the older residents mention it now and then.

Before long, Rhodes thought, there wouldn't be anything left of Clearview's past. Well, change was supposed to be good. If that was so, a lot of small Texas towns were better than they'd been years ago, even though it didn't always seem that way to Rhodes. Sometimes he felt as if little pieces of himself were disappearing and no one would ever see them again.

The old jail was the same, though. Rhodes parked in front of the low chain that ran in front of the parking spaces. Clearview was one of the few towns left in Texas that didn't have a big new jail with all kinds of modern equipment. The commissioners occasionally talked about building a new jail, but as long as the old one met the state's standards and wasn't overflowing, they funneled the money into other projects. Rhodes didn't mind at all. The old building met the needs of the county and the town just fine. The prisoners might have preferred some more conveniences, but Rhodes wasn't excited at the prospect.

Hack and Lawton pounced almost before the door had closed

behind Rhodes. They were too smart to ask him for information about Berry. Instead Hack said, "I guess you heard about the chickens."

Rhodes shook his head. He hadn't heard about any chickens except the ones he'd made up for Weeks's benefit.

"You better write up your reports," Hack said. "You don't want to be worryin' about chickens."

Rhodes sat at his desk and turned on the computer. He'd learned to write reports on it, but that was about all he used it for. He got out his notebook and started typing.

"Yep," Lawton said. "You never know about chickens. First there's one or two of 'em on the loose, and then there's more and more. Next thing you know, they're runnin' the town."

Rhodes sighed and swiveled his chair around. He looked at Lawton, who pretended to be sweeping the floor. He looked at Hack, who appeared to be absorbed in something he saw on the computer screen.

"All right," Rhodes said, knowing he'd be sorry, "tell me about the chickens."

Hack turned to look at him. "You know how you had me call Royce Weeks this morning about if any of his chickens had gone missin'?"

"I remember," Rhodes said. "He said all his chickens were safely in the pen."

"Yeah, he did, but there's other chickens in town."

"Lots of 'em," Lawton said. "And some of 'em aren't in their pens."

Hack didn't like it when Lawton tried to get in on the storytelling. Rhodes was sure that Lawton knew it and interrupted just to aggravate Hack.

"Some of 'em ain't even in town," Hack said, taking back the floor.

"Where are they?" Rhodes said, knowing even as he said it that he wouldn't get a straight answer. Hack and Lawton didn't have many ways to amuse themselves, so they took advantage of every opportunity to have fun.

"If they ain't in town," Hack said, "then they must be—"

"Out of town," Lawton said, earning himself a world-class glare from Hack.

"Out of town," Rhodes said. "Somewhere out near where Seepy Benton lives, I'm guessing."

"Right," Hack said, signaling that the game was over. "You remember Larry Crawford, don't you?"

"How could I forget?" Rhodes said.

The double-wide Crawford had shared with his brother had blown up not so very long ago, beginning a series of events that had led to some harrowing times for Rhodes, including an encounter with his old nemesis, a biker named Rapper. Rhodes couldn't think of any connection with chickens, however.

"Somebody else's put a trailer on the piece of property where Crawford lived," Hack said.

Now Rhodes was catching on. "And they have chickens."

"Had," Lawton said, getting another glare.

"Something got into their chicken pen last night," Hack said. "Prob'ly a coyote."

There were a lot of coyotes in the county. They troubled everybody who had any kind of livestock.

"All the chickens went crazy," Hack continued. "Flew out of the pen and ran all over the place. Some of 'em got back in, and some of 'em didn't."

Rhodes knew that this wasn't the main part of the story. Hack was just telling this to lead up to the important part. To encourage him, Rhodes said, "Nobody calls the sheriff's department to tell us that a bunch of their chickens got loose." He had another thought. "Surely they didn't expect Alton Boyd to go out there and round them up."

"Nope, nothin' like that."

Rhodes waited. So did Hack.

"All right," Rhodes said, giving in. "What happened?"

"One of those chickens tried to cross the road," Lawton said.

Rhodes almost said *why?* Luckily he caught himself in time. He might have let himself in for an endless stream of jokes.

"What happened?" he said.

Hack and Lawton both looked disappointed, as if they'd been primed for him to say *why?* Rhodes grinned at them. For once he didn't feel as if they'd gotten the better of him.

They were so deflated that Hack didn't bother to string the story out any further. "One of 'em flew into the windshield of a car."

"Whose car?" Rhodes said.

"That Benton character's. He was goin' home after school and splattered a chicken. He called us about it because he thought you'd like to know."

"How does he know where the chicken came from?"

"He did some investigatin'. He kinda thinks of himself as one of your deputies now. That academy you had was a good idea for gettin' folks involved. We're gonna cut down on chicken crimes, for sure."

"Whose chicken was it?"

"Hard to say for sure. All those chickens look alike."

"You said it came from the property where Crawford had his double-wide."

"That's what Benton says. The owners don't necessarily agree with him, but they admitted they had a problem with their chickens."

"Who's this they you keep talking about?"

"Couple of truck drivers," Hack said. "Hugh and Lance Eccles. You know 'em?"

Rhodes slumped a little lower in his chair.

"I know them," he said.

When Rhodes got to his house, Ivy was already there, and she had some news for him.

"The movie deal's off," she said.

"What movie deal?"

"The one for *Blood Fever*."

"Oh," Rhodes said. "That movie deal."

Several years ago, two women, Claudia and Jan, had come to Blacklin County for a writers' workshop. They'd planned to write an article about crime in rural Texas, but they decided to write a novel instead, and they claimed they'd based their main character on Rhodes. The truth was that Rhodes and Sage Barton, the handsome, crime-busting sheriff in the book, had nothing at all in common, except that Barton had a black cat.

To say that Barton's life was a tad more exciting than Rhodes's own was a considerable understatement. Barton exercised regularly, chased serial killers, had romances with FBI agents, and fired ten times more shots on one page than Rhodes had done in his entire career.

"Seemed perfect for a movie to me," he said. "I was thinking they could get Brad Pitt to play Sage Barton. Because of the resemblance."

"Resemblance?" Ivy said. "To Sage Barton?"

"No. To me."

"You're about a foot taller than Brad Pitt."

"Better-looking, too."

Ivy smiled. "Well, now, I wouldn't say that. Anyway, you might become even more famous because the next book's been accepted by the publisher. Claudia and Jan are excited about it."

"I thought they'd about used up all the bad things that could happen in the first one."

"Not terrorists," Ivy said. "This one has terrorists."

"I was afraid of that," Rhodes said. "We get a lot of those around here. Blacklin County's a prime target for them in the War on Terror. I'm sure it'll have a lot of explosions in it. That'll make it a cinch movie sale."

Ivy laughed, then sobered. "We don't get many terrorists here, but we do get murders. I heard about Lloyd Berry." Ivy worked at a downtown insurance office and had access to local gossip. "Got any clues yet?" she asked.

Rhodes sat at the kitchen table while Yancey, the Pomeranian, yipped around the base of the chair. Sam, the black cat, lay in his favorite place in front of the refrigerator where warm air came out of the vent. He watched from across the room with his yellow eyes. Yancey was thoroughly intimidated by Sam and wouldn't go on that side of the room unless Rhodes or Ivy did, probably in the belief that if Sam attacked, the humans would protect him.

"No clues," Rhodes said. "I've just been talking to people."

"You always talk to people."

"It's the best way I've found to get to the bottom of things. Sooner or later everything I hear will make sense."

"You mean it doesn't make sense to begin with?"

"Sure it does," Rhodes said, "but not everything fits together. That's the hard part, getting things to fit."

"You'll do it eventually."

Ivy looked at Sam, who was slinking across the floor in Yancey's direction. Sam, as if he hadn't noticed her glance, went back and lay down in his place.

"Maybe," Rhodes said, grinning at the antics of the cat. "Did you hear about the alligator?"

Ivy hadn't heard that story, so Rhodes told her.

"Where would an alligator have come from?" she said when he'd finished.

"That's what I'd like to know."

"Is it illegal to own an alligator?"

Rhodes didn't know, but he didn't think it was, not out in the country, at least. In town it might be a different story. Or maybe owning alligators was just fine, for the time being, like owning chickens.

"Well, I think it should be illegal," Ivy said. "Not that I'm worried about alligators. What are we going to do about dinner?"

That meant she didn't have anything planned, so Rhodes suggested that they give Max's Place a try.

"First, though, we'll have some entertainment," he said.

"What kind of entertainment?"

"Musical."

"That sounds good. I'll get ready while you feed Speedo."

Speedo was their outside dog, a border collie. Rhodes had met him in the course of an investigation and then adopted him. He'd picked up Sam and Yancey pretty much the same way, but at different times.

Rhodes stood up, and Yancey ran to the screen door, jumping and yipping, alive with excitement. He wanted to play with Speedo, so Rhodes opened the door and let him out. Sam watched everything with cool disdain. He clearly wasn't going anywhere, especially not if dogs were involved.

Once outside, Yancey ran straight to the silenced squeaky toy, a green frog, that Speedo regarded as his own. Yancey snatched it up in his mouth and took off. Speedo, who was ten times his size, charged after him. Rhodes knew that Speedo would never hurt the smaller dog, who apparently believed himself to be at least as big as Speedo. They had never let the size difference bother them.

Rhodes made sure that Speedo had food and clean water, then sat on the top step of the little porch to watch the dogs play. While they romped around the yard, Rhodes thought about Lloyd Berry. He didn't seem to have any close friends, but he'd had at least one bad enemy. Whoever that had been was walking around Clearview right now, thinking he'd gotten away with killing Berry, and he was right. At least for the moment. Rhodes had no doubt that he'd find out who the killer was. It would just take a while.

Rhodes sorted through all the conversations he'd had that day, trying to figure out exactly what he'd learned that might be helpful to him.

Someone had killed Lloyd Berry with a pipe-cutting wrench. Whoever had done the killing hadn't been seen by anyone in the strip center where Berry had his shop. Or at least not by anyone who'd admit it, even though everybody had heard about Berry's argument the previous day with Cecil Marsh.

Cecil had it in for Berry because of a singing valentine that Cecil may or may not have paid for.

Darrel Sizemore and Berry had quarreled about the amount of money Berry was paying for music to be used by the Clearview barbershop chorus.

Berry and Wilks seemed to have been better acquainted than Wilks had admitted to Rhodes. They'd had lunch together and sat at the same table. Rhodes wondered what they'd talked about. Rhodes knew that Berry had never complained about the gambling that was going on at the other end of the center, and as far as Rhodes could tell, Wilks was staying within the law. It could be that the two men were just friends and that Wilks hadn't wanted to admit it because he didn't want to be suspected of the murder. Or maybe there was something Rhodes was missing.

He thought he was missing something in the Marsh and Weeks feud, too. It had been obvious during his conversations with Faye Lynn and Royce that the problems went deeper than just shrubs and chickens and all the other things that had come up over the years.

Ivy opened the door and interrupted Rhodes's thoughts.

"Are you ready to go?" she said.

"Sure."

Rhodes stood up and called Yancey, who came running with the frog in his mouth. Rhodes grabbed the frog, and Yancey ran right on in through the door.

"Here you go," Rhodes said, and tossed the frog to Speedo, who snatched it out of the air and ran off to his foam igloo, where he sat down to chew on the toy. It no longer squeaked because Rhodes had removed the metal whistle, but Speedo didn't seem to care.

"It takes so little to make him happy," Ivy said.

Rhodes smiled.

"He reminds me of you," Ivy said.

Rhodes wasn't sure if that was good or bad, so he decided not to ask.

The barbershop chorus met in the Clearview Senior Center, which had once been the Clearview Public Library. There was a new library now, and the old one had been remodeled for a different use. It was a few blocks outside what remained of the downtown area, near a couple of churches.

Not everyone in the chorus was a senior citizen, but the city allowed the group to meet and practice in the building because the members were always happy to sing at city functions or for any group that asked them, and they never charged an admission fee.

"I thought barbershop singing was for quartets," Ivy said as they parked outside the Senior Center, a low, flat-roofed building of redbrick. They were in Rhodes's Edsel, which, like Sam, Yancey, and Speedo, he had come across during an investigation and more or less adopted. Rhodes always seemed to find himself sticking up for the underdog. Or undercar. He was glad the old Edsel was still running.

"You can have barbershop harmony in a chorus, too," Rhodes said. They started up the walk to the front entrance. "Some of the members form quartets, though, and that's part of the problem I'm working on. Berry was in a quartet with Royce Weeks, Darrel Sizemore, and someone else. A baritone, I guess."

"I've heard about baritones," Ivy said. "They're all crazy."

"That's stereotyping," Rhodes told her.

"I was just kidding. They have the junk parts, though, so it takes a special kind of person to sing them. That's what I heard, anyway. Maybe you could sing baritone."

"I can't sing anything."

"They asked you to join."

"Just to break up the fights," Rhodes said, but he wondered if Berry had sensed that something was about to happen to him. Could it be that he'd asked Rhodes to join the chorus because he wanted protection from a killer?

"You're joking about the fights, aren't you?" Ivy said.

Rhodes was about to say that he was, when he pulled open the front door of the Senior Center and they heard the yelling from inside.

"That doesn't sound like barbershop harmony," Ivy said.

"No," Rhodes said. "It sounds like a fight."

As they headed for the practice room, a metal folding chair came flying out the door.

"I think I'll wait here," Ivy said and stopped where she was.

Rhodes stopped as well. "Me, too."

"You can't wait here," Ivy said. "You're the sheriff. It's your job to go in that room."

"Dang," Rhodes said.

11

▼

THE PRACTICE ROOM WAS FULL OF ANGRY, SHOUTING MEN. FIF-
teen or sixteen of them. They were moving around and Rhodes
couldn't get an accurate count.

"All right," he said, "who threw the chair?"

No one paid any attention to him. Royce Weeks and Cecil Marsh
stood toe to toe, shouting, their faces red, their fists clenched.
Rhodes saw Darrel Sizemore, Seepy Benton, Max Schwartz, and
ten or twelve others. Everyone was moving around. Some were
pushing and shoving. Some were jockeying for a good position to
see if Weeks and Marsh were going to hit each other. Rhodes
doubted if any of them even knew he was there. That was what
came of having a voice that didn't project. No wonder he wasn't a
singer.

A podium stood up against the front wall of the room. Rhodes
went over to it and looked around. He saw a coffee cup on a counter

and went and picked it up. Nobody noticed him until he started to bang on the podium with the cup.

When they finally realized that the sheriff was in the room, things began to quiet down. Rhodes stood there watching them until the room was silent. He felt like a grade-school teacher in front of a rowdy class.

"Let's everybody sit down," Rhodes said.

Feet shuffled, chairs scraped. Marsh and Weeks went to opposite sides of the room and took seats, and others dropped into the nearest chairs. After everyone was seated, Rhodes looked at Seepy Benton, who hadn't been taking part in the argument so much as standing aside and watching as if amused. Maybe he was like Speedo, Rhodes thought.

"Dr. Benton, why don't you tell me what's going on here, aside from destruction of public property, assault, battery, and terroristic threats."

"I don't know," Benton said. "The argument started before I got here."

"Did you see who threw the chair out the door?"

Benton looked around the room, as if he thought someone might raise his hand.

Nobody did.

"I didn't throw it," Benton said.

Once again Rhodes felt like a schoolteacher. "That's not what I asked you."

"Hell," Cecil Marsh said, standing up, "I threw it. I was trying to hit somebody with it, and I wish I had."

Rhodes didn't have to ask who he was trying to hit. "I'm calling off the practice."

"You can't do that," Royce Weeks said. "You're not the director."

"No, but I'm the sheriff. I could just arrest the whole bunch of you."

Somebody muttered something about the next election. Rhodes figured he was losing votes, but that was nothing new.

"I'm not going to arrest anybody, but, like I said, practice is over. I don't have time to fool with you. I'll just let you all go on home. Except for you, Cecil. I need to talk to you. The rest of you can get your stuff and leave."

Rhodes stood at the podium and listened to the mumbling and grumbling as the men gathered up their music, but before anyone could leave, Max Schwartz spoke up.

"We can all go to my restaurant," he said. He was still wearing his big cowboy hat. "We can have an afterglow."

"What's that?" Rhodes said.

Schwartz turned to address Rhodes. "We sit around and sing, maybe have some cobbler and ice cream."

People seemed to like the idea. Seepy Benton said, "How can there be an afterglow when we haven't even glowed?"

That was exactly the kind of question Seepy would ask, Rhodes thought.

"What difference does it make?" Rhodes said.

Benton looked hurt. "Besides," he said, "we should do something to remember Lloyd by. He was our director, after all."

"We can honor him by singing," Max said.

That seemed to satisfy Seepy, and he left the room without saying anything more. The other members of the group followed him, except for Cecil, who stayed in his chair, and Schwartz.

"You going to come out for some barbecue later, Sheriff?" Max said. "We'll sing something for you."

"I'll think about it," Rhodes said.

Schwartz settled his hat on his head and left. Rhodes went over and closed the door.

"So what happens now?" Cecil said. "You bring out the rubber hoses?"

Cecil was a solid man with calloused hands and a wind-reddened face. He was outside more often than not, and Rhodes figured he didn't go in for lotions.

"I don't think the Senior Center has any rubber hoses," Rhodes said. "I'd have to take you to the jail for that."

Cecil didn't appear quite sure whether Rhodes was joking, which was fine with Rhodes.

"From what was going on here, I gather you've heard about Lloyd," he said.

"Yeah," Cecil said. "That's what started the fight. Royce Weeks accused me of being the one that killed him."

"That's why you threw the chair?"

"Yeah. Weeks provoked me."

Rhodes could see how Weeks might be able to do that. On the other hand, throwing a chair out the door seemed to be a bit of an overreaction.

"I was trying to hit him with it," Cecil said by way of explanation. "Not throw it. It slipped out of my hands."

"You realize he could press charges for that."

"He won't, though. He started it, and everybody that was here will swear to that. He was feeling guilty and trying to cover up for it."

"Guilty for what?" Rhodes said.

"He's the one that paid for that singing valentine for Lindy Gomez."

Rhodes wasn't convinced of that. He needed some kind of proof.

"Do you know that for sure?"

Cecil looked amazed that Rhodes would even have to ask. "Who else would've done it? Weeks has been out to get me for years, and he thought this would be the way, maybe break me and Faye Lynn up. He's almost done it before."

So there was no proof, just suspicion. Rhodes needed more than that.

"I know that Royce, Lloyd, and Darrel were in the quartet," he said. "Who sang baritone?"

"Wade Turner."

Rhodes knew Turner vaguely. He'd been pushing and shoving with the others earlier.

"How did the payment for the valentine get to Lloyd, anyway?"

"It was in a letter, supposedly from me. Even the signature was printed. An obvious fake."

Maybe, Rhodes thought, or the printed signature could have been a way for Cecil to have a plausible excuse if word got out that he'd sent a valentine to Lindy. Rhodes didn't think Cecil would admit it, so he went in another direction.

"Let's talk about alligators," he said.

Cecil seemed taken aback by the abrupt change in subject. "Alligators? What about alligators? What do alligators have to do with anything?"

Rhodes told him.

"Well, it might have been across the road from my place, but I don't have an alligator. I've *never* had an alligator. Besides, what if I did have one? Is there any law against it?"

Rhodes shrugged. "Not that I know of. It's not a good idea to have dangerous animals roaming loose, though."

"I wouldn't put it past Weeks to plant an alligator on me. On my land, I mean. Did you ask him?"

"No," Rhodes said.

He didn't plan to, either. No matter how odd the feud between the two men was, Weeks wouldn't go that far. Probably.

"Did you happen to drop in on Lloyd today?" Rhodes said.

Cecil stood up. "You're about to make me mad, Sheriff."

"You going to hit me with a chair?"

Cecil sat back down. "No, I wouldn't do that, but I don't like being accused of killing anybody."

"I didn't accuse you of anything. I just asked a question."

"Then the answer is no."

"You worked in Obert today. You had to drive right by Lloyd's shop."

"Faye Lynn told me you'd come snooping around. I don't like that."

"Just doing my job."

"Yeah, and I'll bet you liked it. Anyway, Lloyd's shop was out of my way, and I didn't go by there. I went straight to work. Did anybody say I was at Lloyd's?"

"No," Rhodes said. "Nobody said that."

"It's a good thing, because it would have been a lie. You ought to be talking to Darrel, not me, anyway."

"Why?" Rhodes said, though he knew what Cecil would say.

"Because they've been fighting over the music. Darrel thinks Lloyd might have been dipping into the till."

Rhodes hadn't known after all, or not everything. No one had mentioned that Darrel thought Lloyd might be taking money from the group's coffers.

"Is that what he said?"

"Not in so many words, but it's what he meant." Cecil stood up again. "Maybe I was the only one who took it that way, though. Can I go now?"

"Why not?" Rhodes said.

"One thing I can say for you," Ivy told Rhodes when he came out of the practice room.

"What's that?"

"When you promise entertainment, you deliver. It wasn't quite as musical as I'd thought it would be, though."

"Sorry about that."

"No, you're not. You think it's funny."

Rhodes knew there were times when it was best to keep quiet. This was one of those times.

"That's all right," Ivy said. "I think it was kind of funny, too. Are we still going to eat barbecue?"

"Sure. I think I can still promise you musical entertainment, too."

"Great," Ivy said. "I hope I don't get hit by a flying chair."

"I can't promise that," Rhodes said.

When Rhodes and Ivy walked into Max's Place, they saw Jackee behind the counter and heard a close-harmony version of "Amazing Grace" coming from the big room that was reserved for private parties. Rhodes had never heard it sung quite like that. He took a look inside. Most of the people from the practice were there, but not Cecil Marsh. Rhodes thought that was a good thing. Much less chance of a fight starting.

After the group finished "Amazing Grace," they started in on "My Wild Irish Rose."

Max Schwartz looked over and saw Rhodes. He stopped singing and came to the door. "How does it sound?"

"Good," Rhodes said. "Who's directing?"

"We don't need a director for an afterglow. We just sing polecat songs. Except for 'Amazing Grace.' That was our tribute to Lloyd."

"What are polecat songs?" Ivy said. "Those sound smelly."

"Think barber poles," Max said. "Polecat songs are the ones that every barbershopper knows by heart. You run into three barbershoppers in Alaska, and along with yourself you'll have a quartet that can sing those songs."

"Speak for yourself," Rhodes said.

"You could join us, Sheriff. We'll take anybody."

Rhodes wondered if Schwartz meant that the way it sounded. He hoped not.

"I think I'll just have some barbecue," he said.

Max waved at Jackee. "Show them to the best seat in the house."

Jackee came out from behind the counter with a couple of menus.

"Right this way, Sheriff," she said with a smile. "Every seat in Max's Place is the best seat in the house."

Rhodes glanced back at Max, who was grinning with pride.

"I didn't even have to tell her to say that," Max said. "She's a natural."

* * *

The barbecue was better than Rhodes had expected, and the beans and the slaw weren't bad, either. He wanted the cobbler and ice cream, but he refrained. He had enough trouble buttoning up his pants as it was.

"It's the sauce," Ivy said as they were leaving. "It's really good."

"It's Max's secret recipe," Rhodes told her.

The chorus was still singing as they left. The song was "Sweet Adeline."

"Nice harmony," Ivy said.

Rhodes nodded, wondering when the next fight would break out.

12

▼

RHODES AND IVY MADE IT HOME IN TIME FOR THE TEN O'CLOCK news. A story from Houston caught Rhodes's attention.

One problem in dealing with the eight-liners was that if law enforcement did prove that illegal gambling was going on, the machines were confiscated. In cities like Houston, there wasn't enough space to store them, so places like Rollin' Sevens were fairly safe even if they didn't follow the law.

"Not anymore," said the newscaster, a telegenic young woman with long black hair. "A Houston judge has given permission to the Harris County Sheriff's Department to destroy the confiscated machines. Here's what's happening."

Her image was replaced with film of a giant claw picking up an eight-liner and crushing it, then dumping the remains into a truck to be hauled away.

"I'll bet you wish you could do that," Ivy said.

"Not especially. The only place in town is following the law. Or at least I think it is, and a lot of people enjoy it." Rhodes thought of the Eccles cousins. "Some of them are protective of the place."

"You don't think gambling hurts people?"

"I know it does. Some of the ones in Rollin' Sevens don't have the money to throw away. I don't like it that they do, but unless somebody's breaking the law, I can't shut the place down. If Wilks steps over the line, though, I will."

"How will you know if he does?"

"Somebody will tell me," Rhodes said. "Somebody always does."

The first thing Rhodes did the following morning was call the jail and ask Hack if Ruth had located a next of kin for Lloyd Berry.

"Your friend Randy Lawless called," Hack said.

Rhodes wasn't sure what that had to do with his question. Hack was up to his usual tricks.

"Is Randy related to Lloyd?" Rhodes said, knowing that he wasn't.

Randy Lawless was the defense attorney who had built the Lawj Mahal. He and Rhodes had met in court more than once, always on different sides.

"Nope, not related, but he knows who is."

"How does Randy know that?"

"He's a lawyer."

"So?"

"So he's Lloyd's lawyer, or he was. I guess he still is even if Lloyd's dead. Those lawyers can hang on even after their client's gone. So he's still representin' Berry."

"I get it," Rhodes said.

"I figgered you would, you bein' a professional lawman and used to workin' with clues and all like that. Anyway, Lawless has Lloyd's last will and testament, and he's the executor. The sole beneficiary is some cousin in Hawaii. You think he came down here and killed Lloyd for his inheritance?"

Rhodes didn't think so, and he knew Hack didn't, either.

"So that's that," Hack said. "Everything's all taken care of. Lawless will see to the buryin' and notification of the next of kin."

"That doesn't mean everything's taken care of."

"It will be when you arrest somebody for killin' Lloyd. You comin' in to the jail now?"

"Not yet," Rhodes said. "I have a lot of things to do first."

"That's why they pay you the big bucks," Hack said before hanging up.

One thing Rhodes had to do was pay a visit to Lloyd Berry's house. He didn't know what he expected to find, but you never could tell when something helpful might turn up. Rhodes just hoped he'd know that something and its significance if he saw it. He called up a friendly judge and asked him to fill out a search warrant just to be on the up-and-up. After picking up the warrant, he drove to the house.

It was as old as the ones owned by Marsh and Weeks, though in a different part of town. A couple of big cottonwood trees loomed up in the backyard, and dark green arborvitae shrubs flanked the front steps.

The door wasn't locked. Rhodes didn't think anything about that. Some of the older people in Clearview, and even middle-aged ones like Berry, didn't bother to lock their doors. They didn't lock their cars when they shopped, either. They thought living in a small town was still the same as it had been when they were kids, when there was hardly any crime and neighbors looked out for neighbors.

As much as he'd have liked to agree with them, Rhodes didn't think Clearview, or anywhere else, had ever been like that in anything more than people's imagination. He supposed it was only natural that people liked to look back and remember things as having been better than they were now, but Rhodes had seen the old files in the jail, reports going back to times before he was born. He also remembered some of the things that his parents had told him about. If those sources were to be believed, Clearview had never had a Golden Age.

Still, no one had been into Berry's house and taken anything. Rhodes stood in the small living room and looked around. An old TV set on a stand was hooked up to a cable box, a VCR, and a DVD player. A coffee table in front of a couch had a few magazines lying on top. *Kiplinger's, Popular Science, Reader's Digest.* A little stand under a lamp held a pot of ivy with yellowing leaves. There was nothing in the room that looked like a clue.

Rhodes went through the rest of the house. He had no more luck than he'd had in the living room. The only thing of interest was in a small bedroom that Berry had made into a kind of home office with a desktop computer hooked to a printer and scanner.

Rhodes hadn't seen anything in the house that Berry could have been selling on eBay, so he figured the computer had other uses. E-mail, maybe. Or just Web surfing. Rhodes didn't do any of that himself, but he knew what it was.

He knew just enough about computers to find the switch that turned the machine on. He waited until the desktop appeared and then clicked on the Outlook Express icon. The window opened, and Berry's e-mail began to download. Rhodes looked through it and saw nothing personal, only the usual spam messages promising great wealth, cheap Viagra, or an enlarged penis. Rhodes thought that if anyone ever figured out how to combine those three scams, they'd have a real moneymaker.

Closing the e-mail program, Rhodes clicked on the Firefox icon and brought up Berry's Google home page. No clues there, unless learning that Berry liked to play Bejeweled was a clue. It probably was, but not to the murder. The quote of the day was from somebody named Scott Adams. Rhodes thought he'd heard the name, but he couldn't remember where.

Rhodes clicked on BOOKMARKS in the toolbar, hoping that Berry had left some kind of trail that might lead to his killer, but knowing that it wasn't likely.

The drop-down menu listed only a few sites that Berry had considered worthy of saving. Three of them were for big-city newspapers, two were Internet-only news sites, and the others were related to flowers and floral arranging. Nothing Rhodes saw was going to be of any use to him, and he closed the menu.

If there was anything on the computer that would be helpful, Rhodes knew he was going to need someone else to find it. He'd reached the limit of his expertise.

He called Hack on the telephone in the kitchen and asked what Ruth was doing.

"She's workin' a car wreck down around Thurston. Nobody hurt, but a couple of real upset drivers. You need me to get in touch with her?"

"Never mind," Rhodes said. "I'll get somebody else."

Thinking that Benton would be at the college, he called the switchboard and asked for Benton's office. Benton answered on the first ring.

"Benton's the name, and math is my game. What can I do for you?"

Rhodes told Benton who he was and said that he needed some computer help.

"In person or over the phone? The charge is the same for both."

"And how much would that be?"

"I'll give you the famous lawman discount."

"I'm sure you will."

"Which means I'll do it for free. After all, I'm practically a lawman myself."

The academy that Benton had attended was no more likely to have turned him into a lawman than his math classes were likely to produce another Einstein, but Rhodes would be glad to have his help.

"Since it's free," he said, "can you come to Lloyd Berry's house, or do you have a class to teach?"

"I'm doing office hours now," Benton said. "I'm sure the dean would be happy to let me leave campus to assist in the enforcement of the law. We would be enforcing the law, wouldn't we?"

"Close enough."

"Good. So what's the address of that Berry house?"

Rhodes told him.

"I'll be there in ten minutes," Benton said.

He made it in twelve. Rhodes met him at the door and took him to the computer room, where he explained what he wanted him to do.

"Is it legal for me to do that?" Benton asked.

"You don't have to worry. I have a warrant."

"That works for me." Benton sat in the swivel chair in front of the computer. "First, let's see if everything is in working order."

Rhodes watched as Benton typed a URL into the space at the top of the home page: www.docbenton.com. A Web page opened up. In the upper left corner was a picture of some desert scene. Rhodes was surprised it wasn't a photo of Seepy himself.

"Pretty cool, isn't it?" Benton said, leaning back in the chair to admire his handiwork. "Want me to show you the pages on Einstein's Special Theory of Relativity?"

"It would be a real thrill," Rhodes said. "Right now, though, I'm looking for something that might help me find Lloyd Berry's killer."

"Oh. So what would that be?"

"If I knew that, I wouldn't have asked for your help."

"You don't have any idea?"

"Nope. That's what you're here for."

"I'm great with ideas, all right. Did you check his bookmarks?"

"First thing."

"How about his history?"

Rhodes just looked at him.

"People never remember to clear their history," Benton said.

He leaned forward and palmed the mouse. When he clicked on the word HISTORY in the browser's toolbar, a little box opened. Benton clicked on the line at the bottom that said SHOW IN SIDE-BAR, and a long rectangle appeared at the left of the screen. Rhodes saw folders labeled YESTERDAY, TWO DAYS AGO, THREE DAYS AGO, and so on.

"We can look in those folders and see what Web sites Mr. Berry visited," Benton said. "Maybe that's where we'll find a clue."

He clicked on the folder labeled TWO DAYS AGO, and a line of domain names dropped down. Except that it wasn't different domain names. All of them were the same: youcachein.com.

"Is that a clue?" Benton said.

"I think so," Rhodes said. "See what it is."

It was, as Rhodes had guessed, a site devoted to geocaching, which was interesting, all right.

"We can find caches in our area," Benton said. "Want to have a look?"

"Go ahead," Rhodes said.

Benton typed the Clearview zip code into a box and clicked on GO. A list of sites appeared, all identified by latitude and longitude.

"Sure are a lot of them," Benton said.

"How many?" Rhodes asked.

"Fifty or sixty, at least."

Rhodes thought that was interesting and asked if there were any more pages.

"No. That's all."

"Okay. How can we find out whose page that is?" Rhodes said. "Who owns it, or whatever the word would be."

"Whosis."

"Whose," Rhodes said. "Not *whosis*."

Benton laughed. "Whosis is the name of the site where you search for the owner of a domain name."

He brought up the Whosis page, then typed the URL of the geocaching page in the box provided there. Another click and they had the answer.

"It's a corporation," Rhodes said. "I don't guess you can find out the real owners."

"That would be beyond even my considerable abilities. You might be able to trace it, but it won't be easy. Unless they want to be found."

Rhodes didn't think they'd want to.

"How does this help?" Benton asked.

"I'm not sure," Rhodes told him. "Let's just say it's a piece of a puzzle I'm working on. I'll have to think about it and see where it fits."

"Do you need any help thinking?"

"Probably, but I'll just have to blunder through this on my own for the time being."

"Then my work here is done?"

"Not quite. What's this I hear about you having a run-in with a chicken yesterday?"

"I thought that's what you were calling about this morning," Benton said. "Little did I know you needed my help with a computer."

Rhodes didn't want to spend the rest of the day having Benton point out his techie failings.

"About that chicken," he said.

"It was part of a bunch. What's the word for a bunch of chickens? Flock? Or is that sheep?"

"Does it matter?"

"No. I was just wondering. You wouldn't think people would lump sheep and chickens together like that, though, so maybe there are different words."

"We don't need to know that right now," Rhodes said. "Just tell me about the chicken."

Benton rubbed his chin like David Letterman before a flashback.

"I was on my way home," he said. "Right before I got to my driveway there was a bunch of chickens. Or maybe a flock of them. They got excited when they saw my car and flew up into the air. One of them hit my windshield pretty hard. The windshield didn't break, but the chicken didn't survive."

"And you think the chickens belonged to the Eccles cousins?"

"I drove up and asked them. They said no, but that's because they think I want to put in some kind of claim against them for damages to my car. They did admit that they had some chickens get loose from their pen, though. I think that's where the one the alligator ate must have come from."

Rhodes thought that was a good guess. It didn't explain the alligator, however. He thanked Benton for the computer assistance and told him he'd check on the chickens and see what he could learn.

"I'm glad I could help out," Benton said. "Is there anything else you need from me?"

"Not unless you can think of something on that computer that might be another clue."

Benton surfed around on the computer for a minute or so but found nothing of interest. He went back to the Doc Benton page.

"You're sure you don't want me to explain the Special Theory of Relativity?"

"I'm sure."

Benton looked at his wristwatch, a cheap digital model with a black plastic band.

"It's almost time for my calculus class. I'd better go on back to the college. Feel free to call me anytime you need some more help or want to hear about relativity."

"I'll do that," Rhodes told him.

Benton left, and Rhodes looked around the house a bit more. He didn't find what he was looking for, so he went into the garage. Unlike a lot of people Rhodes knew, Berry had nothing stored inside it except his car. Sitting on the dashboard of the car was what Rhodes was looking for, a GPS receiver. Since the car wasn't locked, Rhodes opened the door, removed the GPS, and took it with him as evidence.

Evidence of what, he wasn't sure.

13

▼

RHODES'S NEXT STOP WAS ON THE COUNTY ROAD THAT WENT BY
Seepy Benton's house. Rhodes looked out the car window at Cecil
Marsh's place when he went by, but he didn't see any more alliga-
tors creeping around. He hadn't expected to.

Rhodes drove on up the road to the hill where the double-wide
owned by the Crawford brothers had been parked until an explosion tore it apart. Sure enough, there was a brand-new trailer
there, sparkling white with a green roof. The silver mailbox by
the open gate had ECCLES painted on it in black letters.

Rhodes drove the county car through the opening and up the
hill. A big red Mack tractor rig with a sleeper cab sat near the
double-wide. ECCLES TRUCKING was written on the doors with silver paint outlined in black. Two Chevy Silverados, one red and
one black, were parked a little closer to the trailer. Both had extended cabs. Rhodes had seen the red one in the parking lot in
front of Rollin' Sevens the day before.

The area around the double-wide had been cleaned up since the explosion. No trace of the Crawfords' trailer remained, or if there was one, Rhodes couldn't see it. He wondered if any of the scrap had been sold to Darrel Sizemore.

In a dog pen near the pickups, a large animal stood at the chain-link fence and stared at Rhodes. It looked like a cross between a leopard dog and a wolf, with maybe something else thrown in, and it didn't look friendly. Leopard dogs were descended from mastiffs, and Rhodes had known a few with bad attitudes, often instilled by their owners.

Before Rhodes was even out of his car, the dog started barking, and when Rhodes's foot hit the ground, the dog began to throw itself against the fence. Rhodes had a feeling this was one animal he wouldn't be developing a good rapport with, even though he had a feeling it wasn't as mean as it tried to appear. Not that he wanted to find out.

Hugh Eccles came through the door of the trailer and started toward the car.

"What're you doing to my dog, Sheriff?" he said.

"I'm not doing a thing," Rhodes said. "I don't think he likes me."

"He doesn't like most people. Just me and Lance. What're you doing here, anyway? This is private property, so you better have a warrant."

Rhodes didn't have a warrant, not that he needed one.

"I'm just here on a friendly visit," he said, looking around.

The dog was still barking, but instead of throwing itself against the fence, it was standing on its hind legs. Rhodes wished the fence were a little bit taller.

"Where's Lance?" he said.

"He's not here," Hugh said.

Rhodes didn't believe him. Both pickups were there, and so was the Mack.

"What do you want with Lance?" Hugh said.

"I wanted to talk to both of you," Rhodes said. "I heard you had some trouble with your chickens."

"Yeah," Hugh said. "A coyote got in the pen and killed some of 'em. That's not any of your business, though."

"It might be," Rhodes said.

"It wasn't one of our chickens that flew into that goofball's windshield," Hugh said. "And even if it was, he couldn't prove it."

Rhodes didn't have to ask which goofball Hugh meant.

"The goofball doesn't care," he said. "He was helping me out. I wanted to know if there were any chickens on the loose around here."

"You can see we got some." Hugh pointed to a pen that was located some distance from the double-wide. "Not as many as we had last night, though. Some got eaten, and some might've got loose. I didn't count."

The chickens in the pen didn't seem too bothered by the barking of the dog. Rhodes, however, was.

"Can you quiet down that dog?" he said.

Hugh didn't do anything for a couple of seconds. Then he walked over to the pen and rattled the gate.

"Hush up, Bruce," he yelled.

The dog stopped barking, but he didn't stand down. He leaned on the fence, watching Rhodes.

Bruce? Rhodes thought.

"Me and Lance had an uncle named Bruce," Hugh said, as if he knew what Rhodes might be thinking. "He was meaner than that dog. Got killed in a bar fight in Comanche County a few years ago."

"Your family likes to fight, I guess."

"Not so much. We don't like being pushed around, though. You tricked me and Lance yesterday, but today I got Bruce on my side. You might want to leave before I open that gate."

Bruce panted as if pleased at the prospect of biting a chunk from Rhodes's anatomy.

"Just a couple of questions before I go," Rhodes said. He looked down the hill to the creek. "You ever been bothered by alligators around here?"

Hugh's eyes narrowed. "Who said anything about alligators?"

"Nobody. I was just wondering because we caught one yesterday morning. It had eaten a chicken." He gestured toward the pen with his thumb. "Maybe one of your chickens."

"We had a coyote here, like I told you. Not an alligator. That all you wanted to know?"

"I was hoping you'd let me have a look around. There's a little stock tank on this property, I think."

"I don't give a damn what you think. What *I* think is, it's time for you to go."

"Not until I have a look at the tank. You want to show it to me?"

Hugh thought it over. Finally he shrugged. "Why not? I don't see what you think you're gonna find."

"Probably nothing."

"We'll go in my pickup," Hugh said. "I don't like the idea of ridin' in a law car."

Rhodes didn't like the idea of being trapped in the cab of a pickup with Hugh any more than Hugh wanted to ride with him.

"You go in the pickup," he said. "I'll follow you in the car."

"If that's the way you want it."

Hugh got into the red Silverado and drove off across the property. Bruce started barking again, but Rhodes didn't pay him any mind.

Rhodes had been on the property more than once, but he'd never looked at the tank. He followed Hugh down a rutted track, and after about a quarter of a mile they came to a tank dam overgrown with weeds. Some were dead, and some were fresh and green.

Hugh stopped and got out of the truck. Rhodes parked behind him.

"There it is," Hugh said. "Not much to look at, though. Water's pretty shallow."

Rhodes couldn't see the water from where he was, so he climbed up on the dam and looked around at the banks. He saw at least two slick places among the weeds where something long and heavy might have made it a habit to emerge from the water.

"You ever go to Florida on any of your hauling runs?" Rhodes said.

"Can't hear you," Hugh said, but instead of moving closer to the dam, he got into his pickup and turned on the radio.

It was tuned to a rap station out of Dallas, and the bass thumped so loud that the truck seemed to vibrate with the sound. Rhodes wondered what kind of speakers Hugh had. They must have been in the extended portion of the cab in back of the front seat.

Rhodes walked down from the dam and toward the truck, wondering why Hugh had felt the urge to turn on the radio and why it was so loud.

It didn't take him too long to figure it out, however. He was covering up another noise.

Rhodes saw the black Silverado headed in their direction. He couldn't hear Bruce barking, but the dog stood behind the cab, his head poked up over the top. He looked thrilled to be riding in the truck. Or it could have been that he was thrilled that he was out of the pen and would have a chance to take a bite out of Rhodes.

Hugh turned off the radio and got out of the pickup.

"Looks like we got company," he said.

Rhodes didn't bother to remind Hugh that he'd said his cousin wasn't around. Instead he wondered what was bothering the two truckers. It couldn't be only the fact that it looked as if an alligator, or maybe two, had been living in their stock tank.

Lance stopped his pickup near Hugh's and slid out of the seat. Bruce leaped out of the bed and stood snarling by Lance's side. The hair along the ridge of his back was standing up, and Rhodes knew he wasn't snarling at Lance.

"You sure do like to push folks around, Sheriff," Lance said. "First at the Rollin' Sevens and now right here on our own property."

Rhodes was at a loss to explain what was going on. The Crawford brothers had operated a whiskey still in the woods near the creek. If the Eccles boys had decided to reopen the business, that might be the reason for their hostility today, but it didn't account for what had happened at the Rollin' Sevens.

Maybe the Eccles boys just didn't like him.

"You don't have to worry about the alligators," he said. "As far as I know, it's not against the law to have one, so you're not under arrest."

Lance and Hugh looked at each other. It was Lance who spoke. "Who said we had an alligator?"

"Nobody, but the signs are there. I think it was an alligator that got into your chicken pen, not a coyote. Bruce would've raised Cain if a coyote had come into the yard, but he might not've been so worried about an alligator. Maybe it was so low to the ground that he didn't even see it."

Bruce heard his name and snarled louder. Lance didn't have a leash on him, and Rhodes thought it might not be too much longer before Bruce decided to have a sheriff for lunch. He hoped not. He didn't want to have to hurt the dog.

"We don't know anything about any alligator," Hugh said.

"When's the last time you made a run down to Florida?" Rhodes said, repeating the question that Hugh said he couldn't hear. "Maybe you had a stowaway on the trip back home."

"That's pretty funny," Lance said. "You must think we're idiots."

That wasn't what Rhodes thought, but he did think the cousins were close to making fools of themselves.

"I think you like animals," Rhodes said. "Dogs, chickens. Alligators."

Lance moved his hand. Rhodes wasn't sure if Lance had done it deliberately to signal the dog or if Bruce had just decided to make his move at that particular moment. The result was the same in either case. The big dog sprang forward, baring his teeth at Rhodes.

Hugh lunged. Rhodes couldn't tell if he was lunging for him or for the dog, but it didn't make any difference to what Rhodes was going to do. Hugh was close enough to reach, so Rhodes grabbed his shirt at the shoulder, pulling him right into Bruce's path.

Bruce collided with Hugh, and they both hit the ground and rolled right into Rhodes's legs, toppling him as well.

Bruce snapped and growled, trying to bite someone, anyone.

Rhodes shoved Hugh aside, but by then Lance was there, aiming a kick at Rhodes's head with his steel-toed work shoe.

Rhodes caught the shoe in his hands and twisted. Lance fell and landed on Bruce, who bit his arm and ripped the sleeve of his shirt.

Rhodes shoved away from the pile and stood up, reaching for the pistol he wore in an ankle holster. Bruce didn't give him a chance to pull the weapon. He threw himself into Rhodes's chest and knocked him back against the tank dam.

Bruce fell to one side, but he was on his feet before Rhodes could get to the pistol, slavering and barking. Rhodes scrabbled around with his hand, and his fingers clenched around a stick. He hit Bruce sharply on the end of the nose with it, and Bruce jerked back.

Rhodes sat up. "That's enough of that," he said, shaking the stick at Bruce. "You just sit right where you are."

Bruce snarled and tensed his muscles to pounce.

Rhodes shook the stick at him. "If you jump me again, I'm going to have to hurt you. You stay. Stay right there."

Bruce stayed, but he growled low in his throat.

"That stick might scare Bruce," Hugh said, coming at Rhodes, "but it doesn't bother me."

Rhodes threw the stick at Hugh, who was distracted just long enough for Rhodes to pull up his pants leg and draw the pistol.

"Now hold on, Sheriff," Lance said, seeing the gun in Rhodes's hand. He rose from the ground. "You don't need to go shooting anybody."

"Put your hands on top of your head," Rhodes told him. "You, too, Hugh."

124

"You wouldn't shoot us, Sheriff," Lance said. "We didn't do anything."

Rhodes had to laugh. "You don't really think a judge would believe you instead of me, do you?"

"I guess not," Lance said, putting his hands atop his head.

Rhodes patted his shirt pocket. His reading glasses were intact. The Eccles cousins would be in big trouble if they broke his glasses.

"That stick hit me in the face," Hugh said. "You could've put my eye out." He rubbed his cheek. "I think I'm bleeding."

"I'll get you some medical attention at the jail," Rhodes said.

Bruce growled.

"We don't have a cell for dogs at the jail," Rhodes said. "Lance, you put him in your truck. The cab, not the bed. Make sure the window's down an inch or two so he can have some air."

Lance had trouble getting Bruce to obey, but after a little cajoling and a bit of a struggle, he shut him in the cab of the black Silverado.

"Now you two put your hands behind you," Rhodes told the cousins. "I'll get some cuffs."

"You really gonna take us in?"

"I really am."

Rhodes got a couple of disposable plastic handcuffs from the county car and cuffed Lance, then Hugh. He ushered them into the vehicle.

"Who's gonna take care of Bruce?" Hugh said. "You can't just leave him there."

"Don't worry," Rhodes told him. "The county has an animal control officer now."

"You're not gonna give Bruce the gas pipe, are you?"

"Not a chance," Rhodes said. "You and Lance, now, that's a different story."

Hugh didn't say another word all the way to the jail.

Rhodes got Lance and Hugh booked and printed with a minimum of interference from Hack and Lawton. He put the GPS from Lloyd's house in the evidence room and was about to leave again when Jennifer Loam arrived.

"Anything new on the Lloyd Berry murder?" she said.

"There's a dog shut in a truck out on the place where the Eccles cousins live," Rhodes said. "Hack, you'd better call Alton and let him know about it. He needs to put it back in its pen and be sure it has food and water. The Eccles cousins might not be home until tomorrow."

"Wait a minute," Jennifer said. "What's this about the Eccles cousins?"

"Dog story's usually better'n some aggravated assault story," Hack said. "People like readin' about dogs."

"Aggravated assault?" Jennifer said. "What happened?"

"Dog's a better story," Lawton said. "Then there's the alligators."

"Alligators? What alligators?"

Rhodes let himself quietly out the door. The way things were going, it would be late afternoon before Jennifer got a story of any kind out of Hack and Lawton.

Since it was a little past noon, Rhodes thought he'd stop and have something to eat. He didn't want barbecue again, but he thought it might be a good idea to drop in at Max's Place. He might see Wilks there and have a chance to talk to him again.

He was driving over the overpass when Hack called on the radio.

"You need to get over to Happy Franklin's place," Hack said.

"I was going to eat," Rhodes told him.

"Yeah, but somebody tried to kill Happy. He says it was Billy Joe Byron."

"I'm on my way," Rhodes said.

14
▼

HAPPY FRANKLIN HAD BEEN BORN IN CLEARVIEW BUT HAD moved away as soon as he graduated from high school. He'd pretty much stayed away, visiting only occasionally, but he'd moved back several months ago to take care of his mother, who had developed symptoms of dementia. He'd been retired for a while, from what Rhodes didn't know, and he occupied himself with a hobby that had made him well known to a lot of people in Clearview.

Every Tuesday and Friday, the regular days for trash pickup, Happy cruised the streets and alleys of town in his little green Ford Fiesta hatchback as he looked for items that he considered useful or collectible. Rhodes had seen the Fiesta loaded with lamps, bookcases, framed pictures, plants, computer monitors, and just about anything else that someone might leave out on the curb for pickup. Rhodes had no idea what Happy did with the things he found. For all Rhodes knew, Happy was selling them on eBay.

Billy Joe Byron had been around Clearview ever since Rhodes could remember. He lived alone in a little house near the city dump, or, to be politically correct, the city's sanitary landfill. He occasionally retrieved things from people's trash, and while Rhodes couldn't imagine that he wanted to kill Happy Franklin for intruding on his territory, he might have been resentful at a newcomer's assumption that he could help himself to the pickings that Billy Joe had considered rightfully his for many years.

The old Franklin house was just outside the city limits on the south side of town, on the state highway that led to a big coal-burning power plant. Once the Franklin family had farmed the land and had a few cattle, but now everything was overgrown with mesquite trees. Rhodes had heard all his life that spring hadn't really arrived until the mesquites had put out their bright green leaves. If that was true, it was fully spring.

The house looked as if it would surely fall down in the next strong wind. It needed paint, and a new roof wouldn't have hurt, either. Rhodes saw that a couple of bricks were missing from the top of the chimney.

Franklin's Fiesta was parked in front of an old tin barn out back. The barn was so old that rust seemed to be the only thing holding it together. When Rhodes pulled off the highway, Franklin came out of the barn and waved to him. Rhodes drove on back and parked.

"Glad to see you, Sheriff," Franklin said, using a greeting that Rhodes didn't hear often.

Rhodes got out of the car and asked about Franklin's mother.

"She's doing as well as can be expected," Franklin said. "Sometimes her mind is clear as can be, like today. She's inside, watching some soap opera."

Franklin was short and skinny. He wore wire-rimmed glasses, a pair of old jeans, and a paisley shirt that Rhodes thought might have been rescued from someone's discards.

"I didn't call you about my mother, though," Franklin said. "I called you because I'm in fear for my life."

"Hack mentioned something about Billy Joe Byron trying to kill you."

"It was terrible. Here, I'll show you."

Franklin turned into the barn. Rhodes didn't know how Franklin was going to show an attempt on his life unless he had video in the barn, but he followed the little man into the rusty building.

Light came in through several windows and through spaces where tin was missing on the sides. Rhodes saw piles of what he assumed was junk hidden under blue plastic tarps, but some things were out in the open: little tables, short shelves, a couple of tricycles, metal holders for floral wreaths, a lot of plastic kids' toys, and a TV set. A few black plastic bags appeared to hold nothing other than trash, but Rhodes knew that one man's trash could be another man's treasure. He asked Franklin about the bags.

"Flowers. Sometimes Lloyd throws them away with his trash. I can use them."

Rhodes didn't ask what he used them for.

Franklin led Rhodes to one of the windows in the rear of the building. A table sat under the window, and an old radio with a wooden case was on it. Some of the insides of the radio lay on the table beside it, dusty tubes and wires that were older than Rhodes.

Looking out the window, all Rhodes saw were mesquite trees thick as the hairs on a dog's back, but it wasn't the scenery that Franklin wanted to show him.

"Right here it is," Franklin said, putting a finger next to a hole in the tin. He had to reach up well above his head. "That's where the bullet came through."

It looked like a bullet hole to Rhodes, sure enough. The edges flared inward and were shiny, indicating that the hole was recent.

"Here's the other one," Franklin said. He showed Rhodes another hole not far from the first but a bit higher. "I was working here by the window. Those bullets came spanging through there and nearly scared me to death."

Somebody had put a couple of shots through the tin, all right, probably that very day.

"You think Billy Joe Byron tried to shoot you?" Rhodes said.

"That's right. He's been upset with me because I get some of the good stuff, but he lives out by the landfill. He gets everything people take out there all to himself. I never bother about going out and pawing through it, so I don't know what his problem is."

"Did you talk to him about it?"

"Talk to him? You know how he is, Sheriff. How could I talk to him?"

Rhodes knew how he was. A conversation with Billy Joe was possible, but it wasn't easy.

"Did you see him fire any shots at you?" he asked.

Franklin looked out the window. "No. You can't see anything out there, but it must have been him. Who else would it be?"

Rhodes suppressed a sigh. Everybody knew who killed Lloyd Berry, but nobody had any evidence. Now Happy Franklin knew that Billy Joe Byron had taken a shot at him, but he hadn't seen him and couldn't prove a thing.

"Let me show you where the bullets hit," Franklin said.

Across from the window stood something tall, covered by one of the blue tarps. Franklin showed him two holes in the tarp.

"What's under there?" Rhodes said.

"Bookcases," Franklin told him.

Rhodes wasn't sure a bookcase would stop a bullet, but when he pulled the tarp back, he saw that the shelves were lined with books. Not the kind that Weeks sold. These were all Reader's Digest Condensed Books, and they'd stopped the bullets. Rhodes didn't dig the bullets out, however. He reached above his head and took the books out to the county car, where he tagged and bagged them. Then he went back inside.

"I'll take a look out back and see what I can find," he told Franklin. "You don't have to worry about getting shot at again while I'm here."

"What about after you leave?"

"It might be a good idea if you didn't stand too close to the windows. Better yet, stay inside the house and watch TV with your mother."

"You're supposed to protect the public," Franklin said. He looked anything but happy. "It's your job."

Rhodes wondered how many people in the county thought it was the sheriff's job to be sure that they were safe from harm at all hours of the day and night. Most of them, for all he knew.

"If I decide there's a legitimate threat," he said, "I'll see what I can do about some protection for you. I don't have enough deputies to give you a round-the-clock guard."

"Hummpf. Seems to me that's what you ought to do."

"Let me have a look around first and see if there's anything out there that would give me an idea of who shot at you."

Franklin nodded. "I'll stay here and work on the radio. I don't guess anybody would try to kill me with you around."

Rhodes wasn't nearly as certain about that as Franklin was, but it was interesting that the shots had come through the tin so high above Franklin's head. It was also interesting that they'd come in through the tin at all. Why not through the window, where Franklin would have been framed like a perfect target? It was more like someone was trying to scare Franklin, or warn him, rather than kill him.

Outside among the mesquites, Rhodes tried to avoid the thorns while he looked for some evidence that the shooter had been there. Whoever it was would have needed a clear shot at the window, so Rhodes looked for an opening through the mesquite branches.

He found one and followed it for about fifty yards until he came across a place where the grass and weeds were mashed flat. Someone had stood there for a while, concealed among the mesquites.

Rhodes didn't find any other clues. No brass, no cigarette butts, no pieces of clothing caught on a mesquite thorn. He did see where someone had walked through the bushes, and he followed the path down to a dirt road that ran parallel to the railroad tracks. He could see where a car or pickup had pulled off and parked beside the road. No houses were in sight, so no one would have noticed the car unless someone had happened to drive by. Finding that someone would be next to impossible, even if the someone existed.

One thing was for sure, however. Billy Joe Byron hadn't fired the shots. He didn't have a car. He couldn't even drive. So he wasn't the one who'd taken a couple of shots at Happy Franklin.

Not only that, as far as Rhodes knew, Billy Joe didn't have a rifle, so to have fired the shots, he'd have had to get his hands on one somehow. While that wasn't out of the realm of possibility, it was about as likely as Rhodes sprouting wings and flying back to Franklin's barn.

Franklin was still at the table when Rhodes returned, walking because the wings had failed to sprout. Rhodes asked all the usual questions about enemies and arguments. Franklin had none of either. Rhodes asked if any homeowners had objected to Franklin's removing their trash from their curbs. None ever had. They were all happy to see it gone, and they didn't care how it got taken away.

Rhodes knew he was missing something, but Franklin was no help at all. Rhodes finally told him that he was probably perfectly safe in the barn.

"Just don't make yourself a target. Whoever shot at you must have been worried about being seen, or he'd have stayed around to finish the job. I doubt that he'll come back."

"That's not very reassuring," Franklin said. "What about that guard?"

"I'll have a deputy check by often enough to let anybody watching you see that there's a lot of police activity around. I don't think you're likely to have any trouble."

Rhodes wasn't certain if what he'd said was true. How could he be? Somehow, though, he felt that Franklin was out of danger. He'd have felt even better about it if he'd had any idea what was going on, but he didn't.

He left Franklin in the barn and got Hack on the radio. He told the dispatcher to tell Buddy to make an hourly pass by the Franklin house, both back and front. Hack said he'd relay the message, and Rhodes drove back to town.

15
▼

Darrel Sizemore's scrap metal business was on the southwest side of town, near an old cotton warehouse that stood next to the railroad tracks that went on south behind Happy Franklin's house. Rhodes didn't think there was any connection, but it would have been easy enough for Sizemore to drive a few blocks on the city streets to where the dirt road began and follow it out to the Franklin place.

The cotton warehouse was, like so many old buildings in Clearview, about to fall down. At one time, more than a hundred years ago, Rhodes thought, nearly all the cotton in Texas had been produced within a couple of hundred miles of Clearview. Cotton farming was the way of life of most of the population then, but that was all over now.

Rhodes couldn't remember the last time he'd seen a field of cotton in Blacklin County. He'd been little more than a kid, though, and while he knew people who claimed they'd seen the warehouses filled with bales of white cotton, Rhodes didn't remember having seen that at all.

To hear those who recalled it tell the story, boxcars were pulled off on the short spur by the cotton warehouse while men wheeled bale after bale into the cars.

The timbers that composed the floors of the warehouse were thick and solid, strong enough to hold up tons of cotton bales. They weren't likely to rot or crumble anytime soon, Rhodes thought, even if the corrugated tin of the roof and sides rusted away. They still retained some of their silver paint, but it was slowly flaking away and would sooner or later be completely gone.

Rhodes didn't know who owned the old buildings, and he wondered what would happen to them. Maybe Darrel Sizemore would buy the tin for scrap. The timbers might still be useful for building. Someone would take them. They'd disappear, and no one would even remember that the warehouse had been there. Not long after that, Rhodes thought, no one would remember that cotton had been farmed in Blacklin County and that in the fall the gins had run day and night to keep up with the harvest. Most people had forgotten it already, or if they remembered, they didn't care. Rhodes shook his head. He supposed it didn't matter.

Sizemore's office was in a small building by the scale that weighed the vehicles bringing metal to sell. Sizemore was inside, looking through some papers on his crowded desk. He looked up when Rhodes came through the door.

"Good afternoon, Sheriff," he said. His big voice echoed off the walls. "Got any scrap to sell me today?"

"How about some copper?" Rhodes said. "I might be able to get you some aluminum, too."

Sizemore's mouth hardened. "That's not funny, Sheriff."

Sizemore's one brush with the law had come a few years back when he'd been cited for receiving stolen goods. Copper prices rose, making the metal a hot commodity, and people were stealing it anywhere they could, taking coils from air-conditioning units, ripping down telephone cables, stealing copper pipes from plumbing companies and builders.

Aluminum had been rising in value, too, and the main target of the thieves in that case was rain gutters. Rhodes had investigated a couple of drive-by gutter thefts in which someone would wheel a pickup into a front yard and an accomplice standing in the bed would rip the gutters right off the fascias on the house. The pickup would drive away in seconds with the gutters in the bed.

Some scrap dealers never reported nonferrous metals when they bought them, but Sizemore had almost always done it, at least as far as Rhodes was aware. Sizemore had slipped up only once, and that had been because he'd trusted a friend who'd told him that the metal he was selling was all his own property. It hadn't been, and he'd been caught stealing more.

Sizemore had been brought before a grand jury, but he wasn't indicted. Nobody had ever believed he was guilty of anything, but the friend was still serving time in some prison unit or other.

Rhodes hadn't intended to be funny by reminding Sizemore of the incident. He wanted the scrap dealer to be a little off balance and to be honest with him.

"Sorry," Rhodes said, though he wasn't. "I didn't come here to talk about scrap anyway. I want to ask something about Lloyd Berry."

Sizemore didn't ask Rhodes to sit down, but Rhodes sat anyway, in a rickety ladder-back chair that was the only place available.

"What about Lloyd?" Sizemore said. "I'd help you if I could, but I've told you about how I found him. I don't know anything else."

"It's about that music he was buying," Rhodes said. "I was wondering about that."

"We had an argument about it. I told you that, too. I'm not somebody who likes to spend the club's money without a good reason."

"Lloyd had a good reason. He wanted the club to have legal copies of the songs. So I thought there might be more to the story than that."

Sizemore folded his hands on top of the papers on his desk and looked down at them. "There's not anything else to tell," he said, but Rhodes didn't believe him.

"Cecil Marsh thinks you suspected Lloyd of taking the club's money for himself," Rhodes said.

"Cecil. He always thinks he knows more than anybody else, but he doesn't know anything."

Rhodes waited to see if Darrel would continue with that line of thought, but he didn't.

"You want to explain that?" Rhodes said.

"One thing he doesn't know is who sent that valentine to Lindy Gomez."

"Maybe he did that himself," Rhodes said.

"Maybe he did." Darrel's tone was skeptical.

"Right now," Rhodes said, "I'd rather hear if you think Lloyd was stealing from the chorus."

"I never said he was."

"Just tell me about it," Rhodes said. "Make it easy on both of us."

Sizemore sat quietly for a while, looking at his hands. Rhodes didn't say anything, either. Finally Sizemore looked up.

"Okay," he said. "Here's the deal. I thought Lloyd was spending too much money on music mainly because I didn't see the music. He'd give me receipts, but when it was time to practice, he'd say he forgot to bring the new music or that the company had sent the wrong songs and he'd had to send them back. He kept stalling around like that, and I wanted to get a better accounting."

"You never did, though."

"I never did. I don't know why Lloyd would need money. It wasn't that much, just a few hundred dollars. It meant more to the club than it would have to Lloyd."

"Unless his business wasn't doing well," Rhodes said. "Maybe he was having problems."

"Two or three hundred dollars wouldn't help if that was the case."

True. So why would Lloyd have taken the money? Maybe the excuses he'd given Darrel were actually the truth. Or maybe not. Rhodes hadn't seen any stacks of new music when he'd searched the house.

"Lloyd must have been mighty offended when you accused him of stealing," Rhodes said.

"I never accused him of it."

"You hinted at it, though. Cecil Marsh caught it. You could have said more to Lloyd in private."

"If you think Lloyd and I got into a fight and then I conked him on the head, you're all wrong. I could never do a thing like that."

Sizemore might not have been mentally capable, Rhodes thought, but the physical act would have been easy for him.

"I'm not accusing you," Rhodes said. "Just wondering if you and Lloyd had discussed it at any length."

"We might have if he hadn't been dead when I got there," Sizemore said, "but he was."

A bell rang on the wall behind Rhodes, and Sizemore said, "Somebody's on the scale. I know you have a job to do, Sheriff, but I have to earn a living, too."

Rhodes took the hint and left. He wasn't going to get any more out of Darrel anyway. Besides, he was hungry. He wasn't going to miss lunch two days in a row, so he went to the Dairy Queen and had a Heath Bar Blizzard. It wasn't exactly a balanced meal, but it was exactly what he wanted.

Fortified by the Blizzard, Rhodes drove to the jail. He wondered if Jennifer Loam had escaped Hack and Lawton, and he wanted to find out what else was going on in the county. As Roseanne Roseannadanna used to say, it was always something.

16

▼

JENNIFER LOAM HAD ESCAPED THEIR CLUTCHES, BUT HACK AND Lawton were primed for another victim. The big news was that the man doing the jumping jacks in the nude had returned to the Lawj Mahal.

"He wasn't wearin' a jockstrap this time, though," Hack said.

"Nope," Lawton said. "He's a lot more fashionable now."

Both men were grinning like possums eating persimmons, so Rhodes knew the story had taken a bizarre turn, as if it weren't bizarre enough already.

"How does fashion enter into it?" Rhodes said.

"Not so much fashion," Hack said, "as style. Ain't that right, Lawton?"

"That's right. Style. I shouldn't've said fashion. It's definitely style we're talkin' about here."

Rhodes hated to break up the act, but he figured they'd had their fun with Jennifer Loam and could afford to cut things short.

141

"What was he wearing?" he said.

Sometimes Hack and Lawton would respond to a direct question with a direct answer, though not always. This time they were willing.

"Panty hose," Hack said. "And heels."

"Stilettos?" Rhodes said.

"Nope," Lawton said. "Not that kind of heels."

"What kind, then?"

"Cowboy boots," Hack said. "You can bet Buddy burned rubber when he got the call, but the fella was gone by the time Buddy got there."

"And nobody recognized him?"

"Nobody's lookin' at his face," Lawton said. "There's not that many people downtown anyway, and it's the getup that grabs the attention of the ones that are, not the fella's face."

"Have Buddy talk to Lawless about it," Rhodes said. "I think Lawless knows more than he's telling us."

"He hasn't told us anything," Hack said.

"That's what I mean. He must know why somebody would pull a stunt like that. He might even know who it is."

"He won't tell if it's a client. Anyway, whoever the fella is, that's the most excitin' thing to happen downtown since the last building collapsed."

"That's a pretty sad commentary," Rhodes said.

"Yeah, but that's the way it is. I hope the fella gets away with it."

"Lots more important stuff for us to worry about," Lawton said.

"Like Lloyd Berry," Rhodes said. "I think I'll work on that a little more."

"You mean you don't have anybody arrested for that yet?"

"You'll be the first to know when I do," Rhodes said. He stood up and started for the door.

"Where you goin'?" Hack said.

"School," Rhodes said.

Clearview Elementary, HOME OF THE CATAMOUNT CUBS! according to the marquee out front, was located on the northeast side of town, not too far from the local cemetery. It was a new building, or at least not a very old one, with a lot of amenities that had been missing in the school Rhodes had attended, which of c-ourse had been torn down years ago. A housing development had sprung up on the old playground where Rhodes had played softball and touch football.

Rhodes parked in a slot marked VISITORS in the school parking lot, thinking that almost everywhere he'd been lately had reminded him of somewhere else, somewhere that either didn't exist anymore or wouldn't be around for much longer. He was beginning to feel like an exhibit in Jurassic Park.

The security in the school building only made that feeling grow stronger. When Rhodes was a youngster, parents and friends could come to the school, walk through the front door, and go straight to a classroom. Not anymore. Even the county sheriff had to stop by the principal's office, get a visitor's badge, and stick it on his shirt.

That is, that's what he'd have to do if he were planning to visit a classroom. Rhodes wasn't there to do that. He was there to see the principal, and for some reason he felt a little wary, the way he'd always felt when he was sent to the principal's office. He looked around and saw the administrative assistant, whose name badge said she was Connie Calder. She recognized Rhodes at once.

"Hello, Sheriff. I read your book."

Rhodes was puzzled for a second, but then he figured it out.

"You mean *Blood Fever.*"

"That's right. I never knew things in Blacklin County were so exciting. I guess I lead a sheltered life."

"Well, it's not really my book," Rhodes said. "It was written by a couple of women from Dallas, and I'm not anything like Sage Barton."

"Now you're being modest."

"I wish. I'm just telling you the truth. And another thing. That stuff in the book was just made up. None of it ever happened, not one single thing."

"Can they do that? Just make things up about us?"

Rhodes figured that by *us* she meant the county. "They don't say the book takes place here. I think they named the county in the book something else."

"I noticed that, but they told a reporter that you were the model for the sheriff. I read it in the *Herald.*"

Jennifer Loam had enjoyed writing that article, Rhodes knew. He thought the tone had been a little sarcastic, but Ivy had told him it was only his imagination.

"I'm only the model for his looks," Rhodes said. "Is the principal in?"

"Sure. You need to talk to her?"

Rhodes nodded.

"She's not in trouble, is she? About that valentine? She seems like such a nice person, and that wasn't her fault. I have to admit that it was kind of romantic. The quartet sounded great. They stood right here and sang to her through the open door."

"She's not in trouble," Rhodes said. "I just need to talk to her."

"All right. I'll tell her you're here."

Connie disappeared into Lindy Gomez's office, closing the door behind her. She came back in a few seconds and told Rhodes he could go right in, which he did.

The office was carpeted, and the desk was shiny black wood. It had a few neatly arranged papers on it, and nothing more. Pictures on the wall showed some of the classes from past years, and in the middle of the wall opposite the desk was a large framed drawing of the school mascot, the Catamount Cub, done in black and white.

Lindy Gomez got up to greet Rhodes. She was almost as tall as he was, with very black hair and eyes. She had on a brown pantsuit with thin white stripes. Rhodes didn't know much about clothes, but he could tell it was expensive. She didn't seem to be wearing much makeup, if any, but Rhodes wasn't very good at being able to tell that kind of thing. She was just on the pretty side of plain, and there was no nonsense about her. She stuck out her hand, and Rhodes shook it. Her grip was dry and firm.

"Did you come to scare my students straight, Sheriff?" she said after they'd introduced themselves.

Rhodes grinned. "I've never been much good at scaring people, even kids. No matter what your administrative assistant thinks."

"Connie really liked that book about you. She thinks of you as Sage Barton."

"Did you read it?"

"I did. I think everybody in the county's read it."

In his darker moods, Rhodes thought the same thing.

"It wasn't about me," he said. "I hope you didn't believe any of it."

"Not for a minute. Why don't you have a seat and tell me what's on your mind."

Rhodes could tell she'd used that line or a very similar one on many parents. She'd be good at dealing with them when they came to call, and Rhodes knew they'd come to call. Parents did that kind of thing now. His own parents had visited the principal only once that Rhodes could remember, and that was because of an insurance problem when he'd been hurt playing football. Will-o'-the-Wisp Dan Rhodes. A lot of years and a few pounds ago. More than a few.

Rhodes sat in a comfortable red leather chair, and Lindy went back behind her desk.

"You don't have any children in school here, do you?" she asked.

Rhodes was a little too old for that. "No. I have a daughter who lives in Dallas. She's an elementary teacher there."

"I'm sure she's a good one."

Rhodes thought so, too, but he didn't like to brag.

"You didn't come here to talk about teaching, though, I'm sure," Lindy said. "I suspect Lloyd Berry's the reason."

"He's one of them."

Lindy's eyebrows went up. "There's another one?"

"Cecil Marsh," Rhodes said.

"Oh. I should have known."

"I'm just trying to get a picture of what's going on," Rhodes said, shifting his weight in the chair. It had looked comfortable, but it wasn't. That was probably deliberate, to keep people from hanging around too long.

"I was very sorry to hear about Lloyd," Lindy said. "You don't think the valentine thing has anything to do with his death, do you?"

"That's what I'd like to find out," Rhodes said.

"This whole thing has been very embarrassing for me."

"I can imagine. Why would Cecil Marsh send you a singing valentine?"

"I just don't know. He did some work at my house when I moved here last summer. He came highly recommended, and he did a good job. But that's all there was to it. I wasn't even there most of the time he was working. We were hardly acquainted."

She sounded sincere, but then an elementary school principal would have had a lot of practice at that.

"What about Royce Weeks? Do you know him?"

"I don't think so. I'm sure he doesn't have any children in the school. He was in the quartet that sang for me, and that's the only time I've ever seen him."

"Did you know Lloyd Berry?"

"I knew he had the floral shop. I've been in there, so I knew him that way, and he was in the quartet. I didn't know him other than that."

Rhodes believed her. "Did you know any other members of the barbershop chorus?"

"I know Darrel Sizemore," she said. "He was in the quartet, and he sings in the choir at the church I attend. He's short, but he has a big voice."

"Do you sing in the choir?"

Lindy laughed. "I can hardly carry a tune. I just like to listen. And if you're asking whether I know Mr. Sizemore any better than I know any of the others, I don't."

That didn't mean that Sizemore might not have his eye on her, however, and he might have had some motive for framing Cecil. Rhodes would have to look into it.

"I wish I could do more to help you, Sheriff," Lindy said, "but I'm as much at a loss to understand what happened as you are."

"I can see that." Rhodes stood up, glad to be out of the red chair. "If you think of anything that might help me, give me a call."

"I'll do that."

Lindy got up to show him out of the office. Connie Calder put her hand on his arm to stop him before he could get out of the building.

"I wonder if you'd do me a favor," she said.

She held her other hand behind her back, and Rhodes wondered what she was up to.

"That depends on what the favor is," he said.

She brought her hand out from behind her back, and Rhodes saw that she was holding a copy of *Blood Fever*.

"I couldn't go to Wal-Mart when you were signing these," she said. "I hoped you'd sign it for me now."

Rhodes didn't mind kidding around about being a handsome, crime-busting sheriff, but he didn't like being a local celebrity, especially since he'd really had nothing at all to do with the book. He was lucky there hadn't been a movie deal. He'd never have been able to live that down.

"I'll be happy to sign it," he lied, and Connie handed him the book.

While he was fumbling it open to the title page, she got a ball-point pen from her desk and gave it to him.

"Would you mind writing something besides just your name?"

"Like what?" Rhodes said.

Connie blushed. "I thought maybe you could say something like 'From the real Sage Barton.' "

Rhodes gritted his teeth silently. "All right. I'll do that."

He put the book down on Connie's desk and inscribed it as she'd requested, then handed her the book and pen. She thanked him and started to ask something, but Rhodes told her he had to leave and escaped the building into the chaos outside.

When Rhodes was young, kids had walked home from school, or ridden their bicycles. Nobody thought anything of it. Now that the elementary building had been moved so far from the center of things, however, walking and riding bikes were things of the past. Big yellow school buses lined the school's drive, and the line of cars driven by parents who'd come to pick up their children stretched for blocks. It was going to be hard for Rhodes to get out of the parking lot.

Luckily for Rhodes, the volunteer traffic director saw his difficulty and stopped traffic so he could pull out onto the road. She saluted him when he drove past, and he saw that she was one of the graduates of the Citizens' Sheriff's Academy. Maybe the academy had been a good idea, after all.

About the time Rhodes got clear of the traffic, Hack came on the radio.

"He's back," Hack said. Rhodes was about to ask who was back, but before he could, Hack said, "This time he has on a cowboy hat."

"And panty hose?" Rhodes said.

"Tighty whities," Hack said. "I think he's in real trouble now. You ever heard about that guy in New York City, the Naked Cowboy?"

"I've heard of him."

"Well, he sued M&M's for copyright infringement, and they didn't look near as much like him as this guy prob'ly does. Not that I've seen him."

"I'm on my way," Rhodes said.

"So's Buddy, but you're both too late."

"Why's that?"

"I just got another call. He's disappeared."

17

▼

WHEN RHODES ARRIVED AT THE LAWJ MAHAL, BUDDY WAS AL-
ready there, standing in front of the building by his parked cruiser.
When Rhodes drove into the parking lot, Buddy walked over to
the sheriff's car.

"I don't know where he goes, Sheriff," Buddy said, resting his
arms on the roof of the car and looking down at Rhodes. Rhodes
didn't have to ask who *he* was. "I don't get it. He can't just vanish
in the air, but I've looked all around here for a car, and I can't find
one. No sign of anybody wearing panty hose, either."

Buddy was so thin he was almost scrawny, with a prominent
Adam's apple that made it hard for him to shave. Rhodes saw a little stubble on his neck.

"You check on Happy Franklin lately?" Rhodes said.

"I did. I let him know I was coming around regularly, too. But
what's that got to do with a man wearing panty hose?"

"Nothing. I just wanted to make sure you were looking in on Happy. Any witnesses to the panty hose guy?"

"Just one. This time it was somebody from in the law offices that called. She said she saw a man out here in his Jockey shorts with a cowboy hat on. Then he ran off."

"Which way did he go?"

"She couldn't say. I guess he took off while she was on the phone."

"Did he leave anything here?"

"Yeah, he did. This is the first time he's done that."

"What is it?"

Buddy pushed himself away from the car and walked to the front entrance of the Lawj Mahal, a wide wooden double door with a heavy coat of clear varnish on it. Rhodes saw something lying in the doorway. It was a piece of cardboard. Buddy picked it up by one corner and held it so that Rhodes could read the hand-lettered sign:

RANDY LAWLESS
STRIPPED ME NAKED!

Rhodes got out of the car. "I'd say that was a clue."

"I say you're right. You think Lawless is involved in some kind of sex ring?"

Buddy's eyes lit up at the thought. Rhodes knew the deputy would like nothing better than to break up a local sex ring, especially if a lawyer was involved. The trouble with that was that as far as Rhodes knew there had never been a sex ring in the county. He wasn't even sure what a sex ring was, but Buddy obviously had a more vivid imagination.

"I don't think the sign means what you think it does," Rhodes said.

" 'Randy Lawless stripped me naked,' " Buddy read. "Says so right there. Couldn't be much plainer than that."

Buddy's imagination didn't extend much beyond the literal, Rhodes decided.

"I have a feeling it's referring to finances and not clothes," Rhodes said.

"You think?"

"Yes, but we can worry about that later. Right now, let's figure out where the guy went."

"Like I said, I've looked everywhere for a car. Nobody sees him drive off, and nobody knows where he goes. It's like he's here one minute, and then, *poof*!" Buddy made a gesture as if he were throwing dust to the wind. "He's gone."

Since that wasn't possible unless they were looking for David Copperfield, Rhodes figured their man was still around somewhere. There was no hiding place near the parking lot, but right across the street was a line of old buildings, a couple of them deserted. To get into one, however, the man would have to go right through the front door. Somebody was likely to see him if he did that.

Across the street in front of the parking lot was a bank, and on down the block more old buildings, some occupied, some not. A man running down the alley behind the buildings might slip into the back of one of them without being seen. He might even have a change of clothes in there, so that he could get dressed, come back out, and not appear to have been scampering around nearly nude only a few minutes before.

Rhodes told Buddy what he thought.

"Could be," Buddy said. "You think he's still inside one of the buildings?"

"Could be. You take the two across the street, and I'll have a look at the ones down the block. If you don't find anybody, you can come help me. If you do find somebody, let me know."

Buddy looked as if he'd prefer the buildings Rhodes had chosen, but he said, "All right," and crossed the street. He looked both ways, even though there wasn't any need. Rhodes seldom saw a car downtown these days, though he could remember a time when the streets had been crowded with shoppers.

He strolled past the back of the bank and a big metal trash container and came to the back of a building that held a jewelry shop and watch repair business owned by a man named Mize. Rhodes didn't think anybody bothered to have watches repaired now. They just threw them away and bought a new one. Maybe Mize just sold a lot of batteries.

Next door was a building that had once been home to a grocery store so long ago that Rhodes didn't remember whether it had been part of a chain or had been locally owned. After the grocery went out of business, someone had put in a furniture and appliance store, but that hadn't lasted long. The place had been vacant ever since.

A small wooden platform with one step sat in front of the back door. A wider metal loading door was to the right. It was spattered all over with rust.

Rhodes looked at the step and wondered if it would hold him or break when he stood on it. He gave it a try, and it seemed sound enough. He put a hand on the doorknob and turned. It moved smoothly, and the door swung open.

Not much light got into the old store, but Rhodes could see all the way to the front windows, which were dusty and cracked. The cracks were taped, and so far the windows hadn't fallen apart, but it was just a matter of time.

Rhodes stepped inside the building, believing that he had reason to suspect that someone he was pursuing was hiding there. He left the door open behind him.

The place smelled of dust and mold. Several of the town's older buildings hadn't entirely collapsed, but the roofs had fallen in. Rhodes hoped that if the roof on this building was going to fall, it would wait until he'd left.

He looked at the dust on the floor. He wasn't a tracker, but he could tell that someone had been there. That didn't necessarily mean that their culprit was the one, but it seemed like a good possibility. Was he still there? And if he was, where was he?

Rhodes looked around the ground floor. It was mostly one big open space, with no place to hide. A couple of cardboard boxes were big enough for a man to stand in, or would've been if they hadn't caved in on themselves. The boxes had held refrigerators years ago. Rhodes wondered where the refrigerators were now.

On one side of the building was a stairway leading up to a loft about half the size of the ground floor. Rhodes didn't much want to go up the stairs, but he couldn't see what was in the loft, and he figured he ought to take a look.

The stairs were on the dark side of the big room, but Rhodes could see well enough to tell that the thick dust on them was gone in most places. Someone had climbed the stairs recently, more than once.

Rhodes had just put his right foot on the bottom step when he heard something at the back door. He swung around, but it was only Buddy.

"Nobody at those other places," Buddy said. "Both locked up tight."

He didn't bother to keep his voice down, so if anyone was upstairs he'd have plenty of warning that someone was in the building. Rhodes waited until Buddy got near him to speak.

"I think somebody might be up there." Rhodes pointed up the stairway. "I'm going up. You stay here in case he gets past me."

"Right." Buddy drew his .38. "If he gets by you, he won't get by me."

"Don't shoot him," Rhodes said. "Judging from the way he was dressed, I'd say he's unarmed."

"I won't shoot him. Just put a little scare in him."

"Put the gun away, Buddy."

Buddy sighed and holstered the pistol.

Rhodes hated to see a man look so disappointed. "If he tries to get past you, you can tackle him."

Buddy nodded, though he didn't look satisfied, and Rhodes went up the stairs. He didn't see any need to be quiet, not after the conversation he and Buddy had just had. Anybody in the loft would have heard them.

The loft was as bare as the ground floor, but there was a section of it partitioned off from the rest. A couple of offices had been there at one time, and windows had been cut in the walls, though they didn't hold any glass. Rhodes saw a man through one of the windows.

"This is Sheriff Dan Rhodes," he said. "You can come on out now."

The man moved around, but he didn't come out or make any reply.

"I have a few questions for you," Rhodes said. "You're trespassing in a vacant building."

The man came out of the office. He wore jeans and a sweatshirt, cowboy boots, and a western hat. His hands were empty, and Rhodes saw no sign of a weapon.

Rhodes recognized him as Neal Carr, who owned the Burger Barn, a little fast food place on the edge of town, or he had owned it. Rhodes wasn't sure he still did. Carr had recently gone through a divorce that had been the talk of Clearview for a while. His wife had received a more than generous settlement, possibly including the Burger Barn, thanks to the work of Randy Lawless on her behalf.

"Hey, there, Sheriff Rhodes," Carr said. "I'm not trespassing. I own this place."

Rhodes hadn't known that.

"I own a couple of these old buildings," Carr continued. "Not just this one. Bought 'em as an investment. One of these days, I'm going to renovate them and get some businesses started, get downtown perked up a little bit." He paused, and his tone changed. "Or that was my plan when I bought 'em. I can't afford it now."

"No need to blame Randy Lawless," Rhodes said, though he knew Carr would never blame himself, even though Lawless had produced copious evidence of Carr's numerous infidelities. It was the infidelities that had led to the divorce, of course. "You still have your buildings."

"Yeah, but only because my wife didn't want any part of 'em. She wouldn't admit they were worthless, though. Got something else as compensation."

"Like I said, you can't blame Lawless for that."

"Who says I blame him?" Carr asked.

"That sign you were carrying, for one thing," Rhodes told him. "You know, you really ought not to be running around undressed. You could catch cold."

"That's an old wives' tale," Carr said. "Viruses give you a cold. You can go around without clothes all day and not catch a cold if you don't give in to the viruses."

Rhodes had seen the Naked Cowboy on TV a couple of times, and going around without clothes didn't appear to have hurt him. He looked healthy as a horse.

"All the same," Rhodes said, "you need to wear clothes when you're downtown. It's the thing to do, and there are better ways to let Lawless know you're unhappy with him."

"I don't think so, Sheriff. I think I got plenty of attention with the way I handled it. Lawless wouldn't even let me in his office to complain. Now I have the sheriff and a deputy after me."

Rhodes heard Buddy coming up the stairs. "Lawless might not even care what you did, but you upset some people in town. My deputy is one of them. He wants to shoot you."

Rhodes turned slightly to be sure that it was indeed Buddy who was climbing the stairs, and also to be sure that Buddy didn't have his pistol drawn.

As soon as Rhodes turned, Carr ran back inside the office he'd come from. Rhodes didn't know if Carr was going for a weapon or trying to hide. He didn't know whether to drop to the floor or to go for his pistol. So he just stood there.

Rhodes couldn't see Carr through the office window, and Carr didn't come back out. Rhodes heard noises, but he didn't know what they were.

"What's he doing?" Buddy said at Rhodes's back.

"I don't know, but I'm going to find out. You stay here."

"So he won't get by me if he gets by you."

"You got it."

"What about my sidearm?"

"You'd better be ready to use it."

"You can bet on it," Buddy said, sounding pleased.

"Don't get carried away," Rhodes said.

He moved so he could look through the window from a different angle. He thought he saw Carr climbing up the wall.

Rhodes ran into the office. A plank ladder was attached to the wall, and Carr was at the top of it. He pushed up a trapdoor in the roof and went through.

Rhodes didn't remember having seen a fire escape on the back of the building, but Carr must have had a plan. Rhodes went up the ladder after him.

The top of the building was flat, covered with a thin coating of tar on top of something else. A few pieces of newspaper blew around in the wind, and Rhodes wondered how they'd gotten up there.

A low wall edged the roof, and Carr was climbing over the barrier that separated his building from the next one in the block, another one that was vacant. For all Rhodes knew, Carr owned that one, too.

Rhodes had no idea where Carr was headed, but evidently Carr did.

Carr ran across the roof of the second building, bent down, and pulled. Another trapdoor opened up.

Rhodes went after him, giving some thought to jumping the low wall. It would look good in a movie, and it was what Sage

Barton would have done. Rhodes, however, knew he was no Sage Barton. He shook his head and climbed over the wall. In the movie, there'd be a stunt man to do the jumping.

Carr disappeared and pulled the trap down behind him. Rhodes hoped he hadn't secured it, and he hadn't. Rhodes pulled up the door and looked down.

The interior of the building was, if anything, darker than the one Rhodes had just left. He could see the top of a ladder, but that was all. He couldn't see Carr.

He went down the ladder anyway. When he reached the bottom he looked around. He still couldn't see much, but he could hear Carr shuffling across the floor.

Rhodes stood still until his eyes had adjusted to the dimness and he could see Carr not far ahead of him.

This building had a broad stairway that led to the ground floor from the middle of the loft. Carr clomped down the stairs and stumbled about halfway down.

That's what he gets for wearing boots, Rhodes thought, glad that he had on rubber-soled shoes.

Carr rolled over a couple of times, bumping and cussing until he hit the bottom of the stairs. Rhodes was careful and got down without falling. Carr lay still on the floor.

When Rhodes bent over to check on him, Carr grabbed his shirtfront and jerked him down, butting Rhodes's forehead with the top of his own head.

Rhodes fell, stunned, and Carr rolled over on top of him. Rhodes bucked him off, put a foot in his chest, and shoved.

Carr fell backward, landing on his tailbone, but he wasn't hurt. He jumped up and ran for the front door.

Rhodes caught him and took hold of his sweatshirt. Carr

whirled around and slammed Rhodes on the side of the head with his fist.

Rhodes reeled but didn't let go of the sweatshirt. They spun across the dusty floor in an awkward mambo. Carr drew back his hand to swing again, but before he could land a blow, Rhodes flung him across the room and into the front window.

The windows in this building were also taped and cracked. They didn't slow Carr down at all. He went crashing through in a jangle of breaking glass. The shards fell outward and shattered all over the sidewalk.

Carr wasn't hurt. He jumped to his feet and found himself staring into the barrel of Buddy's .38.

Buddy stood with his feet spread, the .38 held securely in a two-handed grip.

"Do you feel lucky, punk?" Buddy said.

Rhodes grinned. He figured Buddy had been waiting all his life to say that.

"Well, do you?" Buddy said.

Carr evidently didn't feel lucky. His shoulders slumped.

"Thanks, Buddy," Rhodes said. "You want to cuff him?"

"You think he'll run?"

"I won't run," Carr said. "I didn't want to cause all this trouble."

Rhodes didn't believe him for a second. Carr knew perfectly well that his arrest would generate a lot of publicity in Clearview. In fact, Rhodes thought that was why Carr had run. Being jailed for something like being a public nuisance would be something of a joke, but now he'd resisted arrest and assaulted an officer. Jennifer Loam might even want to do a jailhouse interview. Front-page stuff for the *Clearview Herald*. Plenty of column inches for Carr to air his grievances. Rhodes was tempted not to charge him.

Buddy holstered his .38 and cuffed Carr, who was perfectly docile now.

"You want me to run him in?" Buddy said.

"Book him, Buddy-O," Rhodes said.

Buddy looked blank. Not a fan of the classic TV crime shows, Rhodes decided.

"Run him in," Rhodes said. "This case is closed."

"Yeah," Buddy said. "Too bad they aren't all this easy."

Rhodes thought about Lloyd Berry and felt the little knot of anger flare in his stomach.

"Too bad is right," he said.

18

▼

RHODES LET BUDDY HANDLE THINGS AT THE JAIL. THAT WAY, he could avoid dealing with Hack and Lawton, who naturally wanted to know all about Carr's arrest. Buddy's version of it was much better than the one Rhodes would have told, and besides, Rhodes had Alton Boyd to deal with.

"You gotta do something about that Bruce," Alton said, chewing on his White Owl stub. "He's not happy bein' cooped up, and he's gonna eat us out of house and home. I think it's time you got yourself a new dog."

Rhodes thought about Speedo, Yancey, and Sam. They'd never take to Bruce, and Bruce wasn't a town dog anyway. His rough-and-ready ways weren't suited to life inside the city limits. First thing you knew, he'd be stealing Royce Weeks's chickens. That is, unless the city council voted that he couldn't keep them.

"Well, Sheriff," Alton said, "he's a mighty fine dog. What do you say?"

Rhodes didn't say anything. He could always drop the charges against the Eccles cousins and let them go home, but that didn't seem like a good idea. They still had a story or two to tell, not the least of which would be about the alligator. Rhodes also wanted them to explain their relationship with Guy Wilks.

"I can't take Bruce home myself," Alton said. He removed his cigar stub and gave it a critical glance. It must have passed inspection, because he jammed it right back in his mouth. "I already got three, and my wife put her foot down about me having another one, even for a visit. So it's up to you. It's not like you'd have to keep him long, just till the Eccles boys get out of jail."

Rhodes didn't think it was up to him, and he knew it would be a while before the Eccleses would be leaving since they didn't seem eager to make their bail. Rhodes did, however, have another idea.

"Let me make a call," he said.

Rhodes went with Alton to deliver Bruce to his new, possibly temporary, home. Seepy Benton was standing in his front yard, waiting for them.

"I don't see why you think I need a dog," Benton said when Rhodes got out of the van.

"Look around," Rhodes said. "A man living out here alone needs a watchdog. You never know when an alligator will drop by."

"Too late," Benton said. "That's already happened, and it wasn't so bad."

"Next time could be worse. You could get one of those mutant alligators, like the one in that movie. *Lake Placid*, that was the name of it."

"I think that was a crocodile," Benton said.

"Whatever. You need a good dog to keep watch for you, and this is a good dog. He'd keep you company out here, too, all alone in the country like you are."

"I'm not alone. I'm just barely out of town. People drive down this road all the time."

"It's not the same as having a dog around, though," Rhodes said.

While Rhodes and Benton were talking, Alton got Bruce out of the van. Bruce strained against the leash that Alton had on him. He wasn't used to anything like that.

"That's a big dog," Benton said when Alton walked up with him. "He looks . . . mean."

As if to emphasize the point, Bruce made a short lunge in Benton's direction and started to bark. Alton held on tight to the leash, and Bruce dragged him forward several inches.

"I think he likes you," Rhodes said.

"I think he wants to eat me," Benton said.

"Bark's worse'n his bite," Alton said around the cigar stub. "He's a little excited right now, but he's nice and gentle."

Bruce stopped barking and trembled at the end of the leash. Alton tightened his grip.

"Gentle as a wolf," Benton said.

"You have a good place for him, though," Rhodes said. "A big fenced backyard will give him some room to run around, and you can take him for a walk down the road every day. You two are a perfect match."

"If I can keep him from running away with me. He might drag me down the road."

"You do a hundred push-ups every day. You're a lot stronger than he is. Did I mention that Deputy Grady loves dogs?"

For the first time, Benton showed real interest. "She does?"

"She does. I'm sure she'd like to come out and visit Bruce now and then, see how he's getting along."

Alton looked at Rhodes out of the corners of his eyes. Rhodes avoided his glance. Both of them knew Ruth wasn't all that fond of dogs and wasn't at all likely to come to check on Bruce.

"I suppose we could let him stay overnight," Benton said. "To see how he likes the place and to see if we can get along together."

"You'll be soulmates within an hour," Rhodes said. "Alton and I even have a surprise for you."

"You mean *another* surprise."

"All right, another one. We went by and picked up some dog food for Bruce so you wouldn't have to worry about that. I paid for it out of my own pocket."

"Feeling guilty, were you?" Benton said.

"Just doing you a favor. I'll get the dog food while you and Alton introduce Bruce to the backyard."

Rhodes went to the van, and the other two men went around the house with the dog, Bruce in the lead. Rhodes got the bag of dog food and put it on Benton's porch. Then he returned to the van for two more surprises.

When Rhodes got to the backyard, Alton had taken Bruce off the leash, and the big dog was sniffing around the base of the wooden fence. Any second now and he'd start marking it.

"Here you go," Rhodes said to Benton.

Benton turned toward him, and Rhodes tossed him a large rawhide bone.

"Bruce will love that," Rhodes said.

Benton held it in his hand and stared at it.

"Heads up," Rhodes said, throwing Benton a big rubber ball.

Benton dropped the bone and caught the ball.

"You and Bruce will have a lot of fun with that," Rhodes said.

"You know a lot about dogs?" Benton said.

"A couple of them live at my house. You and Bruce are going to enjoy each other's company."

Benton looked skeptical. "I wish I was as sure of that as you are."

"Trust me," Rhodes said. "I wouldn't steer you wrong."

"No," Benton said. "After all, you're an officer of the law, and officers are our friends."

"You got that right," Alton said.

Rhodes was sure he'd done the right thing by Bruce and Benton both. Bruce would have a good home while the Eccles cousins were in jail, and Benton would have some company.

"You don't really think Ruth's gonna go by there to see about that dog, do you?" Alton said when he let Rhodes out at the jail.

"She might," Rhodes said. "You never know."

"You're mighty sneaky, Sheriff, and that's all I got to say about it."

"Sometimes that's what it takes," Rhodes said.

After Bruce was taken care of, Rhodes had a few more stops to make before he went home. The afternoon was almost gone, but he thought he had time see the two people he wanted to talk to.

Tom Fulton was behind the counter in his store, cheerful as ever, when Rhodes walked in.

"Welcome back, Sheriff," Fulton said. "You decide you needed a good GPS to tell you where to go?"

Rhodes didn't reply.

"That's another joke, Sheriff. A little more GPS humor. 'Tell you where to go.' You get it?"

Rhodes got it. He wasn't sure he wanted it, however. He said, "I have a question for you."

"Fire away. As you can see, I'm not exactly surrounded by customers here."

Rhodes wondered how Fulton managed to pay the rent on his store. It could have been that he was just having a slow week. He did have customers now and then, and so did the other shops in the center. Rhodes still couldn't quite understand why nobody had seen anyone go into Lloyd's place.

"When I was in here yesterday," Rhodes said, "you told me that Lloyd Berry came by occasionally."

"That's right. He did. We'd talk a little, maybe I'd tell him a GPS joke or two."

Rhodes hadn't thought there could possibly be more than two GPS jokes. "There's more?" he said.

"I got a million of 'em," Fulton said with pride.

Rhodes wasn't so sure it was anything to be proud of, and anyway he hadn't come there to talk about jokes. He said, "Lloyd didn't always come by just to talk, did he?"

Fulton looked puzzled. "What do you mean?"

"I mean he had a GPS in his car. I didn't find a receipt for it when I searched his house, but I thought he must have bought it from you."

"I'd have to check my records on that," Fulton said. "I don't remember him buying one."

It seemed to Rhodes the kind of thing Fulton should have remembered. Having so few customers, he'd certainly be likely to know if a shopkeeper in the same strip center had bought a GPS from him.

"I'm not the only one who sells these things," Fulton said. "Wal-Mart's got 'em, and you know how that goes. They undercut everybody on the price, and some folks don't care about supporting their local businesses if they can get what they want for a dollar less. Just look at what's happened to the downtown."

Rhodes had looked at downtown enough for one day. He knew what it was like, though he wasn't sure it was all Wal-Mart's fault.

"Why don't you check your records," he said. "Just to humor me."

"You don't have to get touchy, Sheriff. I'll take a look."

Rhodes didn't think he'd been touchy. Fulton was the one who'd seemed that way to him. Fulton pulled back a green curtain and went into his office. He sat down at a desk and started doing something with a computer.

After a while he came back out. "He didn't buy it from me. Like I said, he must've got it at Wal-Mart."

That surprised Rhodes, who'd thought that Lloyd would support the other businesses in the center. Unless, of course, he had a reason not to buy from Fulton. Rhodes wondered what the reason might be. To save a dollar? Or was there more to it than that?

"If I'd been buying flowers, I'd have bought them from Lloyd," Fulton said. "Wal-Mart sells flowers, but I wouldn't have bought them there. I guess Lloyd didn't feel the same way I do about things."

"I guess he didn't," Rhodes said. He thanked Fulton for the information and went next door to Rollin' Sevens.

The crowd looked pretty much the same as it had the day before, except that Hugh and Lance were missing. Rhodes still wondered about those two. They'd had no real reason to get feisty with him yesterday, and even less reason to attack him that morning. There was more to it than chickens and alligators, Rhodes was sure, but so far the cousins weren't talking. He hoped that after they'd spent a night in jail, they'd change their minds.

Wilks came out of the back room before Rhodes had gotten more than a couple of steps inside the front door of Rollin' Sevens. Unlike Fulton, Wilks didn't seem at all happy to see Rhodes again.

"Are you trying to ruin me, Sheriff?" he said.

His tone wasn't aggressive, but it was clear he thought Rhodes was out to get him.

"You've come in here two days in a row," Wilks continued. "I think that's a little excessive. I run things right here, and I don't appreciate it."

He turned around and walked back to his office. Rhodes followed along behind.

"Are you still here?" Wilks said when he turned and saw Rhodes enter the office. "I thought you'd be leaving."

"Not until we talk," Rhodes said.

Wilks walked around him and looked out into the gambling room. Rhodes turned and looked, too. A couple of people were already leaving.

"You're harassing me, Sheriff," Wilks said. "You're trying to close me down, and I haven't done anything wrong."

"I didn't say you had," Rhodes told him.

Wilks went behind his desk and sat down. "If you're not trying to shut me down, what do you want?"

Rhodes sat in the wooden folding chair. "I want to ask you about the Eccles cousins."

"What about them?"

"They jumped me yesterday after I finished talking to you."

"I'm not responsible for those two. They're just people who like to play the games, and they didn't like having you run everybody off."

"I didn't run anybody off. All I came in for was to talk about a man who'd been murdered. Just like now."

Wilks shook his head. He wasn't interested in hearing about the murder or Rhodes's reasons for dropping in.

"And all my customers are leaving again," he said. "Before long, they'll be afraid to come in at all. It's not right, Sheriff."

Rhodes wondered if Wilks had seen the story on the news about the Houston police crushing the eight-liners. He supposed a story like that would make Wilks a little too quick to take offense where none was intended.

"I went out to see the Eccles boys this morning," Rhodes said. "They jumped me again."

"And that's supposed to be my fault? I can't help it if they don't like you."

Rhodes got the impression that Wilks believed the Eccles cousins were just showing good judgment in attacking Rhodes. In fact, Wilks looked as if he wouldn't mind having them do it again, preferably where he could watch.

"You didn't ask them to cause trouble, did you?" Rhodes said.

"Of course not. Why would I do that? It's bad for business."

That wasn't necessarily true. If the gamblers thought that Rhodes could be intimidated, they'd be less likely to worry if he showed up at the Rollin' Sevens.

"I didn't come here about the Eccles boys anyway," Rhodes said. "I came about Lloyd Berry."

"I thought we'd covered that yesterday," Wilks said.

"Things have changed since then," Rhodes said. "I've talked to a few other people. What they said didn't quite jibe with what you told me."

Wilks leaned forward on his desk. "So you think I didn't tell you the truth? How about these 'other people'? They could be mistaken, you know."

"Sure they could, but I believe them."

Wilks pushed himself up so that he was leaning forward with his arms braced on the desk. "Are you calling me a liar?"

"No," Rhodes said, "but I do think you might want to reconsider what you told me and see if you could have been mistaken."

"I don't even know what you're talking about," Wilks said. He sat back down in his desk chair.

"I'll tell you what I mean," Rhodes said.

He took his little notebook out of his pocket and flipped through the pages. He couldn't really read what he'd written there without his glasses, but he didn't bother to put them on. It didn't matter. The notebook was just for show. Rhodes remembered very well what he'd written. He stopped flipping the pages and put his finger on one, pretending to read it to himself. After a second, he looked up at Wilks.

"Yesterday you said you didn't really know Lloyd very well. You mentioned that you'd seen him a time or two at Max's Place, though."

"That's right. I eat lunch there now and then. It's a new place, so it's a change for me."

Rhodes wondered if it was the place that was the change or if Wilks thought the barbecue was better than at the other local spots. Rhodes thought it was at least as good and that Max had a chance to make a success of the restaurant.

"You didn't tell me that you sat at the same table with Lloyd," Rhodes said. "You didn't mention that you were friends."

Wilks dismissed that idea. "Who said we were friends? When that place first opened, it was crowded. I couldn't take one whole table for myself, so maybe I shared. That doesn't make me somebody's friend."

"It's funny you didn't say anything about sitting with Lloyd, that's all. Seems like you'd have mentioned that."

"I must've forgotten it. It didn't make any impression on me."

Rhodes was sure that Wilks was lying. Rhodes didn't know why, but he could tell something was out of kilter.

"Now that I've refreshed your memory," he said, "do you happen to remember what you talked about?"

"Sports, maybe. It was a while back. We didn't share anything intimate, I can tell you that much. If we had, I'd remember that."

He sounded convincing.

Rhodes didn't believe him anyway.

19

▼

RHODES WENT BACK TO THE JAIL AND HIT THE LAW BOOKS, looking for something about alligator ownership. It wasn't the kind of legal question that occurred every day, and he still wasn't clear about it.

Neither was the law, he discovered. The legislature had tried to do something about it around the turn of the new century by having the state's counties enact their own laws, so Rhodes had to look into the county book. As far as he could determine, Blacklin County had so far taken no action regarding the scaly reptiles, which meant that as far as he was concerned Hugh and Lance were in the clear when it came to having the alligator on their property.

"They still assaulted you, though," Hack said when Rhodes told him what he'd been looking up in the law books.

"Sicced their dog on you, too," Lawton said. "Don't forget that."

Rhodes wasn't forgetting anything. "They assaulted me twice. I let them get away with it once, so maybe the second time was my fault, in a way."

"That's what they're sayin'," Lawton told him. "They've hired Randy Lawless to get 'em out of here."

"All they have to do is post their bond," Rhodes said. "Then they can go home."

"They don't want to post their bond," Lawton said. "They want the charges dropped."

"You sure are gettin' to be a friend to the felons," Hack said. "Givin' 'em a shoulder to cry on and all."

Lawton bristled. "I didn't give anybody a shoulder to cry on. I happened to hear what they were sayin' to each other while I was cleanin' the cell next to theirs, that's all."

"You gonna talk to the DA and ask him to drop the charges, Sheriff?" Hack said, ignoring Lawton.

"No." Rhodes pushed the law books away. He took off his reading glasses, put them in his shirt pocket, and stood up. "Or maybe I will. I have to talk to Lance and Hugh first. If they cooperate, I'll see what I can do about helping them out."

"They might've decided they like it here," Hack said. "We run a nice operation."

"Nobody likes being in jail," Rhodes said. "No matter how nice it is."

"Puttin' dangerous criminals back on the street's not gonna get you any votes in the election," Lawton said.

Rhodes wished they'd quit bringing up the election. "That's next year," he said, "and the Eccles boys aren't dangerous. Just misguided."

"Misguided." Hack shook his head. "That's what all you bleedin' hearts say."

"I'm not a bleeding heart."

"That's what you claim, but you wait till those Swift-boaters get hold of you. You'll look like you voted for Vladimir Putin in the last election."

"I didn't even know he was running," Rhodes said.

"That was just kind of an example of what they'll do to you," Hack said. "You get the idea."

"I get the idea, but I don't think my opponents will stoop to that kind of thing."

"Sure they won't," Lawton said. "Do you even know who they are?"

"How could I know? I keep telling you that the election's a year away. More than a year, if you don't count the primary. Nobody's even running against me yet."

"That shows what you know," Lawton said.

Rhodes was taken aback. "You mean I already have opponents and don't know it?"

"I ain't sayin' you do, and I ain't sayin' you don't."

"I'm saying I don't, then. I think you two are getting a little carried away. Maybe you're worried because you think a new sheriff would make a clean sweep of this place and get him some new help around here."

"Fine with me," Lawton said. "I been thinkin' it was time for me to retire."

"Far as I can tell, you retired about six years ago," Hack said.

"Look who's talkin'. You haven't hit a lick at a snake since I've known you."

Rhodes decided that the best thing he could do was let them fight that one out among themselves. While they were distracted, he left the office and went back to the cellblock.

The Eccles cousins shared a cell, and both of them lay on their bunks. Hugh was in the upper, staring at the ceiling. In the lower, Lance stared up at the bottom of his cousin's bunk. They lay flat on their backs, their hands crossed on their chests, almost as if Clyde Ballinger had laid them out for burial. All they needed was their Sunday suits instead of the swanky orange jumpsuits furnished by the county.

Rhodes tapped on the bars and said, "You fellas doing all right in here?"

"Sure," Hugh said without moving. "We got ourselves three hots and a cot. Beats driving a truck."

"I thought you wanted me to ask the DA to drop the charges so you could go home."

"You hear that, Lance?" Hugh said. "I told you that old coot was listening in on us."

Rhodes grinned when he thought of how Lawton would feel about being called an old coot. Lawton could call himself an old coot, but he wouldn't like it even a little bit if someone else did.

"I hear you have a lawyer, too," Rhodes said.

"That's right. We made our phone call to Mr. Randy Lawless. He's never lost a case."

Rhodes knew better than that. Lawless had defended several people Rhodes had arrested. None of them were back on the streets yet.

"He did Janine Carr's divorce," Lance said, raising his voice. "Took Neal for everything he had."

"I heard that," Neal Carr said. He was in the next cell, and

Lance had obviously known that. "I hate that son of a bitch Lawless."

"You gotta admit he's a good lawyer," Hugh said.

"He's scum, is what he is," Carr said. "I had a good business at the Burger Barn. I had big plans, and things were going good for me before that skunk got hold of me."

"You were running around on Janine, is what I heard," Hugh said.

"That's a lie, made up by that snake Lawless to get my money."

"He must be pretty good, then," Lance said. "Just the kind of fella we need on our side."

"I wanted to talk to you about your side of things," Rhodes said. "I've looked into the alligator laws, and you're in the clear there."

Lance sat up and swung his legs over the edge of the bunk and sat up. He had to lean forward because there wasn't enough clearance for him to sit up straight.

"We aren't in here because of the alligator," he said. "We didn't have one on our land, and even if there was one, it wasn't ours."

"You're right," Rhodes said. "You're not here because of the gator. You're here because you assaulted me and sicced a dog on me."

"I wish I'd had a dog," Carr said.

"You be quiet," Rhodes said. "I'm not talking to you."

"You want something from us, don't you, Sheriff," Hugh said. He still lay on his back, looking up at the ceiling. "I wonder what might it be."

"It might be that if you cooperate with me a little, you won't have to spend the night here."

"That reminds me," Lance said. "What about Bruce? He might

die locked up in that truck where you left him. He needs some-body to look after him."

"Bruce has a good foster home. You don't have to worry about him."

"Maybe we'll just leave him in the foster home. He eats too much, and he didn't do anything to save our chickens from that damn ga—that damn coyote."

Hugh turned over on his side. "You never did get around to say-ing what you wanted, Sheriff."

"Cooperation," Rhodes said. "I mentioned that."

"Cooperation. That's just a word. What's it mean?"

"It means I want to know what made you two so contentious at the Rollin' Sevens yesterday," Rhodes said.

"You pissed us off," Hugh said. "Comin' in there like that, like you owned the place. We wanted to relax and play a few games, and you busted things up, chased people out, spoiled the fun."

That wasn't what had happened, and Hugh must have known it. Rhodes pointed it out anyway. "Then," he said, "when I came out to your place today, you acted the same way. If I were thin-skinned, I'd think you two didn't like me."

"We like you fine, Sheriff. You shouldn't intrude where you aren't wanted, that's all. If you'd mind your own business, we wouldn't get upset with you."

"That's what I say," Carr piped up from the neighboring cell. "What business is it of yours if I want to protest my treatment by that goober Randy Lawless?"

"It's not the protesting," Rhodes said. "It's the way you did it."

"How'd he do it?" Lance said. "The protest, I mean."

"He wore panty hose."

"Hoo-ha! A man in panty hose. Now that's something to think about, especially here in the jailhouse."

"He had on tighty whities, too," Rhodes said.

"Not that there's anything wrong with that," Hugh said.

Rhodes would never have guessed that Hugh was a Seinfeld fan.

"Don't you two get any ideas," Carr said. He stood at the front of his cell, his hands gripping the bars. "It was part of the protest, and that's all it was. It was symbolic."

"I bet it was," Lance said. "You still got 'em on?"

This was worse than Hack and Lawton, Rhodes thought. He said, "Carr, I told you once to be quiet. Go sit on your bunk and don't say anything. Not a word."

Carr tried to look tough, but he couldn't pull it off. He went and sat on the bunk.

"Now," Rhodes said when Carr was out of the way. "Do you two want to help me out, or do you want to stay here for a while?"

"We'll stay," Lance said. "We got the best lawyer in Blacklin County. He's gonna make you wish you'd never arrested two honest men like me and my cousin."

"Yeah," Hugh said. "Two honest men, locked up for no reason at all."

Rhodes could see he wasn't going to get anything out of them, but he still thought something was going on between them and Wilks. He didn't know what, but he'd find it out, even if it took a while.

"If that's the way you want it," he said. "You can get in touch with me any time you change your minds."

"We won't be doing that," Hugh said and rolled over on his back.

"Yeah," Lance said. He lay back down and looked up at the bottom of his cousin's bunk.

Rhodes left them there like that.

When Rhodes got back to Hack and Lawton, they weren't speaking. Hack was watching Judge Judy on his little TV set, and Lawton was sweeping the floor.

Rhodes didn't ask what was going on. He didn't want to know. He hoped to get out and on his way home before they said anything, but he didn't quite make it. He had his hand on the doorknob when Lawton spoke up.

"You want to tell Hack about his TV?" he said.

Rhodes didn't turn around. This was a new argument, and he didn't want any part of it. He had to make a response of some kind, however, so he said, "What about his TV?"

"About how it's not gonna be any good in a little while."

"This little TV works fine," Hack said. "I don't care what you say."

Rhodes knew then what the problem was. Lawton had brought up the fact that TV signals would all be digital soon, and Hack's little TV, an old analog model, wasn't going to be able to receive the signals. They'd talked about this before, and Hack knew very well what the situation was. However, he was deep in denial. Rhodes didn't know how they'd gotten onto the topic from their earlier argument, but it didn't take much for a conversation between those two to jump the rails.

"We'll see about getting you another TV if that one doesn't work any longer," Rhodes said.

"Took forever for me to get this one," Hack said. "I doubt I'll ever get another one."

"If the county won't buy it, I'll take up a collection."

"Don't count on me to put anything in the plate," Lawton said. "A man talks to me like Hack did don't deserve a TV."

Rhodes didn't ask how Hack had talked to Lawton. He said, "That TV is like the election. It's something we don't have to worry about right now."

"I never said I was worried," Hack told him. "That was Lawton."

"You'll see I'm right about it," Lawton said. "You just wait."

Rhodes opened the door and got out before Hack could say anything. The two of them would be at it for a while. Rhodes didn't know why Hack needed a TV set anyway. He had more fun arguing with Lawton than he did watching television.

Rhodes didn't want to argue with anybody. He wanted to spend some time relaxing at home while he tried to sort out everything he knew about Lloyd Berry's murder. He kept thinking there were some things he'd heard or seen that hadn't quite registered with him. If he had time to think, maybe the pieces would fall into place.

But of course he didn't get any time.

At first things went just fine after Rhodes arrived at home. Ivy had gotten off from work a little early, and she'd made her famous meatless meatloaf. The first time she'd made it, Rhodes asked if meatless meatloaf wasn't an oxymoron.

"Like government intelligence," he said.

Ivy hadn't thought it was funny, and Rhodes hadn't brought it up again. He still didn't believe you could have meatloaf without meat, but it wasn't bad. In fact, it was pretty good. Maybe it was the sauce, which was tasty and tangy and disguised the flavor of whatever meatless ingredients were in the dish. Rhodes had never asked what they were.

Sam watched them eat from his place near the refrigerator, while Yancey, calm for once, lay by the back door, waiting for Rhodes to finish eating and then take him out to play with Speedo.

That's what Rhodes would have done if the telephone hadn't rung.

"You want me to answer it and tell them you're in Timbuktu?" Ivy said.

The ringing excited Yancey. He jumped up and ran to Rhodes's chair, where he started to yip and dance. Sam eyed him with suspicious disdain.

"How do you know it's for me?" Rhodes said.

"It's always for you."

She had a point, and for a fraction of a second, Rhodes was tempted to let her answer and see if anyone would believe he was in Timbuktu. Or, even better, Kathmandu. However, his sense of duty got the better of his momentary whimsy.

"I'll take it," he said.

Hack was the caller. "What's that noise?" he said.

"One of the dogs. He's excited."

"He needs to calm down. You might want to get over to Cecil Marsh's place right quick. There's a fight goin' on. Shots fired. One of the neighbors called it in. Duke's already headed that way."

"Me, too," Rhodes said.

20
▼

Duke Pearson's county car pulled to the curb in front of the Marshes' house, and Rhodes pulled in right behind him.

"I drove in from Happy Franklin's place," Pearson said when Rhodes got out of the car. "Everything's quiet out there. What's going on here?"

Pearson was a big, cheerful man whose thick black hair was turning gray. He hadn't been with the department long, but he wasn't new to law enforcement. He'd been a deputy in west Texas before he and his wife had moved to Clearview, her hometown, to take care of her mother. Rhodes felt lucky to have another experienced officer on his staff.

"I think Cecil Marsh and Royce Weeks are at it again," Rhodes said.

"Again?"

Pearson hadn't been in town long enough to know all the details of the feud, and Rhodes didn't have time to fill him in on everything.

"They don't like each other," Rhodes said. "Never have. They've had arguments before, bad ones, but up until now there hasn't been any shooting."

As he spoke, he heard raised voices, two men yelling at each other.

"Doesn't sound like shooting," Duke said. "Guess we should be careful, though."

"Absolutely," Rhodes said, and both men drew their sidearms, Rhodes taking his from the ankle holster and thinking again that it might be time to change its location. Maybe he'd return to using the middle-of-the-back holster, but that was hard to hide if he didn't wear a coat, which he never did in the summer.

"Sounds like it's coming from over there," Duke said, pointing with the pistol barrel in the general direction of Weeks's chicken coop.

"Better take flashlights," Rhodes said.

It was already getting dark, and heavy clouds hung in the north. The wind was picking up, and it looked as if rain was on the way.

"Right," Duke said.

Before they could get the lights from the cars, Faye Lynn Marsh came down her front walk.

"Sheriff, is that you?" she said.

"It's me," Rhodes answered. "And Deputy Pearson. What's going on here, Faye Lynn?"

"It's Cecil," she said. "He's trying to kill Royce's chickens." Her voice cracked; she sounded as if she might start crying at any second.

"What got them started this time?" Rhodes asked.

"The chickens were fluttering around and getting ready to roost. Cecil was already upset, for some reason, and the chickens do make a good bit of noise. Cecil said he couldn't stand it any longer. That's when he got the shotgun. It's a little four-ten loaded with birdshot."

Rhodes considered that good news. A four-ten wasn't a formidable weapon even against a chicken when it was loaded with birdshot. That didn't mean it wasn't dangerous, but at least Cecil wouldn't be as likely to kill somebody with it as he would with a bigger-caliber gun.

"Do you want me to talk to him, Sheriff?" Faye Lynn said.

It was a little too late for that, Rhodes thought, now that Cecil was running around with a shotgun in his hand.

"I don't think so," Rhodes said. "I'll do the talking."

Faye Lynn looked at the pistol Rhodes held down at his side against his leg.

"You aren't going to shoot Cecil, are you?" she said.

Rhodes noticed that she hadn't mentioned anything about not shooting Weeks.

"We're not going to shoot anybody," Rhodes said. "We're just being cautious. Come on, Duke."

Rhodes and Pearson headed in the direction of the yelling, Rhodes a little in the lead. When they got closer, Rhodes waited for a lull in the argument and then announced that he and his deputy were there and that they were coming to talk.

"You can't talk to this big lunk," Royce Weeks said. "You better watch him, Sheriff. He has a gun."

Rhodes was close enough to see the two men now. Cecil did indeed have a gun, a single-shot four-ten. Rhodes was glad to see that it was pointed at the ground and open at the breech.

The chickens were still disturbed. Rhodes heard them clucking and fluttering around in the henhouse as they tried to get settled. It wasn't a bothersome noise, at least not to Rhodes. A gunshot would have been much more disturbing.

"Hey, Cecil," Rhodes said. "Deputy Pearson's going to take your gun. It's not loaded, is it?"

"Not now," Cecil said. "Why should I let him take it?"

"Because I said so and because you don't want him to have to take it away from you. Too risky. You could get a broken finger that way."

Rhodes kept his pistol trained on Cecil. Duke holstered his own sidearm and stepped up to Cecil. Cecil didn't put up any resistance. He handed Pearson the four-ten. Duke checked to be sure it was unloaded and nodded at Rhodes.

Now that Cecil was disarmed, Rhodes and Duke turned on their flashlights.

"Well, now," Rhodes said. "Here's what's going to happen. Duke is going to take Cecil home to his house, and I'm going to take Royce home to his. Deputy Pearson will talk to you, Cecil, and I'll talk to Royce. After that, we'll switch around, and after that, we'll decide what to do with the two of you."

"You can't do anything to me," Cecil said. "I didn't shoot at Royce, just his chickens. Maybe you should arrest Royce for disturbing the peace."

"Discharging a firearm in the city limits is a misdemeanor," Rhodes said. "You'll get a citation for that, and we'll decide if that's all there is to it. Maybe so, maybe not. You go with Deputy Pearson, and I'll go with Royce."

Cecil didn't like it, but he went. Rhodes watched him and Duke walk away to be sure Cecil didn't try anything. Nothing happened.

Cecil seemed docile enough. Rhodes holstered his pistol and turned to Royce. "All right. Let's go have that talk."

They walked to the front of the house, Rhodes lighting the way with his flashlight.

"Cecil's crazy, Sheriff," Royce said. "You know that, don't you?"

"No, I don't know that. He's a little excited about those chickens, but that doesn't mean he's crazy."

"This isn't about chickens," Royce said as they passed between the arborvitae bushes and went in through his front door. "There's more to it than that." He flipped a light switch. "Watch out for the books."

Rhodes had been prepared for the clutter, and he didn't step on any books as he entered the room.

"You can sit down if you want to," Royce said, taking his own seat at the computer desk.

Rhodes looked at the chair where he'd sat previously. The seat was covered in books, just as it had been on Rhodes's last visit. The one on top was an old paperback called *Lust Is a Woman*. Rhodes moved the books to the floor and sat down.

"Tell me about the chickens," he said.

"It's more than the chickens."

"I know. You told me. But I want to hear what caused the ruckus the neighbors called me about. Seems it had to do with shooting at chickens."

"I hope they don't blame me for it," Royce said. "I didn't do any shooting."

"I don't know who they blame," Rhodes said. "If you'll tell me about it, maybe I can sort it out."

"Okay, here's what happened. I was sitting right here at the computer, looking at some of my auctions, and I heard Cecil outside. He was yelling something, and then he fired off the shotgun. I jumped up and ran out there, and he fired off another round before I could get to him. I started hollering at him, and he broke open the gun. He didn't reload, but you saw that. He yelled something about my 'damn chickens,' and that's when he got crazy."

"About the chickens?"

"No. That's what I've been trying to tell you. It's not about the chickens. It might've started out that way, but that's not it any-more. Not all of it, anyway."

"What is it then?" Rhodes said.

"It's Faye Lynn."

If there was one thing Rhodes knew about conversations like this one, it was that he never knew what kind of turn they were likely to take. Sometimes things were straightforward enough; sometimes there was a twist that he just wasn't expecting. Faye Lynn's name coming into it was that kind of twist.

"What about her?" he said.

"He accused me of having an affair with her."

Rhodes was so surprised he couldn't say anything for a while.

"Kind of surprised you, didn't I, Sheriff?" Royce said.

Rhodes admitted it. "I thought that after all these years of fuss-ing and fighting, you and Faye Lynn were enemies just like you and Cecil."

Rhodes thought back to his earlier conversation with Faye Lynn. He couldn't think of a thing she'd said that indicated any kind of affection for Royce. Just the opposite, in fact. Of course, that might have been because she was covering up. On the other hand, Cecil might really be crazy.

"We don't like each other as far as I know," Royce said. "I told you Cecil was nutty. If that accusation doesn't prove it, I don't know what will. I think the county ought to lock him away where he won't hurt anybody. Next time he might use that shotgun on me instead of just trying to kill my chickens."

"Did he kill any this time?"

"I don't think so. You'd have to hit one in the head with that four-ten to kill it. I don't think he's that good a shot. He wished he was shooting at me, though, I can tell you that."

"Did he give you any reason for thinking you and Faye Lynn were fooling around?"

"How could he? We weren't fooling around. Cecil might be nuts, but I'm not."

"What did he say, exactly?"

"Exactly? I don't know He was yelling. So was I. It was pretty confused."

"Approximately, then."

Royce looked thoughtful. "He said something like 'I know what you've been up to with Faye Lynn.' He called me a name or two. He said the evidence was clear, or something like that. I don't have any idea what he was talking about. I just know he's crazy."

Rhodes was beginning to think Royce had a point. He said, "Is that all you can remember about it?"

"Look, Sheriff, he had a gun. For all I knew he was going to shoot me, and that birdshot stings even if it doesn't kill you. Instead of listening to Cecil, I was wondering why I ever went out there in the first place and wishing I'd stayed in the house. I wasn't too worried about the nonsensical ravings of a lunatic mind, but I was worried about the gun. So no, I don't remember anything else that Cecil said."

Something Royce said had a familiar ring to it.

"*Young Frankenstein,*" Rhodes said. "I didn't know you were a movie fan."

"Only of certain movies. Anyway, the line seemed to fit Cecil pretty well. He's a lunatic, for sure."

"Maybe not," Rhodes said. "I'm going over to ask him about all this. You stay right here. Deputy Pearson will be coming over to talk to you."

"I don't have anything else to say. You have it all."

Rhodes didn't bother to explain that he wanted to see if Royce would tell essentially the same story to Duke or if things would change. He just said, "You might think of something."

"I don't think so."

"We'll see," Rhodes told him.

21

▼

WALKING OVER TO THE MARSH HOUSE, RHODES WONDERED about what he'd just heard. Was it possible that Marsh was right about his wife and Royce? If he was, it might explain why Weeks had sent the singing valentine to Lindy Gomez. He could have been trying to show Faye Lynn that Marsh was being unfaithful, so there was no reason why she shouldn't be.

There were a few problems with that idea, however. Rhodes didn't know that Royce was the one behind the valentine, and he'd gotten the impression that the affair, if there even was one, had been going on for a while. At this point, Faye Lynn wouldn't need any persuasion. Besides, Rhodes believed Royce was telling the truth and had never had any kind of romantic relationship with Faye Lynn.

Duke Pearson came out the Marshes' front door and met Rhodes on the sidewalk.

"I didn't get much out of either one of them," he said when Rhodes asked. "I never knew of anybody to get so upset over a bunch of chickens, though."

"Supposedly there's more to the story," Rhodes told him. "You go talk to Royce and get his side of things while I see what the Marshes have to say. Then we'll go to the jail and sort through it."

Duke said that was fine by him. Thunder rumbled in the north, and lightning flashed in the thick clouds.

"We're going to get wet if we aren't careful," Duke said and went over to Weeks's house.

Rhodes knocked on the Marshes' front door and entered without waiting for either of them to come let him in, which was just as well since neither of them did.

Rhodes found them sitting in the living room. The copy of *Southern Living* was still on the coffee table beside the *Harmonizer*, and the big yellow candle was still unlit. This time, however, it was Cecil who sat in the swivel rocker. Faye Lynn was on the couch. Neither of them said anything to Rhodes, so he sat on the end of the couch opposite Faye Lynn.

"Okay," he said, "who wants to start?"

"Start what?" Cecil said.

"Start telling me what the heck is going on here. Shooting chickens, rousing the neighborhood, yelling at the top of your lungs. There must be a good reason."

"Those damn chickens bother me," Cecil said.

Rhodes looked at Faye Lynn, who was looking at the candle as if it were the most fascinating thing she'd ever seen.

"So you didn't make any accusations against Royce?" Rhodes said.

"Did he tell you I did?"

Rhodes hadn't expected this to go well, or easily, and he'd been right.

"Yes. He said you accused him of—"

"Never mind what I accused him of. He's a liar and the truth's not in him. You can't believe a word he says. I went over there to shut those chickens up, and that's all there is to it."

"Shooting at them just got them excited," Rhodes said. "It made things worse instead of better."

"If I'd had a twelve-gauge, I'd have shut them up."

"You'd better be glad you didn't have one. You'd be in worse trouble than you already are." Rhodes paused. "Faye Lynn, I sure could use a glass of water if you wouldn't mind getting me one."

Faye Lynn jumped up from the couch as if she'd been waiting for the chance. "I'll get you a glass of ice water," she said. "I'll be right back."

When she was out of the room, Rhodes said, "Okay, Cecil, do you want to tell me what you and Royce were arguing about now, or do you want me to take you to the jail?"

Cecil looked around the room as if he expected Faye Lynn to pop back in without warning. Rhodes had a feeling that wasn't going to happen.

"Maybe I said something to Royce," Cecil said after assuring himself that Faye Lynn was nowhere around. "I don't remember for sure."

"Your memory's not that bad, Cecil," Rhodes told him.

"That's what you think. It's got to where I can hardly remember my name."

"A sure sign you're getting older. You can remember what you said to Royce, though."

Cecil looked down at his hands and laced his fingers together. Rhodes waited. Finally Cecil said, "I accused him of having an affair with Faye Lynn. I didn't want to say that. I hope you're satisfied."

Rhodes didn't feel any particular satisfaction, but he was glad Cecil was cooperating.

"Why would you accuse him of something like that? They don't even like each other."

"That's what you'd think, but you never can tell. Living right next door to each other, and me being gone all day. Faye Lynn gets lonesome, and Weeks is over there by himself, playing around with that computer of his. Things can happen."

"You're wrong about that, Cecil. Nothing ever happened between those two."

Cecil shook his head. "How come you know so much about what goes on around here?"

"I talked to Royce. He says nothing happened, and I believe him."

"Well, I don't."

"You must have more than just your suspicions."

"I'm not saying anything else."

"I think you'd better. Just to clear the air before your wife gets back in here. Otherwise, you'll have to talk about it with me *and* her. I'm not leaving until you tell me."

Cecil unlaced his fingers, cracked his knuckles, and rolled his shoulders.

"This is my house," he said. "You'll leave if I tell you to."

"It may be your house, but I'm the sheriff," Rhodes said. "I'm investigating a complaint from your neighbors. You can't just throw me out."

"I could try." Cecil flexed his fingers, which were thick, strong, and calloused from using a hammer. "I might not be able to, but I might have fun trying."

"It wouldn't be as much fun as you think. Don't forget that I have a pistol."

"You wouldn't shoot me, Sheriff. I know that much about you. I'm an unarmed man. That other cop locked up my shotgun in his car."

"You're right. I won't shoot you. You won't try to throw me out, though, because deep down you want to tell me what's going on. So go ahead and do it."

Cecil relaxed his hands and looked around the room. "Sure is taking Faye Lynn a long time to get you that drink," he said.

"She knows we need to talk. So talk."

Finally Cecil did. He said, "Here's how it is. I found things in the house, stuff I didn't give Faye Lynn. That's how I know."

"What kind of things?" he said.

"The kind of things a man might give a woman if he was courting her."

Rhodes seemed to remember that when he was in school, his English teacher always told him to be specific. Cecil must have had a different teacher.

"Candy?" Rhodes said. "Flowers? Love poems?"

"None of that stuff. What I found was toys. Those kind of soft little animals that kids like. You know the kind of thing I'm talking about?"

Rhodes nodded.

"She had a lot of them hidden in her closet. That's where I found them."

Rhodes didn't ask why Cecil was going through his wife's

closet. Instead he asked why Cecil suspected Royce of being the one who gave Faye Lynn the toys.

"Because he's right here, right next door, and he's just the kind of rat who'd sneak around and do something like that to get back at me."

He might have said more, but Faye Lynn came in with a glass of ice water in one hand and a napkin in the other. She wrapped the napkin around the glass and handed it to Rhodes, who didn't really want a drink. He took a couple of sips and handed the glass to Cecil.

"I could use a refill," Rhodes said.

Cecil wasn't one to take a hint gracefully, but after giving Rhodes a look that would peel paint, he took the glass and left the room.

"Your turn," Rhodes said to Faye Lynn. "I guess you heard pretty much everything we said."

Faye Lynn sat on the couch. "I heard. I can't believe Cecil could be that dumb. He should know I'd never run around on him, certainly not with Royce Weeks. What was he thinking?"

Rhodes couldn't tell her. Sometimes a man didn't think, at least not rationally. Instead, he did stupid things, like shooting at his neighbor's chickens with a four-ten shotgun.

"So you and Royce aren't friendly?" he said.

"Good Lord, no. We don't like each other even a little bit. That's just some notion of Cecil's."

In spite of her denial, Rhodes got the sense that she wasn't telling him everything.

"And you don't get lonesome here in the house by yourself all day?" he said.

Faye Lynn didn't have anything to say to that. She looked at the door through which Cecil had left the room.

"I never said that."

So maybe she had been fooling around, but not with Royce. Rhodes waited for her to go on.

"I don't get lonely, though. That's not it. I just get bored. Did you ever try to watch TV during the day?"

Rhodes had at one time enjoyed TV in the afternoon, but it had been twenty years or more since the afternoon movie had been worth watching. For that matter, there wasn't an afternoon movie to watch anymore.

"All that's on is talk shows and judge shows," Faye Lynn said, and Rhodes thought of Hack. "I hate those things. I read some-times, and I do a little yard work, but I still get bored."

By now Rhodes thought he knew exactly where things were headed, but he waited for Faye Lynn to tell him.

"What happened was that somebody told me about this place where there was gambling," she said. "Not like Las Vegas or any-thing, but you could win a little prize, like a stuffed animal."

"Rollin' Sevens," Rhodes said.

"So you know about it?"

Rhodes told her that he did indeed know about Rollin' Sevens.

"Then you know what it's like. It's kind of a family atmos-phere, and it's not like you're really gambling. They even have door prizes, but I never win one."

Rhodes didn't remember having seen Faye Lynn in Rollin' Sevens, but there was a good reason for that.

"I haven't been in a while," she said. "Cecil was looking for an old work shirt of his that he thought might've gotten put in my closet, and he must have found my stuffed animals. He didn't mention them to me, and I never told him I was gambling. I knew he'd think it was a waste of money." She paused. "Maybe it was, but I liked having something to do with my time."

"You never thought about getting a job?"

"Cecil's old-fashioned about that kind of thing. He says a wife's place is in the home. But we never had any kids to take care of, and there was never that much for me to do. After all those years, I had to get out for a while. Just had to."

Rhodes could have offered her some more suggestions. She could have joined a club. She could have done some volunteer work at the hospital. Or any number of other things. He didn't think she'd listen to him. She'd found her outlet without his help.

He started to tell her anyway, but he thought of something else he wanted to ask.

"Do you ever see the Eccles cousins there?" he said.

Faye Lynn smiled. "Those two redheaded truck drivers? They're there now and then. They're luckier than I am."

"Do they ever give anybody any trouble?"

"Why, no. There's never any trouble. It's more like they take care of the place to make sure of that."

While Rhodes was thinking about that, Cecil came back into the room with the same glass of water. The ice was mostly melted, and the napkin was soaking wet.

Cecil handed the glass to Rhodes, who dutifully took a drink.

"Gambling," Cecil said. "I should have known."

Faye Lynn couldn't very well accuse him of eavesdropping. After all, she'd done the same thing. She said, "Would it be better if I'd been having an affair with Royce? Why didn't you just ask me about those stuffed animals?"

"I don't know," Cecil said. He looked at Rhodes. "What would you have done?"

"Hard to tell," Rhodes said. "I'm pretty sure I wouldn't have gone out and tried to kill some chickens, though."

Cecil didn't think that was funny. "Why don't you write me a ticket and be done with it? Faye and I need to talk."

"Sounds like a good idea to me," Rhodes said.

Rhodes left the Marshes there to hash out their problems, which now included a citation for Cecil, and drove to the jail. Duke Pearson had brought in the shotgun and filled Hack in on the details of the encounter, saving Rhodes no end of trouble and giving him a chance to ask Pearson what he'd learned from Royce Weeks. Duke's report didn't add anything to what Rhodes already knew, and Duke left to make another run by Happy Franklin's place.

Hack filled Rhodes in on some of the other things that had happened that day. The only one of interest was that Happy Franklin's mother had called just after Pearson took off to see about Weeks and Marsh. She'd claimed that someone kept trying to tear her house down, so she was just going to have to move.

"She ever called about that before?" Rhodes said.

"Not that I remember. She's called about stampedin' cattle, and once about a pack of wild dogs, but that's about it."

"It could be that someone's prowling around out there," Rhodes said. "Did you tell Duke?"

Hack gave him a hurt look. "You think I'm too old for the job and my memory's shot? 'Course I told him. He's on his way out there right now, ain't he?"

Rhodes ignored the sarcasm. "Did she mention Happy?"

"Said he was out in that workshop of his. Barn's more like it. He oughta be in the house with her, especially after dark."

"Especially after somebody's taken a couple of shots at him," Rhodes said. "I wonder who Happy's gotten so upset."

"Don't know. I'm just the dispatcher. I don't get paid to worry about stuff like that."

"What about our prisoners?" Rhodes said.

"What prisoners? Carr bonded out, and Randy Lawless came by and bonded out the Eccles boys."

"I thought they were planning to stay."

"I think Randy convinced 'em that was a bad idea. Anyway, they're gone."

"I'm gone, too," Rhodes said, thinking it was time he got home.

He was halfway to the door when the radio crackled. It was Duke, letting Hack know that he was at the Franklin house and that he thought something was going on. Rhodes stopped to listen.

"Somebody tryin' to tear the house down?" Hack said.

Duke said something that Rhodes couldn't hear, and Hack said, "The sheriff's right here. Want me to send him out there for backup?"

Again Rhodes didn't hear the answer, but he didn't have to. He knew what it would be.

"Tell him I'm on the way," he said.

22

▼

THE RAIN STARTED JUST BEFORE RHODES GOT TO HIS CAR. IT wasn't much of a rain, just enough to be annoying. Rhodes got in the car and turned on the wipers. They smeared the dust around for a few seconds before clearing the windshield. As soon as he could see, Rhodes took off.

Driving toward Franklin's place, he thought over what Weeks and the Marshes had told him. He knew he'd failed to follow up on something that might have been important, but he couldn't think what it was. He hoped Cecil and Faye Lynn got their problems worked out. Maybe all they really needed was to have a good talk to get things out in the open. Or not. Rhodes didn't feel qualified to be a marital counselor.

Cecil's problems with Royce Weeks weren't going to go away no matter how much talking got done, even if Faye Lynn convinced Cecil that his ideas about her having an affair with Royce were wrong.

More aggravating than that, Rhodes was no closer to finding out who'd killed Lloyd Berry, but right now he was worried about what was going on with Happy Franklin. He couldn't figure out why anyone would shoot at Happy or prowl around his house after dark. Maybe Duke had caught the prowler, and Rhodes would get his questions answered.

It didn't work out like that, however.

Rhodes saw that there was a light on in the barn, so he drove there and parked beside Duke's car. Duke and Happy were inside talking. Rhodes got out and joined them.

"What's going on?" he said.

"We don't know," Duke said. "Happy didn't hear anything or see anything. His mother swears she did, though."

Rain rattled down on the tin roof of the barn, sounding much louder than it would if they'd been inside a shingled building.

"My mother's not exactly the best witness in the world," Happy said. "She sees and hears things that aren't there."

Rhodes remembered a time before Happy had moved back home. Mrs. Franklin had called the sheriff's department to report that someone had sabotaged her washing machine. As it turned out, the only problem had been that the load of clothing in the machine was unbalanced. Rhodes had redistributed the load, and all was well. He didn't think that this was a repeat of something similar, though.

"Those bullet holes are there," Rhodes said, pointing at the wall.

"Yeah, they are," Happy admitted. "I'm not saying nobody was here. I'm just saying I didn't see them. Didn't hear them, either."

"What about you?" Rhodes asked Duke.

"I didn't see anybody, but I heard somebody running through those mesquites out back of the barn when I got here."

"Are you sure you didn't hear anything?" Rhodes said to Happy.

"I can barely hear *you* with that rain beating on the roof. How could I hear anybody outside?"

Rhodes believed him. "How's your mother's hearing?"

"Her hearing's not a problem. She can hear a dust mite walk across a powder puff."

Since she was under an insulated roof, she might have heard something Happy hadn't. She might have seen something, too.

"You go talk to her, Duke," Rhodes said. "I'll check the pasture."

"Are you sure?"

Rhodes was sure. He didn't like getting wet, and he knew it would make Ivy unhappy with him, but, as much as he hated to admit it, he *liked* being the one who got to do the more dangerous jobs.

"There's probably not anyone there," he said. "I'll check it out and come right back."

"Probably not anyone anywhere," Happy said. As I said, "my mother's not the most reliable witness."

"We'll ask her anyway," Rhodes said. "Go on and talk to her, Duke."

Duke left the barn, and Rhodes got his flashlight from the car. He put on a rain slicker while he was at it. It wouldn't help a lot, particularly below the knees, but it would be better than nothing. It might even be thick enough to keep him safe from mesquite thorns.

After checking to be sure that Happy was still safely in the barn, Rhodes slogged off through the mesquites. Their wet leaves brushed his face, and he tried to avoid running directly into one of the trees.

The heavy clouds made it difficult to see where he was going, but he didn't want to turn on the flashlight and give anyone a warning or make himself a target. His training was that if you used the light, you held it out to the side so that if someone shot at the light, you'd be safely out of the way. The problem with that was in trusting in the fact that whoever did the shooting could hit what he aimed at, and Rhodes wasn't that trusting. He'd always thought that someone shooting at the light would miss and hit him.

Whoever had shot at Happy earlier that day hadn't even come close. Just the kind of person who'd miss the flashlight by a mile.

Rhodes got to the railroad tracks without falling down or getting scratched by a thorn, a major accomplishment. On the other hand, he hadn't seen or heard anyone, which wasn't much of an accomplishment at all.

He decided it was time to risk the flashlight. He held it well away from him and turned it on.

The yellow beam reflected from the raindrops, but it wasn't strong enough to cut through the darkness. It didn't reveal anything. No car sat beside the road. No one was hiding in the ditch. The only sound was the pattering of the rain on Rhodes's slicker.

Beside the railroad tracks and off to his left, the remains of an old roundhouse loomed in the darkness like the ruins of Dracula's castle. The roundhouse hadn't been in use in over sixty years, Rhodes was sure, probably a lot more than that. The tracks had long since been torn up and either melted down or used elsewhere, and Rhodes suspected that hardly anybody in Clearview even remembered the roundhouse was there. It was the only hiding place around, other than the thick mesquites, so Rhodes thought he'd have a look. He turned off the flashlight and started toward the rubble.

He hadn't gone far before he heard something, a scraping noise as if someone had started running on the other side of the round-house.

Rhodes started to run, too. Big mistake. The ground was uneven, and before he'd gone twenty yards, he stepped on a stick that somehow flipped up between his legs, tripping him. He fell into a shallow depression that had begun filling with water. He dropped the flashlight and splashed around looking for it. By the time he found it and got up, whoever had been running away, if indeed there had been anybody, was long gone.

Rhodes stood where he was for a while. He didn't think he could get any wetter. Cold water had gotten under the slicker and into his shoes. His socks were soaked.

He wasn't quite sure what he was waiting for, but after a couple of minutes, he heard a car start somewhere down the road. A couple of headlights appeared, and then the car sped past. Rhodes couldn't even tell what make it was, much less read the license plate. The red taillights disappeared in the murk of the night.

Rhodes thumbed the button that turned on the flashlight. He pointed the light at the ground and picked his way back to the barn, being careful not to fall into any more puddles.

"She heard somebody outside a window," Duke was telling Happy when Rhodes walked in. "She thinks he was ripping boards off the house with a hammer. That's all she knows."

"Maybe the first part of that is true," Happy said. "I don't think the last part is. We'd be able to tell if any boards were missing. She does have dementia, after all."

"Somebody was here, though," Duke said. "There are tracks in the mud. Did you see anybody, Sheriff?"

"I got a glimpse of somebody, I think, but he got away." Rhodes looked at the water pooling at his feet. "I fell in a puddle, and he got away."

The rain had slowed almost to a stop outside, but it still made noise on the tin roof.

"I don't get it," Happy said. "Why would anybody come creeping around here? I don't know that many people in town. I've never had a problem with anybody except Billy Joe Byron, and you say it's not him."

"He can't drive, and he doesn't have a gun," Rhodes said. "Whoever's slipping around has a car. And a gun. Maybe you've offended somebody by accident."

"I wish I knew who it was so I could apologize."

"I don't think he wants an apology," Duke said. "Not the way he's acting."

"What *does* he want, then?" Happy said. "If he'd tell me, maybe I'd give it to him."

It occurred to Rhodes that maybe Happy had hit on the problem.

"Have you picked up anything valuable lately?" he said. "Anything that somebody would want back?"

"Not that I know of, and nobody's asked for anything. Wouldn't they ask instead of trying to kill me?"

"You'd think so, wouldn't you?" Duke said.

Rhodes wasn't sure now that anyone was trying to kill Happy. It was more like someone was trying to scare him. They discussed it a little longer, but they couldn't come up with anything helpful. Duke agreed to drive by the house and to check the back road every half hour or so, though Rhodes didn't think anyone would be coming back that night. It was too wet and too dark. Nevertheless, he didn't want to take any chances. After they'd settled on that plan, Rhodes went home.

The ten o'clock news was just starting when Rhodes walked into his house. Rhodes had hoped Ivy might be in bed already, but she was waiting for him. So was Yancey, who went into his happy dance, skittering around Rhodes's feet as if greeting someone who'd returned from six months' travel.

"You're wet," Ivy said.

"It's raining," Rhodes said. "Or it was."

"Not that much," Ivy said.

Rhodes decided he might as well tell her the whole story. Just as he'd thought, she got a good laugh from the part where he fell down.

"Here I am," she said, "worrying about you getting your head blown off, and the worst thing that happens is that you fall in a puddle. Serves me right. You, too."

Rhodes knew that Ivy worried about him. She'd gotten better about it since the first few months of their marriage, but she'd never gotten used to the fact that he was sometimes in danger.

"Nobody shot at me," he said. "Nobody even hit me with anything."

"You look like somebody tried to drown you."

Rhodes looked down and saw water was oozing out of his shoes and dripping off his pants. Yancey stopped larking around and lapped at the water droplets that beaded up on the floor.

"You don't know where that's been," Rhodes told him.

Yancey kept right on lapping the water. Sam walked over to see what was going on. Yancey saw him and ran to the other side of the kitchen. Sam sniffed the water and walked back to his usual spot. He turned around a couple of times and lay down, resting his chin on his front paws and looking at Yancey with his yellow eyes. Yancey whimpered. Rhodes sneezed.

"You're going to catch cold," Ivy said.

"Not me. It's not the cold and wet that causes problems. It's viruses. A prisoner told me that today."

"He's right, but if you get wet and cold, you help out the viruses. You need to take a hot shower and get to bed."

"I'm not sneezing because of viruses, either. It's that cat. I'm allergic to him."

"You're not allergic to Sam. It's all in your mind."

She always said that. Rhodes wasn't convinced.

"It's the cat," he said.

"Even if it is, you need a hot shower."

"My gun got wet. I have to clean it."

"You can clean it after we shower," Ivy said.

"Well," Rhodes said, "Since you put it that way . . ."

23

▼

THE WEATHER FRONT PASSED THROUGH DURING THE NIGHT, AND the next morning was bright and dry. Rhodes went to the jail with the feeling that during the course of the past couple of days he'd gathered pretty much all the information he needed, but he still hadn't put it into any coherent order. Hack and Lawton were no help.

"Guess you heard about Elvis," Hack said when Rhodes walked in.

"I heard long ago," Rhodes said. "He's been dead for years. I'm not that far behind the times."

"Not that Elvis," Lawton said, and Rhodes knew he was in trouble even though it was still early in the morning. Still, he had to ask.

"Which Elvis are we talking about then?"

"The one that lives with old Miz Coggins," Hack said.

"Oh," Rhodes said. "That Elvis."

The Elvis that lived with Ms. Coggins wasn't a person, even though Ms. Coggins might have considered him one. Elvis was a neutered male dog, a mixed breed. Nobody knew just which breeds were mixed in him, but there were several, none of them attractive except to Ms. Coggins.

"Elvis's got woman trouble," Lawton said.

Rhodes didn't see how that was possible, considering Elvis's neutered state, but again he couldn't resist asking.

"What kind of woman trouble?"

"Not the kind you think," Hack said.

"I'm not thinking of any particular kind. I was just wondering."

"Woman's stealin' him blind," Lawton said, earning a dirty look from Hack.

"What can a woman steal from a dog?" Rhodes said.

"Food," Hack said. "That's what."

"A woman's eating dog food?" Rhodes said. He knew how unlikely that sounded, but stranger things had happened in Clearview. "Is it canned food or dry food?"

"You're gettin' the wrong idea," Hack said.

And it was no wonder, Rhodes thought. With those two, it was a miracle that he ever got the *right* idea.

"Why don't you tell me exactly what's going on," he said, and to his surprise, Hack did.

"It's a female dog that's stealin' his food," Hack said. "Miz Coggins puts it in a bowl on the back porch, and this female dog comes around ever' mornin' and eats it. Elvis is scared of her, won't go around his bowl till she's gone. By then, all the food's gone, too, Miz Coggins says."

"Elvis's gettin' all shook up over it," Lawton said, and that was enough to get him dirty looks from both Rhodes and Hack.

"Did you send Alton to catch the female?" Rhodes said.

"Won't work," Hack said. "That dog's not a stray. Miz Coggins knows who she belongs to. It's Lew Chandler."

"Why doesn't she call Lew?"

"Says it's up to us to be sure Lew's dog don't get out."

"That's Lew's job, but if Alton brings her in, that should get Lew's attention. Call Alton and put him to work on it."

Hack said he'd do that.

"Anything else going on?" Rhodes said.

"Just the usual. Nothin' you need to worry about."

Elvis hadn't been something Rhodes needed to worry about, either, but Hack and Lawton couldn't resist an opportunity to give Rhodes the business.

"All right," Rhodes said. "Since everything's under control, I'm going to do some more investigating. Be sure to have Ruth check on Happy Franklin's place every half hour, and give me a call if you need me."

"Don't I always?" Hack said. "Where you goin'?"

"Lloyd Berry's house," Rhodes said.

Rhodes went through Berry's house again, but he didn't find anything he'd overlooked the first time. So he called Seepy Benton.

"Benton's the name, and math is my game. What can I do for you?"

Rhodes identified himself and told Benton he needed to work on a new greeting.

"I'll do that, Sheriff, and what can I do for you today? You need somebody who can bend reality with his bare hands? I'm your man."

"I need somebody with a GPS. Do you have one?"

"Actually, the GPS is up in orbit. So I don't have one. I have a GPS receiver, though. In fact, I have two, one for the car and one I can carry around."

That came as no surprise to Rhodes.

"I'm writing a song about a GPS," Benton continued. "You remember Lou Reed's 'Satellite of Love'?"

Rhodes had to confess that he didn't.

"Great song. Anyway, I'm writing one called 'GPS of Love.' It's going to be even better than Lou's."

Rhodes said he was sure that was true. "Can you come to Lloyd Berry's house and bring your GPS with you? Your receiver, I mean."

"Anything to help out the law, you know that. I'll let my department chair know where I'm going and be there in a jiffy. Or in a car. One or the other. Or both."

"I'll be waiting," Rhodes said.

Benton arrived in a jiffy and a car. Rhodes met him at the curb and asked about Bruce.

"He's doing fine," Benton said. "I bought him one of those igloos at Wal-Mart. I had to get a really big one, but I think he likes it. He eats a lot, but that's okay. I think he and I are going to be good friends."

"How good?" Rhodes said.

"He likes me. I like him. That good. Why?"

"You might be stuck with him. The Eccles cousins mentioned something about leaving him in his foster home."

Rhodes hoped they'd do it. Bruce would be better off with Benton, who'd already seen to a better shelter for the dog than any-thing Rhodes had seen at the Eccles place. Benton would probably feed him better, too.

"He's welcome to stay with me," Benton said. "I don't want to steal him from his rightful owners, but if they don't want him back, he's right at home in my backyard." He paused. "I thought maybe Deputy Grady would come by and check on him, but she hasn't."

"She's been pretty busy," Rhodes said. "I hope you didn't take Bruce just because you thought she might drop by."

"No, no. I wouldn't do a thing like that. I like Bruce as a per-son. Or as a dog. You know what I mean."

Oddly enough, Rhodes did know.

"That's good," he said, "because Bruce may be living with you for a long time."

"I hope so," Benton said, "but you didn't call me out here to talk about Bruce."

"No. I want to have a look at some of those locations that Lloyd had in his computer history. Can we do that?"

"Sure. I'm fully armed with GPS receivers. They're both in the car."

Benton opened the door of his car and got a small portable re-ceiver out of the glove box. Rhodes noticed it was a Garmin and asked if it was from Tom's TomToms.

"I bought it online," Benton said. "I know I should support lo-cal businesses, but I got this before I moved to Clearview."

Rhodes told him not to feel guilty about it, and they went inside to check the computer coordinates. After Benton had programmed three of them into the Garmin, they left to find the sites.

The first one was in Obert, down a county road that went past the college and the rock crusher. Rhodes had investigated crimes at both places, but the location they were looking for was at the foot of an old wooden bridge that was due for replacement soon. It took them a while to find the exact site, even with the receiver leading them, and when they did, there was nothing there.

"Someone's moved the cache," Benton said. "They're not supposed to do that. You just record that you found it, or if you take what's there, you replace it with something else."

So Benton knew the rules of geocaching, too. Again, Rhodes wasn't surprised. Benton seemed to know about everything.

"Let's try another site," Rhodes said.

The next location was a block away from what had once been downtown Obert, near the remains of the old Obert school. Not the college but the public school, which had shut down in the 1950s when the school district had consolidated with Clearview. The redbrick building was nothing more than a brick facade now, with no roof and no glass in any of the window openings. When Rhodes and Benton found the cache location, they again found nothing.

"That's funny," Benton said. "I don't know what the game is, but it's not geocaching."

"We don't know for sure," Rhodes said. "Doesn't it take three points to make a line?"

"Yes, but this isn't a line. It's a game with rules."

"I still want to check one more site."

"Fine with me. I can avoid doing any actual work that I'm being paid for."

The third site was at an old roadside park on the highway back to Clearview. The park looked as if no one had used it in years. The concrete benches on both sides of the concrete picnic table were cracked, and the table was covered with dirt, along with leaves and sticks that had fallen from the big oak tree that spread over it.

The cache was at the base of the tree, by the top of one of the thick roots that sank into the ground, and nothing was in it.

"You have a real mystery here," Benton said. "But a professional crime-solver like you isn't going to be baffled by a little thing like this."

"That shows how much you know about professional crime-solvers like me," Rhodes said. "I'm as baffled as you are."

"You'll figure it out. Just like I can solve any math problem."

"We'll see," Rhodes said. "Have you talked to any members of the chorus lately?"

The leaves of the oak rustled above them, moving spots of sunlight and shade over the table and ground.

"I talked to Max today," Benton said. "He's thinking he might be a good director. I encouraged him."

"Isn't he too busy with his restaurant and his music store?"

"He has more energy than three normal people. He can handle it."

"What about Lloyd? Has anybody mentioned him to you?"

"Darrel Sizemore called today. He's still worried about the money. He says that there should be a lot more music than there is."

"He still thinks Lloyd was stealing from the group."

"He hasn't put it that way, but that's what he thinks. Did you find any music when you searched the house? Maybe he had it stuck away somewhere."

"If he did, it was stuck where I couldn't find it. Like whatever was in these caches."

"Just another mystery for you to work on. It probably doesn't matter in the long run. Nobody killed Lloyd to steal sheet music."

"No, but it's funny that the music would disappear."

"He may never have ordered it. Darrel thinks he faked the receipts."

"There are a lot of things about all this that don't make any sense at all," Rhodes said, more to himself than to Benton.

"Maybe Lloyd was like me, able to bend reality with his bare hands."

"That would explain it," Rhodes said.

24

▼

RHODES WAS BUCKLING HIS SEAT BELT WHEN HACK CAME ON the radio.

"Randy Lawless wants to know if you can come by his office," Hack said. "He has some clients who want to talk to you."

"Which clients would those be?" Rhodes said, though he had a pretty good idea.

"The Eccles cousins. Randy wants to thank you, too. He's glad to have Neal Carr off the streets."

"I thought you said he'd bonded out."

"Yeah, I did. But so far he's not prancin' around in front of the law offices in his panties, and Randy's glad of it. You better go on over there. Maybe he'll give you an endorsement in the election."

"Not likely," Rhodes said. "He's not one of my biggest fans. Anyway, like I keep telling you, the election's not until next year. I might not even run."

"You'll run. What else you got to do? You don't collect baseball cards or paint pictures of bluebonnets."

Hack had a point, but Rhodes wasn't about to admit it. He signed off and drove downtown.

The Lawj Mahal gleamed white in the sun, looking more like a national monument than ever. A small monument, true, but an impressive one in a place like Clearview. It was the only building in town that Rhodes felt vaguely uncomfortable in, as if he didn't quite belong. He wasn't sure whether it was because the building was so new or because he was intimidated by its grandeur.

Less intimidating than the building were the two pickups parked in front. Rhodes recognized them as the two he'd seen at the Eccles boys' place, and they meant that the Eccles cousins were inside the Lawj Mahal, where they'd feel even less at home than Rhodes.

Lawless's secretary, dressed to the nines, told Rhodes to go right on into the attorney's office, an antiseptic place that harbored no dust or clutter.

Lawless stood up behind his clean desk when Rhodes came through the door and said how pleased and happy he was to see the sheriff.

"I want to thank you for catching that prankster, Neal Carr," Lawless went on. "He was bad for business."

The Eccles cousins sat in a couple of big maroon leather chairs, wingbacks the same color as the bindings of the law books that lined one wall of the office. They wore their baseball caps and jeans. Just as Rhodes had thought, they looked uncomfortable and out of place, certainly more out of place than they had in the jail cell. Then again, Rhodes couldn't fault them for that. He was more comfortable in a jail cell, too.

"Just doing my job," Rhodes said, with a glance at Lance and Hugh to let Lawless know that Rhodes had been taking care of business when he arrested them, too.

"You do a fine job for the county and the town," Lawless said. "Everybody knows that."

The Eccles cousins looked at each other and smirked, not caring if Rhodes saw them. Lawless should have coached them better.

Rhodes took a seat in a third wingback chair, and Lawless got right to the point.

"Sheriff," he said, "my clients have decided that they want to be of assistance to you in an investigation you're conducting."

Rhodes had figured that was what the meeting would be about. A little time in jail had given Lance and Hugh a new perspective on things.

"What do they want from me in trade?"

"They're hoping that for their cooperation you'll consider asking the DA to drop the charges against them."

"I might," Rhodes said, "if they have anything I can use. It'll have to be good."

Lawless leaned back in his chair and relaxed. "Why don't you tell him what you know, Lance. Then he can decide if it's of any help."

Lance looked at Hugh, who nodded as if to give him permission to speak. Lance cleared his throat.

"Okay, Sheriff," he said, "here's the deal. Me and Hugh got a pretty good hauling job lined up. It's gonna take us way outta state, and if we take it, we can't stay around the county. We need the money, and we'd like to get things settled so we could take the job."

Lawless looked as if he were suffering from severe gas pains, but he didn't try to stop Lance from laying out his position.

"You're kind of weakening your argument," Rhodes said. "Knowing how important this is to you, I'll have too much leverage."

"Hey, you haven't heard what we got. You'll be willing to make a deal. I guarantee it."

Lance sounded confident, and Rhodes got a little more interested. He'd thought all along that the Eccles boys had a story to tell, and maybe now he was finally going to hear it.

"Get on with it, then," he said.

"Well, me and Hugh don't just gamble at the Rollin' Sevens. We kind of keep an eye on the place for Guy. Mr. Wilks, I mean."

"You're the bouncers," Rhodes said.

"When we're there, we are. Not that the place needs us much. That's why we said we'd do it. See, we're peaceable guys, me and Hugh. We don't like getting into confrontations, but if it's part of the job, then we will."

"How was getting into a confrontation with me part of your job?"

"We just do what Mr. Wilks tells us," Lance said.

Rhodes was disappointed. He'd thought they'd do better than the old *I was only following orders* defense.

"Not good enough," he said. "You'll need a lot more than that."

"We got it," Hugh said, taking over from Lance. "See, we know the reason Wilks wanted us to get after you. I'll bet he didn't tell you that Lloyd Berry used to come in the Rollin' Sevens."

Wilks hadn't told him, but Rhodes wasn't surprised to hear it. He remembered what Max had told him about Wilks and Berry sitting together in Max's Place. Wilks had denied knowing Berry, but he'd obviously been covering up.

"Wilks didn't tell me that," Rhodes said, "but there's nothing wrong with Lloyd having a little relaxation in a homey family atmosphere like the one at Rollin' Sevens."

Hugh gave Rhodes a suspicious glance. "Are you making fun of us?"

"Not me. I'm just saying that there's nothing wrong with a man having a little fun."

Hugh looked skeptical, but he said, "You got that right. There's more to it than that, though. See, Wilks and Berry had a big falling-out a couple of days before Berry got killed."

That got Rhodes's attention. "What about?"

"Don't know that, but they had a big argument in Wilks's office. I think it had to do with money. Lloyd stormed out, and Wilks told us not to let him in if he came back."

"How about that?" Lance said. "Good enough for you?"

Rhodes thought it over. If Lloyd had been stealing from the chorus, as Darrel Sizemore suspected, he might have been using the money to gamble. Rhodes didn't know how much money Lloyd had taken, but music was expensive. He could have spent hundreds of dollars, which was a lot to feed into eight-liners. Things were beginning to fall into place.

"It's not bad," Rhodes said. "I'm tempted to talk to the DA, but I'm not sure he'd go for the deal. He's a hard man to convince."

Randy Lawless was smiling. Rhodes never liked it when a lawyer smiled, but this time he had a feeling that Lawless was smiling because his clients had even more to tell. That turned out to be the case.

"That's not all we got," Lance said. "We know something else we bet you don't know about. Even Cecil Marsh doesn't know it."

"That's right," Hugh said. "If he did, he'd have killed Berry for sure."

"Maybe he did kill him," Lance said, looking at his cousin. "We don't know. Anyway, Berry was getting mighty friendly with Cecil's wife. He used to give her all those little stuffed animals he won."

"Not that there's anything wrong with that," Hugh said, back in his Seinfeld mode. "Faye Lynn came in now and then, but she hardly ever won. Lloyd gave her his animals because he didn't want them."

"Did it go beyond the animals?" Rhodes said. "How friendly were they?"

"Well," Hugh said, "me and Lance are pretty good with the women, if you know what I mean."

Rhodes knew what he meant, and he didn't believe a word of it. If Hugh and Lance had been good with the women, they wouldn't have been hanging out at Rollin' Sevens.

"So we know what's what," Lance said. "I don't think Berry and Faye Lynn were gettin' it on or anything, but it wasn't because Lloyd wasn't trying."

What they said explained a lot. Faye Lynn had covered for Lloyd by letting Rhodes think she'd won all the animals by gambling.

Rhodes wondered if Cecil had known more than he was telling. What if he'd been putting on an act when Faye Lynn claimed to have won the animals? To Rhodes's way of thinking, Cecil was a suspect again, along with Wilks, who'd joined the list.

Rhodes thought of something else. Could Lloyd have been the one who dedicated the song to Lindy Gomez in Cecil's name? He would have been the one trying to persuade Faye Lynn that Cecil was having a fling, not Royce Weeks. Rhodes suspected that was what had happened, all right. No wonder Lloyd didn't explain exactly how he'd gotten the request.

"You have anything else to offer?" Rhodes said to Lance.

"Outside of that, we don't know a thing. Being public-spirited citizens, though, we knew you'd want to hear what we had to tell."

"Nothing a law officer likes better than public-spirited citizens," Randy said. "Isn't that right, Sheriff."

Public-spirited citizens who'd kept quiet until their own necks were on the chopping block.

Public-spirited citizens who'd sicced their dog on Rhodes when he came out to their house because they thought he was going to arrest them for harboring an alligator.

Public-spirited citizens who'd lied and concealed the truth until it suited them.

"That's right," Rhodes said, "and Hugh and Lance are full of it, all right. Public spirit, I mean," he added when he saw the look on Randy's face. "There's something else I need to know, though."

"My clients will be happy to tell you," Randy said. "They just want to help. Isn't that right, boys?"

Lance and Hugh nodded.

"Just go ahead and ask, Sheriff," Randy said. "They'll be happy to cooperate."

Randy was as full of it as Lance and Hugh, but Rhodes didn't mind. That was Randy's usual approach.

"What about Bruce?" Rhodes said.

"Who's Bruce?" Randy said. He leaned forward, obviously not pleased at not having gotten that bit of information from his clients in advance.

"Bruce is a dog," Rhodes said, and Randy relaxed.

"He's our dog," Lance said. "Mine and Hugh's. The sheriff placed him in a foster home when he threw us in the clink."

"We don't call it 'the clink,'" Rhodes said. "We prefer 'the hoosegow.'"

All three men looked at Rhodes as if he'd lost his mind.

"Let's get back to Bruce," he said.

"Okay," Lance said. "You told us you'd found him a good home, and maybe that's the best thing for him, and us, too. We go on these long trips, and it's always hard to find somebody to come by and feed him. We got a cousin down in Thurston who's been doing it, when he comes to feed the chickens, but he doesn't like Bruce, and Bruce doesn't like him. I think he's scared of Bruce, to tell you the truth. So if you have somebody who wants Bruce and will take good care of him, it's all right with us for Bruce to stay with him."

"Who is it, anyway?" Hugh said.

"It's Dr. Benton," Rhodes said. "He lives right down the road from you."

Hugh was not impressed. "That nutty guy with the math sign?"

"That's the one. He might be nutty, but he likes Bruce."

"I guess it's all right, then," Hugh said. "But you tell him we'll be stopping by to check on how he's treating Bruce."

"Yeah," Lance said. "We want visitation rights."

"I think I can agree to that for Dr. Benton. Do you two have anything else to tell me?"

"That's all," Randy said. "Now about dropping those charges . . ."

Rhodes stood up. "I'll talk to the DA. I'm sure he'll go along with me on it."

Hugh and Lance looked relieved.

"Fine," Randy said. "So Hugh and Lance can take the job and leave the county if they have to?"

"They can," Rhodes said.

Lawless came around the desk and shook Rhodes's hand to seal the deal, and Rhodes left so he could talk to his clients in private. Rhodes wondered if they'd discuss the bill. If they did, Hugh and Lance might not look as relieved when they left as they had when they'd found out they were off the hook.

Rhodes hoped they wouldn't resort to parading in front of the Lawj Mahal in their underwear.

25

▼

Jennifer Loam was waiting for Rhodes when he came out of the Lawj Mahal. She was the only other person in the entire downtown area, as far as Rhodes could see.

"Hi, Sheriff," she said. "Been visiting the opposition?"

Rhodes shook his head. "I never think of attorneys as the opposition. We're all in the business of making life better for the citizens of Blacklin County."

"Wow. Can I quote you on that?"

"Better not. I don't want Randy Lawless to get a big head."

"Okay. That's not really what I wanted to hear from you anyway."

"What did you want to hear?"

"I wanted to hear how the investigation into the murder of Lloyd Berry was going."

"The sheriff's department is on the case, and an arrest is expected at any moment."

Jennifer grinned. "I know better."

"No wonder you're an ace reporter."

"An ace reporter would have a better story about the murder than I do. Don't you have any leads or suspects you can tell me about?"

"I'm still working it out," Rhodes said. "Maybe by tomorrow I'll have something for you."

"Is that a promise?"

"I try not to make promises that I'm not sure I can keep."

"What about in an election year?"

Rhodes wished people would quit bringing that up. He liked his job, but he didn't like having to run in elections.

"Election year promises don't really count, do they? I avoid those, too, though."

"A wise policy," Jennifer said. "Too bad the people running for national office don't follow it."

"They don't ever listen to what I tell them."

"Their loss. What about my story?"

"Right now, there's not one. If there's a story later on, you'll hear about it before anybody else."

"I know I will, but it would be better for my career if I could hear about it now."

"You'll just have to wait, I guess."

Jennifer wasn't satisfied, but she told Rhodes to be sure to call her when he made an arrest.

"Now I have to interview Randy Lawless about his stalker," she said.

"Neal Carr wasn't stalking anybody."

"Oh, so you do have a story for me."

"Nope," Rhodes said. "You'll have to get it from Randy."

Jennifer said she would and went into the Lawj Mahal. Rhodes got into his car and left.

Rhodes drove to the Dairy Queen. He'd decided that what he needed was a FlameThrower GrillBurger to help him think. He ordered the quarter-pound version instead of the half-pound one, feeling virtuous. Then he sat in a booth, trying to get his thoughts lined up. When his number was called, he still hadn't made up his mind about what to do. He got his burger and Dr Pepper and dug in.

The FlameThrower lived up to its name. It had Tabasco sauce, jalapeño bacon, and pepper jack cheese. Rhodes needed two re-fills of Dr Pepper before he was finished.

The heat from the peppers didn't help his brain much, but he did come up with a theory. It was one he'd already come up with, so it wasn't much of a stretch, but it was the best he could do. He bused his tray and left.

Rhodes drove to the Marshes' house and found out from Faye Lynn where Cecil was working that day. He didn't tell Faye Lynn why he wanted to know, and he didn't ask if she and Cecil had set-tled their differences. He did, however, ask about Lloyd Berry.

"Who told you that?" she said.

"I'm the sheriff. I hear things from all over."

"It's not my fault that Lloyd got interested in me. He's been lonesome since his wife died. I've been a little lonesome, too, so we talked some. He got too friendly, and I told him I wasn't inter-ested."

"How much of this does Cecil know?"

"More than I thought. I guess he hears things, too. Is that why you want to talk to him?"

Rhodes couldn't think of a way around it, so he said it was.

"Cecil never hurt anybody in his life," Faye Lynn said. "I want you to know that."

"I'll keep it in mind," Rhodes told her.

Cecil was working that day for Olive Harris, a retired high school teacher who had taught Rhodes English and Spanish. Or had tried to. Rhodes didn't remember much of the Spanish, and he could recall only a few lines of the poetry that he'd been forced to memorize in Olive's classes.

Olive lived not too far from Marsh in a little two-bedroom house that she kept in immaculate condition. The place was so neat that Rhodes hated to park in the street in front, for fear that his car might leak a drop of oil onto the street.

Rhodes parked anyway, right behind Cecil's old Ford pickup, which had ladders and paint cans in the bed. Its sides were dented, and the tailpipe hung down so low that it nearly touched the street. If anybody's vehicle fouled the street, it would be Cecil's.

Rhodes got out of the car. He could hear Olive haranguing Cecil somewhere in the backyard. As he walked around the house, Rhodes admired the neatly trimmed shrubs and the closely cropped grass. He thought about mowing his own lawn, but he pushed that thought out of his head.

Turning the corner at the back of the house, Rhodes saw Cecil using a roller at the end of a long handle to put a coat of red paint on a little storage shed shaded by a big cottonwood tree that was starting to put on a few new leaves. Rhodes saw a bird's nest in one of the low branches of the tree, but he didn't see any birds.

Olive was standing a short distance away from Cecil, offering comments about the way the job was going.

"You're getting paint on the grass," she said. "You need to be more careful."

Cecil kept painting without looking around.

Olive started toward him, but she must have heard Rhodes, because she turned around to see who was there.

"If it isn't Sheriff Danny Rhodes," she said. Rhodes hadn't been called Danny in more than twenty years. "I haven't seen you in a while."

Olive was a short, round woman who wore her gray hair in a bun at the back of her head. She had on overalls, a work shirt, and a pair of brogan shoes with scuffed toes.

"Did you drop by to discuss the new translation of *Beowulf*, or is this business?"

Rhodes hadn't thought about *Beowulf* in years, and he certainly hadn't heard about any new translation of it, but he didn't want to admit that to Olive.

"As much as I enjoy your company," he said, "it's Cecil I came by to see."

Cecil had already turned around. He stood with the paint roller near his head, the end of the handle resting on the ground.

"I hope you're not going to arrest him," Olive said. "He's not finished with the job yet."

In the theory Rhodes had worked out at the Dairy Queen, which was just a reworking of something he'd thought of earlier, Cecil had found out about Lloyd and Faye Lynn, and things had happened as Rhodes had thought earlier. Cecil had stopped by the flower shop on his way to Obert and said something to Lloyd about Faye Lynn, and an argument had started. Things had gotten out of hand, and Cecil had hit Lloyd with the wrench. When he saw that Lloyd was dead, he'd panicked and run away. Everything fit.

The problem was that Rhodes didn't have any evidence, so the neat fit didn't matter. He'd have to get Cecil to confess, and that might not be easy. Cecil didn't look to be in a cooperative mood. The front of his white painter's overalls was spattered with red, and for a second Rhodes thought Cecil looked like a butcher who'd been cutting up fresh beef.

"I don't have anything to talk to you about, Sheriff," Cecil said. "I'm working here. You better just go on back to the jail and leave me alone."

"He's right, Danny," Olive said. "He's working for me, and I'm paying him good money."

If Rhodes knew Olive, she was paying Cecil by the job, not by the hour, and she wasn't paying him much.

"I won't take up a lot of Cecil's time," Rhodes said, "if you don't mind letting me talk to him."

"I suppose it will be all right," Olive said. "Just don't talk too long. It's almost time for lunch anyway, so I'll go inside and make myself a sandwich."

Rhodes watched her go. Cecil watched Rhodes. When the screen door shut behind Olive, Cecil said, "You just can't leave well enough alone, can you?"

"You knew about Lloyd and Faye Lynn, didn't you," Rhodes said.

Cecil's face darkened. "I didn't know a thing till you started coming around with all your questions. This is all your fault."

Rhodes had long ago gotten used to being blamed for the troubles of others. It was part of the job. He didn't let it bother him.

"You're the one who accused her of fooling around with Royce," he said, "but you knew better. You knew all along it was Lloyd who was interested in her."

"You don't know what you're talking about," Cecil said.

"People tell me that all the time."

"I can see why." Cecil kicked at the ground. "You're so ignorant that I don't have anything else to say to you."

"We've established a time of death for Lloyd," Rhodes said. It wasn't true, but Cecil wouldn't know that. If he was like most people, he watched *CSI* or some other forensic fantasy and thought that it was easy to tell the exact moment someone died. "I can ask Chap Morris what time you got to Obert to work on his driveway, and I can ask Faye Lynn what time you left your house. Then I'll know if you stopped off at Lloyd's shop."

"I stopped off, all right, but it was just to get a coke and a sausage biscuit at McDonald's. I wasn't anywhere close to Lloyd's shop."

Cecil would know Rhodes couldn't check on that. Too many people crowded McDonald's in the morning, and Cecil would say he hadn't saved his receipt. Nobody ever saved a receipt at McDonald's. Rhodes decided to turn things around on Cecil.

"Can you prove you were there?" he said.

"No, and you know it. You'll just have to take my word for it."

Rhodes wasn't in the mood to take Cecil's word for it.

"That's not going to work, Cecil," he said. "You're going to have to tell me the truth."

"That is the truth, dammit."

Cecil sounded sincere, but his actions weren't in line with his words. He flipped the paint roller and aimed it at Rhodes like a spear.

Rhodes raised a hand, but he didn't have time to say anything conciliatory before Cecil heaved the paint roller at him.

Rhodes ducked, but he was a little too slow. The roller hit him on the point of the shoulder and sprinkled him with droplets of red paint before falling to the grass. Rhodes thought that Olive wasn't going to like that, and then Cecil barreled into him.

The two of them rolled over a couple of times with Cecil coming out on top. He drew back a fist to hit Rhodes in the face, but Rhodes threw his right leg up and hooked it around Cecil's body. Rhodes heaved up with his torso and back with his leg. Cecil flipped over on the ground.

Cecil landed right by the paint roller, which he grabbed with both hands. He didn't try to get up. Instead he swung the roller and hit Rhodes in the side. The roller end flew off the handle and hit Olive's screen door, rattling it.

Rhodes snatched at the handle and got hold of it with his right hand. He jerked hard and tore it from Cecil's fingers. Rhodes tossed it aside. Cecil kicked him in the ankle and rolled across the yard.

Rhodes limped after him. Cecil came to a stop at the storehouse and jumped to his feet. He looked around for a weapon and saw the gallon can of red paint.

The exercise hadn't done Rhodes any favors, not after the FlameThrower. He didn't feel like any more strenuous activity, so he lifted his pants leg and pulled his pistol. Cecil didn't seem to notice. He swung the paint can by the wire bail, ready to hurl the can, paint and all, at Rhodes, who decided he didn't want to be drenched with red paint or hit by the heavy can. So he pulled the trigger.

The bullet hit the paint can, which flew from Cecil's fingers, showering paint all over the grass, and Cecil, too. A little of it even got on Rhodes.

Cecil stood right where he was, panting.

Olive yelled from the back door, "Danny Rhodes, you're going to have to clean up that mess!"

Rhodes thought the grass would survive. After the paint dried, someone could mow the lawn and get rid of most of it. Rhodes, however, didn't plan to be the one who did the mowing.

"I'm going to have to arrest you, Cecil," he said.

"I didn't kill anybody."

"No, but you assaulted me. I'm getting really tired of being assaulted. It's happening way too much lately."

"No wonder, the way you act."

"Did you hear me about that paint?" Olive called.

"I heard you," Rhodes said.

"Well, what are you going to do about it?"

"Nothing right now."

"Humph. I don't know if I'm going to vote for you again, Danny."

"Yes, ma'am. I understand. Come on, Cecil. It's time for us to go before we do any more damage."

Cecil didn't have any more fight left. He shrugged and walked ahead of Rhodes. The red paint made both of them look as if they'd been seriously bloodied, but Olive didn't have any sympathy for them.

"Who's going to clean up this mess?" she said from the door. "That's what I want to know. Is the county going to send over a crew to clean it up? Will the commissioners pay me to do it? I'm an old woman. I can't do it."

Rhodes thought the commissioners were going to have a problem on their hands if something wasn't done, and then it would become his problem, just the way Cecil's problem had become his.

"I'll send somebody to take care of it," he said, wondering who he'd send.

"You'd better send somebody to finish painting my shed, too."

"Yes, ma'am," Rhodes said.

"And don't leave that junky old truck parked out in front of my house, either."

"Yes, ma'am," Rhodes said.

26

▼

HACK AND LAWTON WERE SO SURPRISED BY THE WAY RHODES and Cecil looked that they didn't have much to say at first. When they discovered that both men were all right and that what they thought was blood was instead just red paint, they became more talkative.

Rhodes, however, didn't banter with them. He got Cecil booked and printed and into a cell, but he wasn't happy about doing it. The more he thought about it, the less he liked his whole scenario.

A couple of things bothered him. One was the fact that he still didn't have any hard evidence against Cecil.

Another was that Cecil hadn't admitted anything. Nothing unusual in that, but maybe, just maybe, Cecil didn't have anything to admit.

Going back over everything from the beginning, Rhodes still wondered why nobody had seen the murderer arrive at the flower shop or leave it. People had seen Neal Carr even in the nearly deserted downtown area. Only a few people, granted, but he'd been seen.

Not many people frequented the strip center where Lloyd's shop was located, but people worked there, and people went in and out of Rollin' Sevens often enough. So why hadn't anybody seen anything?

Rhodes couldn't help feeling he'd missed something important. The pieces of the puzzle were all on the table right there in front of him, but he couldn't make any of them fit together the right way.

He had a prisoner, and the prisoner had motive, opportunity, and means. All that wasn't enough, however. In spite of everything, Rhodes couldn't quite bring himself to believe that Cecil had killed Lloyd.

Things would be different on *CSI*. The cops on that show had all kinds of forensic facts before they made an arrest. About all Rhodes had to work with was his intuition, and at the moment that seemed to have failed him.

The truth of the matter was that he didn't feel right, and it wasn't just that his stomach was still punishing him for eating the FlameThrower. He could've used a couple of antacid tablets, not to mention some solid evidence and a couple of credible witnesses.

Since he had none of those things, and since he wasn't likely to come across any of them except the antacid tablets, at least not without a lot more work, he decided to go with what he was feeling. He told Cecil to call Randy Lawless.

"What for?" Cecil said.

"He'll bond you out, and you can go finish that job for Ms. Harris. You'll need to clean up the yard, too."

Cecil brooded on the bottom bunk of his cell. He didn't look happy with his orange jumpsuit, but it was an improvement over the paint-spattered overalls.

"I don't see why I have to clean anything up," he said. "It wasn't my fault that the paint got all over the place."

"If you hadn't tried to throw the paint can at me, it wouldn't have happened," Rhodes reminded him.

"Yeah, well, you made me do it. You accused me of killing Lloyd."

"Not exactly, but even if I had accused you, you had no reason to throw that paint roller at me and then to go for the whole can. It's going to be a tough cleanup, and you're the one to do it. Ivy's not going to be happy with the way I look, either. You've ruined my clothes."

"I hope you don't expect me to take care of that, too."

Rhodes said he'd take care of it himself.

"What am I gonna tell Faye Lynn about all this? You may think you're in trouble with your wife, but at least you're not in jail."

"I have a feeling Faye Lynn will understand. She never fooled around with Lloyd, if that's what you're worried about. You can believe me on that."

"How do you know?"

"Trust me, I know. I'm the sheriff."

"Right, and I'm the handyman convict."

Rhodes had had enough of Cecil's self-pity. He was trying to give the man a break, and Cecil wouldn't take it.

"Just call Lawless," Rhodes said. "He'll take care of you, and you'll take care of Ms. Harris's yard. Right?"

Cecil waited a while to answer, probably to make Rhodes sweat a little. Finally he said, "Right."

The little strip center hadn't changed a bit since the last time Rhodes was there. He parked in front of Lloyd Berry's shop, moved the yellow crime-scene tape, and opened the door.

If he'd been hoping to spot some previously overlooked clue at his first glance, he was disappointed. Nothing had changed, except that most of the plants looked a bit wilted.

Rhodes went inside. He'd have to bring Ivy out and let her see to the plants. He was certain death for plants. If he touched one, or even tried to water it without touching it, it would die.

He moved through the shop and then went out back to the stairs. Climbing them, he looked out at the cattle in the fields. For all he could tell, they might not have moved since the last time he'd been there. The spring grass was coming in, and that seemed to require all their attention.

The inside of Lloyd's apartment looked the same, too, almost. Rhodes thought that something was wrong, and he realized that someone had been there since his last visit. Ruth had checked it out, of course, after he'd looked it over, but she would never have left the paperback book on top of the nightstand. He was sure of that, but there it was.

Rhodes wondered what someone had been looking for. Money, maybe. If so, they hadn't found any, not unless he and Ruth were a lot more careless than he thought likely.

Looking around the room, Rhodes didn't see anything else that had been moved. He did his own careful search but found nothing that hadn't been there before. He wished he knew what he was looking for. He stood and thought about it, but he couldn't come up with any answers.

After a while, he gave up and left.

Guy Wilks was no happier to see Rhodes than he'd been the last time.

"Who'd you kill?" he said.

"Nobody. It's just paint, not blood."

Wilks looked disappointed and didn't say anything else. He just sat behind his desk and glowered, so Rhodes didn't see any point in making small talk.

"You lied to me about Lloyd Berry," he said.

Wilks relaxed a little. "I never lied about anything. Maybe I didn't tell you all I knew, but I didn't lie."

"You said Lloyd never came in here."

"Not exactly. I said I'd never seen him in here. There's a difference."

"True. But you *have* seen him in here. Right in this office. So why did you lie to me?"

Wilks's eyes narrowed. "Who told you he was in this office?"

"Reliable witnesses," Rhodes said, thinking that he might be giving the Eccles cousins a little more credit than they deserved.

Wilkes puffed out his cheeks and blew out some air. Rhodes wondered if he was counting to ten.

"Okay," Wilks said. "It's true. Lloyd and I had a little discussion. I told him I thought he was spending too much time here. He came down every day after he closed the store, and he didn't win much. I thought it would be good for him to take a break."

Somehow Rhodes hadn't thought of Wilks as being quite so altruistic.

"That was thoughtful of you. I guess he didn't take your advice too well."

"You could say that. I thought it was for the best, though."

"And you never saw him again after that."

"See? That's why I had to lie to you. You think I killed him, but I didn't, and I can prove it. I never left this place the morning he died. We don't have a lot of people in early in the day, but we have a few. They'll all tell you I was right here, and that includes your snitches."

"My snitches?"

"The Eccles boys. It took me a second, but I figured it out. They're the only ones who'd know enough to get you interested in me. So ask them. They'll tell you. I'm in the clear all the way."

Maybe, Rhodes thought. *Maybe not.* Whatever the answer was, he'd need some kind of evidence against Wilks, and he just didn't have it, any more than he had evidence against Cecil. It was something he'd have to think about. Right now, Wilks was at the top of his list of suspects.

"You're going to ask them, right?" Wilks said. "Be sure to do it pretty soon, because they're leaving town, or so they told me. You can bet they won't be coming in here again. I'll ban them for life."

Rhodes wondered who Wilks would get to enforce the ban.

"I'll ask them," he said.

"You do that. And don't hurry back."

"Oh, I'll be back," Rhodes said. "I think you can count on that."

The Eccles cousins were just about to crank up the big red Mack and hit the road when Rhodes drove into their front yard. They didn't look happy to see him. It was beginning to seem as if nobody ever was, not that Rhodes blamed them, particularly not Lance and Hugh. They must have thought he was there to keep them from leaving.

"I hope the other guy looks worse than you do," Lance said when Rhodes got out of the car.

Rhodes was tired of explaining about the paint, so he said, "He does. A lot worse."

It was even true, in a way. Cecil had a lot more paint on him than Rhodes did.

"Good," Lance said. "I hope there's not a problem with me and Hugh. You said we could leave whenever we needed to."

"This isn't about you going anywhere," Rhodes told him. "It's about Guy Wilks."

Rhodes told Lance what he wanted to know about Wilks. Hugh, who was still standing by the truck, listened in.

"Wilks is telling you the truth," Lance said. "Isn't that right, Hugh."

"Maybe. There's a back door to that office. Didn't you see it when you were there, Sheriff?"

"I saw it."

"He could've gone out that way," Hugh said. "While we were playing the games. Wouldn't take him long to walk down to Lloyd's and come back. We might not've seen him go."

"That's right," Lance said. "I don't think he left, but I couldn't promise you that he didn't."

"All right," Rhodes said and thanked them. "You boys have a good trip."

"Any trip away from here's a good trip," Hugh said, mounting the cab.

"Don't bring home any alligators this time," Rhodes said.

"We won't," Hugh said. "I'm not saying we ever did, you understand."

"I understand," Rhodes said.

Hugh climbed into the cab of the truck, slammed the door, and cranked the engine. Lance got in on the other side of the cab and honked the air horn.

Rhodes flipped them a salute, and they drove away.

Ivy hadn't come in yet when Rhodes got home, so Rhodes and Yancey went out in the backyard to go a few rounds with Speedo. Yancey was in fine form. He nabbed the squeaky toy before Speedo even knew he was there and went tearing across the yard with it. Speedo took off in hot pursuit.

It made Rhodes feel good to watch them. For a little while he forgot all about Lloyd Berry, Cecil, and all the rest of it. His stomach felt fine now, and he wondered what he and Ivy would do for supper. Meatless meatloaf leftovers didn't appeal to him much. Even though he'd had a substantial lunch, he wouldn't mind going out for dinner.

His good feeling didn't last long. Lloyd Berry's murder bothered him too much. The more he thought about it, the more convinced he was that Cecil hadn't done it.

But if Cecil hadn't, who had? Rhodes didn't have any idea, and that made him feel even worse. He didn't even cheer up much when Yancey made a sudden spin move and stopped dead, causing Speedo to tumble over him.

* * *

Rhodes heard the screen door open behind him, and Ivy came out.

"Good Lord!" she said when she saw Rhodes sitting on the step. "What happened?"

Rhodes realized that he'd forgotten to change clothes.

"It's not as bad as it looks," he said.

"It looks terrible. I hope that's not your blood all over you."

Rhodes laughed. People kept making the same mistake.

"It's nobody's blood," he said. "It's red paint."

"Red paint? How did that happen?"

Rhodes went through the story, making it as short as possible.

"I'm glad it was nothing worse," Ivy said, and then she told Rhodes that she'd like to try some more of Max's barbecue instead of having dinner at home. Rhodes thought that was a fine idea, even though he wasn't sure what another spicy meal would do to his stomach. He didn't mention the FlameThrower to Ivy, however. He was pretty sure she wouldn't approve.

"You'll have to clean up first, though," Ivy told him. "We can't go anywhere with you looking like that. I don't know how we'll get that paint off you."

"I've heard Vicks VapoRub works," Rhodes said.

Ivy was skeptical. "Where did you hear that?"

"I'm the sheriff. I have a lot of confidential informants who feed me information."

"All right," Ivy said. "Who am I to question a confidential informant. We'll give it a try."

27

▼

THE VICKS WORKED BETTER THAN RHODES HAD EXPECTED, AND by using it along with some soap and water he was able to make himself more or less presentable. Certainly presentable enough for barbecue.

Max Schwartz greeted him and Ivy when they came inside Max's Place, and he had a question for Rhodes.

"Do you know who Joe Bob Briggs is?" he asked. "He writes stuff about movies."

As it happened, Rhodes did know, because Joe Bob liked some of the same kinds of movies that Rhodes had once enjoyed watching so much.

"I'm not talking about movies, though," Max said. "I'm talking about my business."

"The barbecue business or the music store?" Rhodes said.

"This one. Briggs wrote something once about the way to tell if you're getting good barbecue is to go to a place where they don't spell out the word on the sign out front. He thinks the sign should just say BBQ. That's the key, he said. Do you believe that?"

Rhodes said he'd never thought about it. "What difference would it make to how the food tasted?"

For Rhodes, the smoky smell of the mesquite wood in the pit and the thought of ice cream melting on top of hot cobbler were enough to make him hungry. He didn't need a sign. Whatever the sign said, it wouldn't matter to Rhodes.

"Perception," Schwartz said. "It's all perception. People would think the food tasted better, depending on the sign, and if they think it's better, that's the same as if it was better."

Rhodes tried to follow the logic of it, and Max got impatient.

"Should I change my sign or not?" he said. "What do you think?"

The sign out front said MAX'S PLACE. BARBECUE. RIBS. BRISKET. SANDWICHES. Rhodes couldn't see how changing it would make any difference at all, and he told Max so.

"Maybe, but what if this Briggs is onto something?" Max said. "I worry about things like that."

"You have a lot of customers," Rhodes said. "You don't have anything to worry about."

Max was a worrier, however, and nothing Rhodes said would ease his mind. Another customer came in, and Max rushed over to him to ask him about the sign.

Seeing that Rhodes and Ivy were free of Max, Jackee came out from behind the counter and said, "I'll show you to a table. Max will fret about that for a week, and then he'll leave the sign just the way it is."

When Rhodes and Ivy got into the dining room, Rhodes saw Seepy Benton tuning his guitar.

"Entertainment tonight," Ivy said.

"You're not being sarcastic, are you?" Rhodes said.

"Me? Of course not."

"Good. I think that right after Jerry Kergan criticized Seepy's singing, Kergan got smashed by a truck."

"You're not saying there was a connection, are you?"

"You never know," Rhodes said, and something tickled at the back of his mind.

He couldn't bring it forward, but he knew it would make its way there sooner or later if it was important. He and Ivy sat at the table Jackee took them to. It was made of heavy wood, and the oversized chairs were also wood. The floor was thick planking.

Rhodes looked at the menu Jackee set in front of him. Rhodes already knew what he wanted, and so did Ivy. As soon as the server came, they both ordered the small beef plate.

By the time the food arrived, Seepy had started on his first set, beginning with what he called "an old favorite that I wrote a couple of weeks ago, a little number called 'Getting Wasted Is Wasted on the Young.' It's in the key of G, and you can all hum along if you don't know the words. If you can't hum, you can suck on ice cubes in four-four time."

Rhodes didn't know the words, and he didn't hum along. He didn't suck on ice cubes, either. Even his humming was unsatisfactory to him. He'd rather listen to someone else, even if the someone was Seepy Benton. As far as Rhodes was concerned, Benton's bass rumble blended just fine with the clinking silverware and conversations of the other diners, hardly any of whom seemed to notice that Benton was singing.

"That song's not exactly politically correct, is it?" Ivy said.

Rhodes poured some sauce from a little side bowl onto his

brisket and added a dash of habanero sauce from the bottle on the table. Combined with the FlameThrower, this meal would either kill him or make him stronger.

"I don't think Seepy cares about being politically correct," he said. "He just likes the way the words sound."

"You don't think he's advocating drug use by older people?"

"I'll pretend I didn't hear that," Rhodes said, and he started to eat.

The beans needed a little something, so he put some barbecue sauce on them. The coleslaw, potato salad, and brisket were just right.

While he was eating and halfway listening to Seepy Benton's songs, Rhodes's mind kept worrying at the pieces of the puzzle that was Lloyd Berry's murder. Rhodes wondered if he and Max Schwartz weren't a lot alike in a way, both of them worriers of the kind that couldn't let go of something once they started thinking about it, not even to eat or listen to music, if you could call Seepy's singing music.

Rhodes looked up from his plate and across the room of diners at Seepy, and as he did, a few pieces of the puzzle rearranged themselves inside his head and fit right together.

"Bingo," he said.

"Bingo?" Ivy said. "I didn't even know we were playing."

"This isn't playing," Rhodes said. "It's a lot more serious than that."

"Bingo is?"

"Never mind," Rhodes said. "Just eat. Then we need to talk to Seepy."

"About bingo?"

Rhodes grinned at Ivy's confusion. It was too bad he couldn't play Hack and Lawton that way, and he wasn't even trying.

"About the Internet," he said, "and Web sites."

"You're playing bingo on the Internet?"

"Never mind," Rhodes said. "Just eat."

She did, but every now and then she looked at him as if he might be losing his mind.

Seepy finished his first set about the time Rhodes and Ivy finished eating. Rhodes would have liked to get some cobbler and ice cream, but talking to Seepy was more important.

"The tip jar's right there," Seepy said when Rhodes approached him, and sure enough, it was, sitting on a little stool near the stand where Seepy had put his guitar when he finished playing.

"Who put the money in it?" Rhodes said. "I didn't see anybody come over here."

"I've primed the pump," Seepy said. "Now it's your turn."

Rhodes dug his wallet out of his back pocket, located a dollar bill, and dropped it in the jar.

"Thanks," Seepy said. "I'm sure other dollars will accumulate now."

Rhodes didn't see anyone getting up to contribute, but he liked Seepy's optimism.

"People might be too shy to come up while you're here," he said. "Why don't you and Ivy and I go back to Max's office and talk for a minute."

"What about?"

"Bingo," Ivy said.

"Bingo?"

"Don't listen to her," Rhodes said. "Let's go ask Max if we can use his office computer."

Max was still worrying about his sign, but he said it would be all right if they used the computer.

"Just take your pick," he added. "I have three."

"Three?" Rhodes said. "Why?"

"I like computers. I have four in my office at the music store. I pick them up cheap on eBay. Some of them are a little outdated, but they work fine."

"Do you have the Internet?" Rhodes said.

Max looked insulted. "Please. I have DSL here, and cable at the music store. Do I have Internet? I hope I'll never be without it. Not that I'm addicted. I can take it or leave it alone."

Max had so much going on that Rhodes didn't know when he could find time for the Internet, but it didn't matter. All Rhodes wanted was a computer and a connection.

"Come on," he told Seepy. "I have a job for you."

Max showed them into the office, which was more cluttered than Rhodes would have thought possible, since Max had moved in only recently. Rhodes counted six large speakers and three computers with monitors. Books were scattered on shelves, on desks, and even on the floor. It was like being in Royce Weeks's living room except that the books were different. They all seemed to relate to computers and electronics.

Benton looked around and declared that he felt right at home.

"Which is the fastest computer?" he asked, and Schwartz showed him an old Gateway.

"I've added some extra memory and perked it up a little," he said.

Benton logged on to the Internet and asked Rhodes what to look for.

"That site we checked at Lloyd's house. Youcachein, I think. Well, not the site itself. I want to know whose site it is."

"I found that out already."

"I know, but I made a rookie mistake when you told me that it was owned by some corporation."

"What was the mistake?"

"I didn't ask the name of the corporation. I need to know what it is."

It didn't take Benton long to find the answer. "It's something called Whipsnake, Inc."

"Bingo," Rhodes said.

"There you go again," Ivy said. "I wish you'd stop that."

"Whipsnake's the name of the corporation that owns Rollin' Sevens," Rhodes said. "Since they also own that Web site, there's a connection."

"So?" Ivy said.

"There aren't very many caches listed on the Web site," Rhodes said. "Tom Fulton told me there were thousands of them in this general area."

"So?" Ivy said.

"So something's wrong. Why so few caches on the site? I think it has something to do with Lloyd Berry's murder."

"I get it," Benton said. Then he paused. "No, I don't."

"Let's say you wanted to get around the law if you owned Rollin' Sevens," Rhodes said. "Say you wanted to give bigger prizes than the law allowed. People get tired of stuffed animals, after all."

"Not me," Benton said. "I like stuffed animals."

"Normal people," Rhodes said. "Normal people get tired of stuffed animals, and gambling for them gets old. Sooner or later, you want to win something bigger and better, but you can't because it's against the law. So what the corporation does is come up with a scheme. You identify the real gamblers, the ones who can be trusted and who keep coming back, and you give them a door prize. It would be easy to rig the drawing, and the winner would get something that wasn't too valuable, like a one-day rental of a GPS."

Benton looked at Rhodes, who corrected himself. "A GPS *receiver,* I mean. And you program in a location where you've hidden something. Money, maybe, or something worth a good bit more than a stuffed animal. A watch, a ring, whatever. A pretty good prize."

Rhodes liked his theory a lot. It explained why Faye Lynn never won a door prize. She wasn't one of the select gamblers. But maybe Lloyd Berry was. Wilks would be the one who handled the drawings, and he wouldn't have taken anyone into his confidence, certainly not the Eccles cousins, who were just muscle. He wouldn't need muscle to plant the prizes. He could take care of everything on his own.

"What does that have to do with Lloyd Berry's murder?" Max said.

Rhodes had a couple of ideas about that, and they explained why there were no witnesses to Lloyd's death. Not so long ago, Jerry Kergan had been run down behind his restaurant, now Max's Place, where Kergan had been crushed against the Dumpster. Thinking of that had reminded Rhodes of the setup at the strip center.

All Wilks had to do was go out the back door, walk down behind the shops, pass by the Dumpster, and go in Berry's back door. No one would have seen him back there. Only the cows in the pasture would have seen him, and they weren't talking. Or maybe someone else *had* seen him. Rhodes had an idea about that, too.

"Lloyd and Guy Wilks had a big argument," Rhodes said.

"So did Lloyd and Cecil," Max said.

"I don't think Cecil killed him. Wilks is a different story. Let's say Lloyd knew about the caches. He had a GPS device in his car. He might have won some door prizes and collected the stuff from the caches."

"I get it now," Benton said. "That's why there was nothing when we looked at those places from the Web site. Whatever had been there didn't need to be replaced."

"Right. Lloyd had gotten into Rollin' Sevens pretty deep. He may have been stealing from the chorus to support his gambling. When Darrel called him on that, he needed more credit from Wilks. They argued, and when Wilks threatened to cut him off, Lloyd said he'd come to me with what he knew."

"How do you know that?"

"I don't know it. I'm speculating."

"And you think Wilks killed Lloyd?"

"It could have happened that way," Rhodes said. "I can think of another possibility, too. Lloyd might have started to collect prizes that other people were supposed to get by checking the Web site and going to all the locations. Wilks wouldn't have liked that if he'd found out. That would have been reason enough for killing Lloyd."

"Neither one of those reasons seems enough for murder," Ivy said.

"It wasn't premeditated," Rhodes said. "I think Wilks stewed about it for a while, then went to talk it over with Lloyd. They got into another argument, and Wilks got carried away. The wrench was there, and he used it. He probably didn't even think about it."

"That sounds like something Randy Lawless might say in his closing argument, anyway," Ivy said.

"Maybe I should go to work for him," Rhodes said. "Work the other side of the fence for a while."

"I don't think so."

"Me neither," Rhodes said.

When they left Max's office and went back to the dining room, Rhodes was surprised to see Ruth Grady eating at a table alone. He couldn't remember having seen her in civilian clothes in months. He and Ivy went over to talk to her, but Benton also saw her. He slipped past Rhodes and Ivy and got to her first.

"Did you come to hear me sing?" he said.

Ruth gave him a smile. "I thought that it might be fun. Anybody who's as kind as you are to a dog like Bruce might be worth listening to."

Rhodes couldn't believe what he was hearing. Could Benton actually be on his way to getting a date with Ruth?

"I'll do a song especially for you," Benton said.

"Which one?"

Rhodes didn't wait around to hear the title. He said hello to Ruth and got out of there.

"What's the hurry?" Ivy said. "I wanted to talk to Ruth for a minute."

"I need to go to work," Rhodes said, and it was the truth. "I'll take you home first."

"Why not let me go with you?"

"This is county business, and you haven't even taken the academy course yet."

"I've been thinking about doing it, though," Ivy said. "When is it going to be offered again?"

"I don't know. It might be a long time."

"Let me know when you decide."

"I'll do that," Rhodes said, but he didn't really mean it.

28

▼

After he dropped Ivy off at their house, Rhodes drove out to the strip center. All the shops were dark, but there were plenty of cars on the end where Rollin' Sevens was located. The neon sign flashed red and blue over the door.

Inside, Rollin' Sevens looked exactly as it did during the day. Rhodes looked around for the bouncer. He saw a man called Nob Russell at one of the machines near the back. Nob was a shade-tree mechanic who got most of his money from a small inheritance and worked on cars as a sideline. He also worked out with some kind of exercise machine he'd bought at a pawnshop in Dallas. He had the muscles of a lifer in the state pen.

Rhodes went to him and asked if Guy Wilks was in.

"Why are you asking me?" Nob said.

He hadn't shaved in a day or so, and his stubble was thick and black. His eyes were black, too, and so was his buzz-cut hair.

"I thought you might know," Rhodes told him.

"Yeah, I'll bet. Guy's not here. Sammy's pulling the duty to-night."

"Sammy?"

"Sammy Reddington. You might not know him. He's just been around for the last couple of weeks."

"Where's Guy?"

"Don't know. I don't keep up with him. He doesn't work nights, and what he does then is his own business."

Rhodes didn't think there was any need for him to talk to Reddington. He thanked Nob and left.

When he got to his car, he called Hack on the radio and asked if Duke Pearson was still keeping an eye on Happy Franklin's place.

"He's been goin' by ever' so often," Hack said. "I guess it's quiet out there tonight, since he hasn't called in about it. Nobody's tryin' to tear down Miz Franklin's house or anything. Not yet, at least."

"Send Duke out there, and let him know I'm headed out that way. I don't want him mistaking me for one of the bad guys."

"What're you gonna do?"

"Have a look around. I might need Duke for backup."

"What's goin' on?" Hack said.

"I'm not sure," Rhodes told him, which was just the kind of thing that would make Hack even more curious, as Rhodes well knew. It was a perfect situation, so he signed off before Hack could ask anything else.

While he drove toward Franklin's place, Rhodes thought things over. The thought of Jerry Kergan's death had reminded him of the Dumpster in back of the strip center, but it had reminded him of a lot of other things, too, including something he'd seen in

Happy Franklin's barn: two metal easels like the kind wreaths were often placed on at funerals.

Where would Franklin have picked up something like that? Several places came to mind, and one of them was the back of Lloyd Berry's shop.

Franklin might have been making his usual rounds on Tuesday morning about the time Berry was killed. What if he'd seen someone coming out of Berry's back door? It might not even have registered with Franklin that what he'd seen was important, but if Wilks had seen Franklin, it would be important to Wilks. Maybe even important enough for him to take a couple of shots at Franklin in hopes of getting rid of a potential witness against him.

Rhodes didn't know a thing about Guy Wilks other than that he managed Rollin' Sevens, but he had no reason to believe that Wilks was any kind of marksman. He'd missed badly when shooting at Franklin. That didn't mean he wouldn't try again, however, and this time he might not miss. Even a blind hog turned up an acorn now and then.

"We haven't had any trouble today or this evening," Happy Franklin said.

He and Rhodes were in his barn, where Franklin had been working on the old radio when Rhodes showed up. Happy had pulled his worktable away from the window and put it where he couldn't be seen from either the window or the big front door of the barn. The light wasn't good, but working in shadow was better than getting shot.

"Glad to hear it," Rhodes said, and then he asked Happy where he'd picked up the green metal easels.

"I got those in back of Lloyd Berry's shop," Happy said. "I don't know why he got rid of them." He walked over to the stands and put his hand on one. "You can see that this one's a little wobbly, but that's easy to fix with a little tightening up. The other one's got a bad weld, but I can fix that, too."

Rhodes wondered what Happy planned to do with the stands when he got them fixed, but he didn't ask. He said, "How long have you had them?"

"Just got them the other day." Happy paused. "Come to think of it, I guess I picked them up the day Lloyd was killed." He paused again, longer this time. "You think somebody shot at me because of that?"

"Could be," Rhodes said.

"I don't see why. You said Billy Joe Byron didn't do it, and these things were right there for the taking. Billy Joe is the only one who'd care if I got them."

"If you saw somebody coming out of Lloyd's shop, that person would care."

Happy thought about it, then shook his head. "The trouble with that idea is that I didn't see anybody."

"Are you sure? Maybe you did, but it didn't register at the time."

"Nope. I'd know if I saw anybody. There's nothing behind that strip center but the Dumpster. Nothing in back of it except a cow pasture. It's hard to miss anybody if he's there, and nobody was."

"That kind of spoils my theory," Rhodes said. "Maybe somebody was coming out the door of Lloyd's shop and ducked back inside. Did you notice any sudden movements?"

"I was looking for treasures in the trash," Happy said. "Not sudden movements. What I saw was these two green flower stands leaning up against the side of the Dumpster like maybe somebody was going to come out later with more trash and toss them in. That's it."

Rhodes was disappointed to hear it. He'd thought for sure he was on the right track, but now it appeared that if he had been, he'd been headed in the wrong direction. He asked if Mrs. Franklin had heard any more prowlers.

"No," Happy said, "and I'm not convinced she ever heard the first one. You know, whoever put those bullets into the barn might just have been hunting rabbits or something. It could have been just an accident. That kind of thing happens around here now and then, doesn't it?"

It did, but usually during deer season, not when somebody was hunting rabbits. Rhodes didn't think anybody ever hunted rabbits anymore. And since Wilks wasn't in Rollin' Sevens, Rhodes was still going to take a look around, just in case.

"You can do it if you want to," Happy said with a shrug. "I don't mind if you go tramping through the pasture, but it's muddy and wet. You'd better be careful."

Rhodes smiled, thinking about it. "I can always take a shower later. I think a deputy will show up here in a little while. You can tell him what I'm up to."

"I'll do that," Franklin said, and Rhodes left the barn to see what he could see.

Franklin was right about the wet and the mud, not that Rhodes was surprised. He'd known what he was getting into. He squished along, avoiding the mesquites as best he could as he made his way toward the roundhouse. If anybody was lurking about, that would be the ideal place to lurk.

Before he was halfway there, water had soaked through Rhodes's shoes. He feet were cold, and the lower quarters of his pants legs were soaked, too. If he'd been smart, he'd have driven along the road below the pasture and looked for a car. A car could be hidden, however, and probably was. Or so Rhodes tried to convince himself. He'd be better off looking for someone who was hiding in the pasture or the roundhouse, waiting to sneak up to Franklin's barn. If he'd found the car, he'd still have had to check out the pasture.

The moon was out, nearly full, and although a heavy dark cloud crossed its face now and then, Rhodes didn't really need his flashlight. He stuck it into his back pocket and hoped it wouldn't fall out without his knowing it.

As he walked, he listened. Besides his own squelchy footsteps, he heard an occasional car as it passed Franklin's house on the paved road. A barn owl screeched somewhere. That was followed by the thump of something moving in the brush and then rapid thrashing as it sped away. A spooked armadillo, maybe. Certainly nothing human.

By the time Rhodes reached the roundhouse, he could no longer see the light from Franklin's barn. Both the railroad tracks and the gravel road beside them were deserted. Rhodes might have been the only person for miles around.

Somehow, though, he didn't think he was. It was just a feeling, but it was a strong one. The closer he got to the roundhouse, the more cautious he became.

The purpose of the roundhouse when it was operational had

been to turn steam locomotive engines around and head them in the opposite direction, so the huge buildings were built around a giant turntable. Most of the turntable in the one Rhodes now faced had been removed years ago, as had all the windows in the place, along with the roof. The windows had been broken by vandals or the weather, but Rhodes didn't have any idea what had happened to the roof. Maybe there had never been one.

Rhodes approached the ruined building for a closer look, and when he was about thirty yards away, something charged out of the building, skittering on the clinkers where the old tracks had been. Rhodes grabbed for the flashlight, but before he could get it out of his pocket, a small figure resembling a bowling ball with a tail shot past him and off into the darkness. Another armadillo, but this time Rhodes hadn't scared it. Something inside the round-house had.

Guy Wilks hadn't been at Rollin' Sevens, and Rhodes thought he might very well be in the roundhouse. Just why, Rhodes wasn't sure, since Happy Franklin claimed he hadn't seen anyone in the alley behind Lloyd's florist shop. If Wilks wasn't trying to kill a witness, why would he be sneaking around the property? Rhodes would ask him when he caught him.

Rhodes sidled up to the side of the wall near the long vertical window opening. Just as he did, he heard a train whistle from the direction of town.

The southbound tracks crossed six of Clearview's streets at the edge of town, so the train generally slowed down as it passed through. It started to pick up speed as it left, but it would still be going fairly slowly by the time it got to the Franklin place. Rhodes wasn't worried that it would interfere with what he was doing or run over him. The siding that led to the roundhouse was long gone, and the tracks the train ran on were forty or fifty yards away.

Looking back in the direction of the whistle, Rhodes saw the headlight of the train in the distance. He decided that he'd better make some kind of move soon because when the train arrived, it would cover any noises from inside the roundhouse and give Wilks a chance to get away.

Rhodes wished he knew what kind of move to make, but he couldn't think of one.

After a couple of seconds, he took the flashlight from his pocket and turned it on. The beam was strong, and Rhodes, keeping himself protected by the wall, moved the light so that it shone on the interior of the roundhouse. He waved the beam up and down, right to left.

A pistol shot echoed around the walls of the roundhouse. The bullet didn't come close to Rhodes's hand or the flashlight, but the shot got his attention. He jerked his hand back from the window.

As soon as he did, he heard someone moving around inside. Turning off the light, Rhodes moved quickly and stepped through the window opening. On the other side of the ruins, a dark shape disappeared through another opening.

The train had almost arrived from town. Rhodes heard it roaring down the track, and its shrill whistle pierced the night air.

Rhodes started across the roundhouse, remembering just in time that a roundhouse might have a work pit in the middle. He flicked on the flashlight. Sure enough, the old pit was there, filled almost to the top with rubble and trash, but still a danger. He skirted it and came to the window opening where the dark figure had disappeared. Before looking out, Rhodes turned off the light once more.

The train arrived and started to thunder past. Rhodes felt its rumble reverberate in his bones. The ground vibrated under his cold feet.

Rhodes saw someone running toward the train and went after him. He wasn't worried that the man would get away. The train was a long one, and it would block the tracks for several minutes.

What Rhodes hadn't counted on, what he wouldn't have thought of in a million years, was that the man would try to board the train.

But that was what he did. He ran along the track beside a boxcar for a few strides and grabbed hold of the ladder at the end of the car. The train's momentum pulled him off his feet, but he clung to the ladder and after a couple of seconds started to pull himself up it.

Rhodes didn't think there was anything to do but go after him. He jammed the flashlight in his pocket and ran as fast as he could, which wasn't fast at all, not on the muddy ground.

By the time Rhodes reached the train, he was already four box-cars behind his quarry, but he didn't hesitate. He grabbed the ladder of a passing car as the train boomed along.

Rhodes thought his arms would be jerked from their sockets, but they weren't, and for a second he flew along beside the train like a human pennant. Then he flopped down against the car. The toes of his shoes bounced along the ground. He wasn't sure he had enough strength in his arms to pull himself up, and he wished he'd done some weight work over the years.

Too late now.

Rhodes risked a glance back over his shoulder. He saw Duke Pearson standing by the track a good way back. Duke was no dummy. He didn't try to board the train.

He did, however, wave good-bye as Rhodes was hauled away.

29

▼

SOMEHOW RHODES GOT HOLD OF THE NEXT COUPLE OF RUNGS on the ladder and inched his way upward. The train seemed to be going faster, and the wind tore at his clothes.

You can do this, he told himself. *You've seen hundreds of guys do it in the movies.*

It occurred to Rhodes that those guys had been stuntmen with years of training and experience, not to mention a certain amount of athletic ability that Rhodes lacked.

He shook that thought out of his head and climbed the ladder far enough so that he could slip around and get a foot on the coupling between the cars. The swaying of the train, the clickety-clack of the steel wheels, and the force of the wind all made Rhodes nervous. If he fell, he'd be cut in half. Escaping that, he'd be so beaten up that nobody would ever be able to identify the body.

He decided he'd better not fall. He pressed himself against the cold steel of the boxcar and gripped something around the corner. Holding to it with his right hand and to the ladder with his left, he moved his right foot to the coupling. When he was sure he wasn't going to slip, he pulled himself quickly around and found himself clinging to another ladder with both his feet solidly on the coupling.

Now what?

Wilks, or whoever it was, had been four cars forward. Had he stayed there? Rhodes hadn't seen any open cars, so Wilks couldn't have gotten inside one. Rhodes hadn't seen any gondola cars, either. So was Wilks standing on a coupling, waiting for Rhodes, or was he lying along the top of the car? Or had he jumped off?

Rhodes supposed he'd have to find out. The ladder he clung to went right up to the top of the car, so Rhodes took a breath and started to climb it.

When he poked his head over the top of the car, the wind whipped his hair, what there was of it. He remembered a scene from some movie with Charles Bronson, where Bronson had run along the top of a boxcar as nimbly as a squirrel crossing a street on a power line.

Of course Rhodes knew it hadn't been Bronson at all. More likely a stuntman paid to take risks for the star. Rhodes wished he had someone like that working for him. Whoever it was, whether Bronson or a stuntman, he had a pretty good sense of balance, something else Rhodes lacked.

It took him a little while to pull himself atop the car. When he got there, the first thing he noticed was that the car wasn't still. It was rocking a little. Not much, but enough to bother him.

Then he noticed that the top wasn't perfectly flat. It slanted down a bit from the middle on both sides.

Rhodes thought he'd just lie there for a minute. Maybe it was all a dream and he'd wake up at home in his bed with Yancey licking his face.

He closed his eyes. When he opened them he was right there on top of the boxcar.

Okay, if that was the way it was going to be, he'd go along to the next car. But not standing up. He wasn't a stuntman, and he wasn't Charles Bronson. He writhed along on his stomach, stretching out his arms in the hope that he could catch himself if he started to slide off.

He hadn't gone far before he learned that there were ridges about an inch high every few feet. He didn't like having to slide over them, but he was glad to have something to grab. Every cloud has a silver lining.

Rhodes slithered along to the end of the car. Was he going to stand up and jump across the opening to the next one?

Not a chance. He climbed down the ladder from his car to the coupling, sucked in a deep breath, crossed the coupling, and climbed up the next ladder.

The top of this car was flat, with no ridges. Rhodes decided he'd be Charles Bronson. He stood up and started walking, his arms extended out to his sides for balance. The wind buffeted him, but he didn't fall.

He didn't jump to the next car, either. He climbed down and up again. The top of this car was also flat. Again Rhodes walked along it. He felt he was getting better at it. If Hollywood needed new stuntmen, he'd apply. But he wasn't going to make that jump between the cars. Someone with more experience would have to do that.

After more climbing, he was atop the fourth car. Someone was either waiting for him at the next coupling or gone. Rhodes figured that waiting was more likely. He hadn't seen anyone running along on top of the other cars, and he didn't think anyone would have jumped off.

He was getting used to the movement of the train and the rush of the wind now. He walked along almost confidently, feeling certain he wasn't going to fall, or that if he did, he'd just hit the roof of the car and not the ground or the tracks.

The train made a hollow sound as it boomed across a trestle over a small creek that was dry most of the time. It would have a little water in it now because of the rain. Rhodes thought it would be a long way down to the water.

When he got almost to the gap between cars, he stopped and knelt down. Once again a movie memory popped into his head, and he wondered, not for the first time, if he'd seen too many movies in the course of his lifetime. He didn't watch nearly as many now as he once had, but he seemed to remember a little of every one he'd ever seen.

In this case, Rhodes thought of *The Manchurian Candidate* and a scene in which Frank Sinatra fought a villainous Henry Silva between two cars on a swiftly moving train. More likely it was their stunt doubles who'd fought, but Rhodes's memory of the scene was vague. Mainly he remembered Sinatra's toupee. He knew Sinatra had won, but he couldn't recall what had happened to Silva. What he wondered now was how they'd managed not to fall off the train.

Rhodes didn't want to get into a fight with Wilks, because he knew less karate than Sinatra or his double, though neither had exhibited anything like the skill of a real practitioner of the art. Rhodes didn't want to get shot, either, but he didn't want to shoot Wilks. Well, not unless he had to.

He pulled his flashlight from his pocket. It was heavy aluminum, and Rhodes reached out to tap on the rim of the car. The noise of the train on the tracks and the rush of the wind made it hard to hear, so Rhodes tapped harder.

"Are you down there, Wilks?" he yelled.

He got no answer, so he edged closer to the gap and tried again.

"Wilks? This is Sheriff Rhodes. Throw away your gun, and we can talk."

His voice carried better this time because, a few miles past Franklin's place, the tracks turned to make a long curve and started up a little hill. The train had to slow down quite a bit for that stretch, and the noise from the wheels and wind diminished.

Rhodes still got no answer. He lay down on his stomach and risked a look over the end of the car.

Tom Fulton looked back at him.

"You got the wrong man, Sheriff," he yelled.

It took a second for Rhodes to process the information. He hadn't been sure Wilks was the one running from him, but he hadn't thought it would be Fulton. It made a kind of sense, though.

"I have the right man," Rhodes said finally. He turned on the flashlight. "I just had the wrong name. You still have that gun?"

Fulton moved his right hand from behind his back and showed Rhodes a pistol. Then he tossed it into the darkness.

"Not anymore," he said.

"Good," Rhodes said. "I'm coming down."

He was halfway down the ladder when Fulton jumped off the train.

*　*　*

While the train had slowed to a crawl, Rhodes didn't want to follow Fulton. He couldn't help thinking of rocks, sharp sticks, broken bones, crushed skulls, and any number of other terrible things.

On the other hand, he couldn't very well let Fulton get away. He didn't think any more. He tossed away his flashlight, not wanting to hurt himself with it. Then he gathered himself and jumped.

Rhodes landed on his feet, but he wasn't on them long, just long enough for the jolt to travel all the way from his shoes to his shoulders.

After that, his feet slid in the slick mud and he pitched forward, remembering somehow to tuck and roll. He somersaulted a couple of times and then found himself on his side, rolling over a few of the rocks and sticks he'd dreaded.

Eventually he came to a stop and lay still. He thought he could get up, but he didn't want to rush things. He wiggled his fingers and toes, then moved his arms and legs. Everything worked, so he pushed himself up into a crouch. He was dizzy, but he stood up anyway.

It took a little while for his head to clear. When it did, he didn't bother to look for the flashlight. He just started walking back along the tracks. He was covered in mud, and he had leaves stuck all over him.

Another movie came to mind. *Swamp Thing*. Rhodes wondered if he'd meet Adrienne Barbeau.

Not a chance.

The train boomed along beside him for a couple of seconds, and then it was gone. Rhodes could remember when there had been a caboose on the back of a train, but that had been long ago, and there was no caboose on this one.

The rumble faded after the last car passed. Rhodes hardly noticed. He was looking for Fulton, and he wondered what the odds were that Fulton had found the pistol he'd thrown from the train. Slim and none, most likely. No need to worry about it.

Rhodes walked slowly, not wanting to fall again. He was already going to be sore for a while. He didn't want to aggravate the problem.

He estimated that he'd walked less than a quarter of a mile when he saw someone hobbling along ahead of him. It had to be Fulton. Who else would be out there at that time of night?

Rhodes still had his own pistol in the ankle holster, though it was probably a little wet. He figured he wouldn't need it, not if Fulton felt as bad as he did, but there was no use in taking chances. He stopped, bent over, and pulled up his pants leg. The pistol was there, and not too wet in its holster. Rhodes pulled the Velcro straps and got the gun.

"Fulton," he called when he'd straightened back up. "Stop where you are. You're under arrest."

Rhodes always felt a little odd saying that, mainly because nobody ever stopped.

Which was why he was so surprised when Fulton turned around to face him and said, "I'll wait for you right here."

Even in the dimness Rhodes could see that Fulton looked bad, muddy and ashen. Maybe it was just the moonlight.

Rhodes approached Fulton cautiously, but Fulton didn't try anything. He listed to one side, and when Rhodes got closer, he said, "I think I broke my ankle."

"Sorry about that," Rhodes said, though he really wasn't. "You're going to have to walk to the road anyway."

"I don't think I can make it."

Rhodes didn't trust Fulton. He waited a good five yards away to see what Fulton would do, but the man didn't move.

"It's probably just sprained," Rhodes said. "You should've stayed on the train."

"Yeah, that would have been a good idea, now that you mention it. I wasn't thinking."

"Seems like you haven't been thinking for a good while. I'm going to read you your rights now."

Rhodes held the pistol in his right hand while he fumbled in his back pocket with his left. The outside of the pocket was slick with mud.

Rhodes found his wallet and had to use both hands to get out the Miranda card. It was awkward with the pistol in one hand, but he managed.

He couldn't really read the card without a flashlight, and he didn't have his reading glasses on, either. In fact, they weren't in his shirt pocket any longer. There was no need for Fulton to know all that, through. Rhodes had the Miranda stuff memorized right down to the last period.

When he was finished, Rhodes asked Fulton if he understood.

"Yeah," Fulton said.

Rhodes put the card and billfold back in his pocket. He asked if Fulton had any questions.

Fulton didn't say anything. Rhodes looked to his right. He couldn't see the road, but it paralleled the tracks, so it couldn't be too far away. He gestured with the pistol.

"Head that way," he said.

Fulton limped in the direction Rhodes had indicated, groaning now and then to let Rhodes know he was suffering. Rhodes didn't care about either the groaning or the suffering. He was trying to arrange the pieces of the puzzle and fit them together with Fulton in place of Wilks.

It took them about ten minutes to get to the barbed-wire fence that stood between them and the ditch that ran alongside the gravel road. Rhodes made Fulton climb through the fence without assistance. Then he told him to cross the ditch and stand in the road. When Fulton was safely out of the way, Rhodes climbed through the fence himself, managing to catch his shirt on only one barb. He got it free without tearing it and joined Fulton on the road.

"If we're lucky," Rhodes said, "someone will come along and pick us up."

"What if we're not lucky?" Fulton said. "I haven't had a lot of luck lately."

"Sure you have," Rhodes told him. "It's just all been bad."

"You got that right. So what do we do if nobody comes?"

Rhodes looked down the long dark road toward town.

"We walk," he said.

30

▼

THEY STARTED WALKING TOWARD CLEARVIEW, OR LIMPING TO-
ward Clearview in Fulton's case. By then Rhodes thought he had
things figured out.

"You killed Lloyd Berry, didn't you?" he said.

Fulton just shrugged.

"It was the GPS," Rhodes said. "He did get it from you, but he
didn't buy it. He got it as a door prize and didn't return it. You
looked for it in his apartment but didn't find it there. I should have
thought of that thing sooner. It has a serial number on it somewhere, and it can be traced to you."

Fulton kept his mouth shut.

"You went to his shop to get it back. He'd had some kind of
falling-out with Wilks, probably over money, and he'd threatened
to come to me about the GPS scheme. You were in it with Wilks.
Your business wasn't doing so well, and Wilks must have paid you

a little to help him out. Maybe it was even your idea to begin with. You couldn't let Lloyd tell what he knew."

Fulton still wasn't talking.

"The GPS was in Lloyd's car," Rhodes said. "You didn't look there, did you?"

Fulton kept limping but said nothing.

Rhodes was a little worried about the silence. If he didn't get a confession, all he had was the GPS as evidence against Fulton.

At least that was all in the murder case. Rhodes had plenty against Fulton in the attempts on Happy Franklin's life. Except a motive.

"What I can't figure out," Rhodes said, "is why you wanted to kill Happy."

That got Fulton started. "Who said I wanted to kill him?"

"Bullets through the wall of the barn," Rhodes said.

"Ha. If I'd been trying to kill him, he'd be dead. All I wanted to do was get him out of there."

Something clicked into place in Rhodes's head.

"You made the noise at the house, hoping he'd look for you and let you into the barn."

"Yeah, but the old lady called you. That's all they ever did, was call you. You'd think they'd at least go outside for a look around. Don't they have any curiosity?"

"Some people don't," Rhodes said.

"I guess not. I thought I'd try one more time tonight. I wasn't going to shoot again. Just bang on the walls of the barn and get him out of there for a while. I thought maybe I could get in before you got there if they called, but instead you came snooping around too soon and didn't give me a chance."

"What did you want Happy out of the barn for?"

Fulton didn't answer. Rhodes could come up with only one idea. Fulton must have wanted to get something out of the barn when Franklin went to look around. What could he have wanted? Not the flower stands. Rhodes tried to remember what else he'd seen. Black plastic trash bags had been by the stands. If they'd come from behind Lloyd's shop, they might have had some artificial flowers in them. Or if they came from some other place, there might be something else. Receipts? Records?

"You should always shred things when you throw them out," Rhodes said. "I'd say there are even some things you shouldn't keep records of in your business, like who's rented a GPS."

"The damn shredder stopped working," Fulton said.

"So Happy Franklin has the goods on you."

"He grabbed those trash bags. I was talking to Lloyd when he was out back."

"That was before you hit Lloyd."

"Wilks sent me to talk to him. It wasn't my idea. I didn't mean to hit him. He got mean with me. Called me a crook. Said I was as bad as Wilks. I just wanted my GPS. I figured if I had that, I'd be in the clear."

"But you forgot the records."

"They were in the trash," Fulton said. "Another half hour and they'd have been gone to the dump."

"Happy has them now, though."

"Yeah. I guess."

Fulton should never have tried to get them back, Rhodes thought. Happy would most likely have tossed out the receipts or whatever they were without ever looking at them.

"He shoved me," Fulton said. "When we were arguing. That wrench was there, and I grabbed it to protect myself."

"You can save that stuff for your lawyer," Rhodes said.

He saw headlights coming toward them on the road.

"Better get off to the side," he said.

They did, and the car stopped in front of them, its headlights catching them in their beams. Duke Pearson got out of the car and looked them over.

"Some people say a man's made out of mud," he said, and he laughed. "Just an old song that came to mind. You two need a ride?"

"We could use one," Rhodes said. "You can take me back to Happy's, and you can take the prisoner to the jail and book him."

"What charges?"

"I'll make a list," Rhodes said. "It'll be a long one."

Guy Wilks wasn't at home when Rhodes went by. The house wasn't locked, but Wilks's car was gone. Rhodes had a feeling that Wilks was on a long trip and wouldn't be coming back to Clearview, at least not voluntarily. Rhodes would put out an APB on him.

Wilks's hasty departure meant that Rollin' Sevens wouldn't be opening its doors again. Rhodes would see to that. He wondered what he'd do with the eight-liners. He hoped the county didn't have to store them. The Houston solution would be better.

He didn't kid himself that illegal gambling was at an end in Blacklin County. Another place would open soon enough, and whoever opened it would have figured out a way around the law about prizes before the first winner walked through the door. Rhodes thought someone needed to go after Whipsnake, but that wasn't his job.

Rhodes left Wilks's house and drove home. Ivy wasn't stunned at his condition. She'd seen him when he was even muddier, but Yancey got pretty excited about it. Sam, on the other hand, didn't seem to notice or even care that Rhodes was at home.

"You need a shower," Ivy said.

"I need to clean my pistol," Rhodes told her. "And I should call Jennifer Loam and let her have the story."

"Later."

"Right," Rhodes said. "Later."

The barbershop chorus sang at Lloyd Berry's graveside service the next day. They did only one number, "Amazing Grace," and Rhodes liked the way it sounded in four-part barbershop harmony. It was too bad that Lloyd wasn't there to hear it. He'd have been proud of them. Max Schwartz directed the group in Lloyd's place, and as far as Rhodes could tell, he did a good job.

It was a fine day, not too warm but with plenty of sunshine, and from the hill where the cemetery was located Rhodes could see the railroad tracks heading off into the distance both north and south, though the ruined roundhouse was too far away for him to get a glimpse of it.

After the service, Seepy Benton caught up with Rhodes while he was enjoying the view.

"How'd you like our singing?" Seepy said.

Rhodes told him the singing was just fine, and Benton said, "Have you changed your mind about joining us?"

Rhodes hadn't even thought about it. "Lloyd didn't really want me to join. He just wanted some protection from Cecil."

"I don't think that was it."

"Sure it was. If you'd ever heard me try to sing, you'd know."

"Being a member might do you some good at the next election."

Rhodes wished people would quit mentioning the election.

"It's too soon to worry about that," he said.

"If you say so." Seepy paused. "You don't mind if I'm dating your deputy, do you?"

"I didn't know you were."

"Well, I haven't actually asked her out yet."

"Why don't you do that and then ask me how I feel about it. How's Bruce, by the way?"

"He's fine. I think he likes it at my place."

Rhodes was glad to hear it. "I saw Cecil and Royce singing in the chorus. They didn't get into a fight at the rehearsal, I hope."

"No. I think they've settled things, except about the chickens. That's still a problem."

The Marshes had problems besides chickens to worry about. Rhodes hoped they could work them out.

"We'll let the city council deal with the chickens," Rhodes said.

"What about alligators?" Seepy asked.

Rhodes laughed. "Them, too," he said.